I0761431

A Wonderful Christmas Crime

Also available by Jacqueline Frost:

The Christmas Tree Farm Mysteries

I'll Be Home for Mischief

Stalking Around the Christmas Tree

Slashing Through the Snow

'Twas the Knife Before Christmas

Twelve Slays of Christmas

The Kitty Couture Mysteries

(writing as Julie Chase)

Cat Got Your Crown

Cat Got Your Secrets

Cat Got Your Cash

Cat Got Your Diamonds

A Wonderful Christmas Crime

A CHRISTMAS TREE FARM MYSTERY

Jacqueline Frost

NEW YORK

Books should be disposed of and recycled according to local requirements. All paper materials used are FSC compliant.

This is a work of fiction. All of the names, characters, organizations, places and events portrayed in this novel are either products of the author's imagination or are used fictitiously. Any resemblance to real or actual events, locales, or persons, living or dead, is entirely coincidental.

Published in the United States by Crooked Lane Books, an imprint of The Quick Brown Fox & Company LLC.

Crooked Lane Books and its logo are trademarks of The Quick Brown Fox & Company LLC.

Library of Congress Catalog-in-Publication data available upon request.

ISBN (hardcover): 979-8-89242-197-3
ISBN (ebook): 979-8-89242-198-0

Cover design by Rich Grote

Printed in the United States.

www.crookedlanebooks.com

Crooked Lane Books
34 West 27th St., 10th Floor
New York, NY 10001

First Edition: October 2025

The authorized representative in the EU for product safety and compliance is eucomply OÜPärnu mnt 139b-14, 11317 Tallinn, Estonia, hello@eucompliancepartner.com, +33757690241

10 9 8 7 6 5 4 3 2 1

Chapter One

Evan held my bandaged hand as we crossed the lot to Dr. Bright's office. The historic two-story structure resembled a small ski chalet with its floor-to-ceiling windows and high pitched roof. Pine greenery and wide crimson velvet bows draped the railing along the second-floor deck. Collections of larger-than-life sleigh bells in silver and gold hung from the corner posts, jingling in the frigid wind.

I smiled at the backdrop of snow-covered mountains and ancient evergreen trees. I adored my little life in historic Mistletoe, Maine, any time of year, but there was nothing like it at Christmas. Some days it felt as if magic literally glistened in the air.

"Oops!" I pinwheeled one arm as my boots slipped on the ice of a frozen puddle.

Apparently, it took more than magic to keep me upright despite a darn good pair of snow boots.

My husband, ever at my side, moved his grip from my hand to my elbow and waited while I regained my footing. "I've got you."

"Thanks." I stilled with a smile, feeling small, despite my five foot eight inches, at his side.

Evan was tall and broad with miles on me in many ways, like his impeccable balance and walk-and-gawk capabilities. His hair was brown like mine, his eyes a soft, soulful green, and sometimes, when he smiled wide enough, a dimple appeared in his right cheek.

I felt powerful when I made that dimple appear.

"You steady?" he asked.

"Yeah. I was looking at the mountains," I admitted. I wasn't watching where I was going. I had Evan for that.

He held the door for me, head shaking in amusement. I ducked beneath his arm and into the warm, cinnamon-scented waiting room.

The receptionist smiled warmly at our approach. "Hello, Holly," she said, before moving her gaze to Evan. "Sheriff." Her blue eyes seemed to widen as she took in my husband. It was a regular occurrence for women between sixteen and one hundred, as far as I could tell. I didn't blame them. I still did the same thing every time he appeared, and I saw him every day.

I tried to match her pleasant expression, but I wasn't thrilled to be back in the office. I wanted to get on with my day, visit my family, see my friends.

Marina was technically a family friend. She'd worked with Dr. Bright since the practice opened about a year before my birth. My mom visited the office throughout her pregnancy, and I'd seen the general practitioner all my life. Being on the patient roster was a bit of a White-family tradition, but I had yet to convince Evan to make the switch. I supposed that was reasonable since Dr. Bright planned to retire soon.

Evan nodded at Marina and tugged off his gloves as I signed my name on the clipboard shaped like a gingerbread man.

She pushed out her bottom lip in a dramatic pout. "How's the hand? These snowstorms wreaked havoc on the computer systems. I'm sorry you had to come back so soon."

To Peggy King

I smiled as my husband squirmed at my side. "It's no problem," I told her. "We were going out this morning anyway. We just added another stop along the way."

After we checked in, Evan led me to a pair of high-backed, red velvet chairs near the windows. "Have I told you yet today how sorry I am that you were hurt?" He unzipped his slick black coat and loosened his scarf.

I followed suit.

"No," I lied. I kept my face straight while I waited for the kisses that followed. My forehead. My nose. And the gentle brush of his thumb along my chin.

Evan and I had married two years ago in history's most perfect wedding ceremony, but somehow, he seemed to love me more every day. I felt that way too, but I wasn't as outwardly affectionate. Still, I never tired of his doting.

"It was an accident," I reminded him, quietly, and for the thousandth time. "The stitches look good, and the swelling is already going down. Nothing was broken."

He looked at my bandaged hand, then back to me with deep concern in his soft green eyes. "I shouldn't have asked you to help me mount that silly sleigh."

Evan and I purchased a child's sleigh at a flea market in Bangor last summer with plans to fill it with twinkle lights and faux presents and display it on our roof for the holidays. We'd rushed to set it up before dark, always too busy to get the job done by daylight, and that led to trouble. I'd cut my hand on the rusty runner in haste. Then, true to form, I fell from the ladder after jerking away from the pain. I'd only been a couple of rungs high when I got hurt, and I'd landed in a snowbank. Two small miracles. Unfortunately, I'd put my hand out on instinct to soften the fall and added a severe sprain to go with my potential tetanus.

Dr. Bright had examined me fully within an hour of my fall and applied several stitches to the cut, but I hadn't gotten a tetanus shot. The system was down, and we didn't know when I'd received my last dose of the vaccine. She'd suggested visiting Mistletoe General Hospital, but I wasn't a fan of hospitals and didn't mind waiting a day or two for things to come back online here. Besides, my fingers all moved easily enough under my command, even if they were still too swollen to wear my wedding ring.

I was either back for the tetanus shot or something was missing from my file. I supposed I'd find out soon enough.

"Crossword?" I asked, lifting the morning paper from a nearby table and setting it across the arm of my chair.

Evan rose and dragged his seat closer, until it touched mine. He sat again with a smile. "Yes."

We'd developed a routine of playing the daily puzzle together. As two of the arguably busiest people in Mistletoe this time of year, him as the sheriff, and me wearing a dozen hats at my family's tree farm, some days the only time we had together happened as the sun rose. Thankfully, the paper faithfully arrived before that.

Today, we'd stayed in bed until it was time to leave for my appointment. So it felt a little like a gift to me that the puzzle was right here waiting.

"Oh!" I said, delighted at the very first clue. "Two across is all about me."

Evan chuckled. "Mistletoe and blank. Five letters."

"H-o-l-l-y," I dictated as I tapped a finger against each empty square on the paper. I didn't want to write the answers and ruin the game for anyone else.

I snuggled against Evan's shoulder as he held the paper between us.

He smelled of gingerbread and pine. Scents of citrus mingled with the cinnamon I'd noted in the air upon arrival. My stomach growled in response.

"I can't wait for a cup of Mom's wassail," I said. "And a slice of her cranberry gingerbread."

"Soon." Evan checked his watch. "I hope the doctor isn't running behind already."

"Big day?" I asked. The question was wholly rhetorical.

Managing a historic holiday town at Christmastime was an enormous, occasionally impossible job. Mistletoe doubled its usual population annually, usually around Thanksgiving, and often reached quadrupled levels as Christmas drew near. Today, just twelve days before the big day, it'd taken forty-five minutes to make what should have been a twenty-minute commute to the doctor.

Evan rolled his shoulders and met my eye. "Tour buses are destroying the traffic patterns, which is leading to a lot of fender benders and more road rage than I like to deal with, but I hired plenty of additional security to mitigate as much of the chaos as possible."

"Good planning ahead."

One corner of his mouth tipped up at my praise. "The antiques show is hauling in higher numbers of patrons than I expected, but at least they seem to be a calm bunch. I doubt crime will rise based on their presence, unless you count illegal parking and jaywalking. There's plenty of that."

I grinned. Honestly, everyone I knew would be thrilled if those were the biggest problems we had this year. Our precious little town had gotten into an unfortunate routine about five years ago that involved an annual murder. The pattern had slowly drawn the attention of true-crime fanatics, and a podcasting duo showed up last year to cover the story—and my involvement. A bunch of harmless antiquers seemed the unequivocally better option.

"We should go check out the show this week," Evan said.

"I'd love to." I wasn't a collector, but I loved history and everything about it. Seeing pieces of the world from a multitude of eras in one place sounded like my kind of fun.

Evan squeezed my fingers gently. "The mayor was smart with this one. Everyone coming into town for the antiques will spend money on food for the day, lodging if they planned far enough ahead to get a room, and they'll likely spend some cash in the shops as well. It's great for commerce, and so far, it's a manageable crowd."

"The mayor is good," I agreed. Last year's town-wide 150th-anniversay theme had likely gotten the attention of more historians and history lovers than ever before. "Mistletoe deserves some good press this time of year."

"Holly White?" a nurse called from the front.

I rose and hurried in her direction, eager to get the appointment over with. "You don't have to come back with me," I told Evan when he followed.

"I want to," he said. "It's my fault you're here."

The nurse grinned. "Yeah, it is," she said, then turned to lead us down a narrow hall.

Evan and I exchanged looks but kept moving.

A few steps later, we were seated in chairs across the desk from Dr. Bright.

"Hello, Holly, Evan," the older woman said. A mass of curly white hair around her narrow face accentuated her light brown skin. Her dark brown eyes flickered with mischief. "How are you feeling, Holly?"

Evan shifted beside me, looking as if we were in the principal's office or about to receive a citation.

"Good," I fibbed, feeling increased stress from meeting in her office versus an exam room. That wasn't a good sign, right?

"Well, I'm glad," she said with a chuckle. A pair of little green gumdrop earrings danced among her curls. The matching necklace hung loosely around her white turtleneck. I'd made the jewelry pieces years ago. Long before I'd had an inkling that the practice would become a thriving business. She still wore the set every year.

"Do I need a tetanus shot?" I asked.

"Not for a while," she said. "The systems are running again, and I've confirmed you're all caught up on vaccines, tetanus included."

I sagged a little in relief. I wasn't a fan of needles, and the last time I visited, an interning nurse had poked me twice before getting the blood sample Dr. Bright ordered. I still had some minor bruising from her effort.

"Great!" I said, pushing to stand. The faster we got out of there, the sooner my pulse could return to normal. My breaths had become a little shallow as I'd waited to hear the news. Now, as relief rushed in, I felt a little woozy.

Evan's hand snaked out to anchor me in place. "She's not finished."

"Still experiencing lightheadedness?" Dr. Bright asked.

I nodded. "Still no idea why?" I asked.

She smiled. "Actually, today I have two."

I took my seat, curiosity piqued. I'd struggled with fatigue and dizziness since Thanksgiving, but so far she hadn't found a reason, and the symptoms were getting worse. I hadn't told her or Evan, but it was partially the cause for my fall from the ladder. I was sure I could've kept my balance a few months ago, even after pulling back from the cut.

Evan shifted forward, visibly worried, as he had been since my first request for answers failed last month. "Was it Holly's bloodwork?"

I grimaced as I met his terrified gaze, certain I might pass out from the sudden unnamed stress.

Dr. Bright's expression fell. "Yes, but I didn't mean to alarm you," she said. "As you know, I ran a full panel in hopes of casting a wider net when Holly's symptoms of fatigue and dizziness persisted. The more concerning portion of our last visit was her blood pressure."

"What?" I asked. She'd mentioned that before, but we'd chalked it up to stress from the recent fall from a ladder. "You said it was only slightly elevated."

"I'll have another listen in a bit," she said. "Maybe it's returned to normal today."

I highly doubted that.

"Possibly it's a result of your condition, in which case, the elevation, slight as it is, becomes more concerning."

"Condition?" I asked, cheeks heating and stomach knotting. I cast my gaze around the room in search of a waste bin in case I was sick.

"Thankfully this will resolve itself come summertime."

My attention snapped up to meet hers. "What?"

Dr. Bright wore a tight cat-that-ate-the-canary smile. "Congratulations. You're having a baby."

Evan's grip on my hand tightened, and he made a soft, strangled sound.

My ears roared and the world tilted. "I'm sorry, what?" I repeated.

"About ten weeks as far as I can tell," she said. "I almost didn't check, given the date of your latest cycle, but sure enough."

I stood, driven back to my feet by a sudden shot of adrenaline.

Evan followed, his hand on my wrist. "Holly," he whispered, eyes wide with wonder and misted with unshed tears. The instant wattage of his wide, awestruck smile might've blinded me if my world hadn't gone black.

I opened my eyes to the lights of an exam room. Apparently, I'd been moved after passing out.

"Here she is," Dr. Bright sang.

The cuff on my bicep loosened, and I realized she'd taken my blood pressure.

Evan helped me adjust my position on the table while the doctor pivoted on her rolling chair.

"You're going to be just fine, Holly," she said. "Both of you. I'll see to it." She unwrapped my hand and moved it gently between her palms. "Any limited range of movement?"

"No."

She put on her glasses and examined me a little longer. "Swelling and bruising are on track for this many days post-fall. It'll be tender for a while longer. Apply ice and take over-the-counter pain medication as needed. Elevate it when you can."

"Okay."

"Most importantly," she said, rewrapping my hand. "Take it easy."

I followed her gaze to my middle and felt a tear emerge from my eye.

"Both of you," she added.

My hands flew to my stomach as the memory from just before my collapse returned. "I'm pregnant."

"Yes," she said simply. "And passing out is par for the course, I'm afraid. Watch out for the ice this time of year, and anything else that could put you in harm's way."

"How is this possible?"

She chuckled.

"I mean—" I waved a hand. "It's just that there weren't any signs." Then I realized I was wrong. My lightheadedness and nausea were signs of pregnancy. Probably also my brain fog and fatigue. The signs were there, but I'd ignored them when my life carried on as usual month after month, despite our best efforts at conception.

"Many women are much farther along than you before they realize," she said. "You aren't alone."

I swung my gaze to Evan.

He towered over me, hands braced on his hips, utter joy etched on his handsome face.

"Keep an eye on her, Dad," she said. "And monitor that blood pressure."

His Adam's apple bobbed long and slow. He cleared his throat before speaking, apparently balanced on an emotional cliff. "Yes, ma'am."

Dr. Bright stood and shook our hands. "Congratulations to you both. The nurse has a care package with lots of information and samples from local vendors that you can pick up on your way out. Make an appointment to see me again in a month and give me a call if you have any questions in the meantime."

"Wait." I stretched a hand in her direction as she passed. "That's it?"

"For now," she said. She opened the door with a boisterous laugh. "Just wait until I hand you a baby and send you home from the hospital. That's when the real fun begins!"

I gaped.

"Merry Christmas!" she called.

The door closed behind her, and she was gone.

Chapter Two

The walk from Dr. Bright's office was silent.

Evan loaded me into his truck as if I was made of glass, then he shut the passenger door and stared at me through the window.

I stared back.

A moment later, a new car arrived on the lot and snapped him into motion. He marched around the hood to the driver's side and climbed behind the wheel. "You okay?" he asked.

I gave one sharp dip of my chin, the profound feeling of shock somehow holding my tongue.

Evan echoed the movement, started the truck, and drove us through town.

I'd gone in for a tetanus shot and came out with a baby.

Not exactly, I realized, but that was certainly how it felt.

Maybe I actually had tetanus and was hallucinating the whole thing.

My mind raced, but I couldn't speak. I set a hand on my abdomen, processing the possibility. A fizzing, wonderous sensation swept through my body, standing the fine hairs on my arms at attention beneath my coat.

I was in awe.

I looked at Evan, backdropped by my beloved historical holiday town outside his window. My best friend. My confidant. My husband.

He stole glances at me as he drove.

I opened my mouth to say something, anything, but a shuddered breath rattled through me instead.

Evan pulled the truck over and we began to laugh. Joy filled the cab so thickly, I thought I might drown in it.

I unfastened my belt as he did the same, and in the next breath he pulled me across the bench to his lap. I buried my face against his neck, absorbed his strength, the strong wall of his chest, the protective cage of his arms, and the trademarked scent I loved.

He pressed kisses in my hair, against my temple, along my cheek. "She called me Dad," he whispered.

I nodded, and he hugged me.

Snow piled on the windshield and sounds of distant holiday music filtered through the warm, quiet space. Less than two weeks before Christmas seemed like cosmic timing for such perfect news.

A long moment later, I met his awestruck gaze with a smile. "I could sit here all day," I said softly. "But this adorable holiday town can't protect and serve itself."

He groaned.

"And my folks are expecting me."

He let me return to my side of the vehicle and we fastened our safety belts once more.

I waved at familiar faces outside my window as we trundled through town at half the posted speed limit, hamstrung by gawkers and rubberneckers, tour buses, and tourists who didn't know where to go or what they were doing.

At least the view was pretty.

Twinkle lights lined shop roofs and hung in dramatic sweeps above the street. Shoppers stole kisses on street corners beneath balls of mistletoe.

Families held packages on Santa-red benches, waiting for loved ones or rides.

Carolers swayed, chins upturned on corners, belting lyrics to familiar seasonal songs.

There wasn't any better place on earth to raise a baby—except maybe at my family's tree farm, if I was extremely specific.

Evan covered my bandaged hand with his palm and curled his fingers softly around mine. "Are we supposed to wait a few months to tell people?" he asked.

"Not our families," I said, knowing he was thinking about our baby, something I'd likely not stop doing for the rest of my life. "If anything goes wrong, I want our loved ones to know so they can help us through it."

He lifted my hand to his lips and pressed a kiss to my tender knuckles. "Just our folks then," he said. "And Libby."

I smiled. His sister, Libby, had become one of my closest friends after her move to Mistletoe. She'd married my friend Ray in a destination wedding over the summer, and we definitely couldn't leave her out on news this big. "That will mean telling Ray," I said. "And I have to tell Caroline." She was my best friend, after all.

He nodded, patiently navigating the bumper-to-bumper traffic around the square downtown. "And Cookie."

My smile grew. Cookie was a family friend I'd known all my life.

"She'll tell Theodore," he continued, a twinkle in his eye. "And he'll tell his wife."

"This is getting out of hand," I teased.

Evan fixed me with a goofy grin.

Someone honked behind us, and Evan reluctantly pulled his attention back to the road.

"Do you want to stop at home before heading to the farm?" he asked.

"No, I'm good," I said, eager to see my parents.

Evan and I lived in the home he'd bought when accepting the role as Mistletoe's sheriff five years ago. He'd left the Boston PD for a much-needed break, burnt out by endless big-city crimes and craving space to enjoy his career again.

I tried not to be thankful for the criminals who drove him here, but some parts of me would always want to send them a basket of cookies when I remembered why he came.

Someday, when we had enough money, we planned to build a new place on the acre of land my parents had carved out for us, a stone's throw from the inn I once managed and the house where I'd grown up. In my perfect future, Evan, the baby, and I would walk over for coffee with my parents every morning. Until then, we had a big truck and solid snow tires to help us safely make the trip.

Traffic thinned as we reached the country road outside town. Tidy rows of homes decked out in their holiday best slowly gave way to rolling hills and fields of snow.

My gaze caught on a white Boston Red Sox logo Evan placed at the corner of the windshield. I imagined buying baby pajamas with the same image and later taking the toddler to their first game.

Soon the familiar crunch of gravel under tires sent a fresh thrill along my spine. We passed beneath the hand-carved Reindeer Games sign at the tree farm, and Evan parked at the Hearth, the farm's small café.

We traded mischievous smiles, then hurried into the icy day.

Mom appeared outside the building and waved an arm overhead for us to hurry. "What took you so long?" she said. "We were starting to worry!"

"Sorry," we called, picking up our pace across the heavily salted lot and hurrying inside.

Rich aromas of hot chocolate and melted caramel met us as we crossed the threshold. We stomped our boots on the thick welcome mat, leaving tufts of snow to melt beneath the blowing heater.

"Come along," Mom said, striding toward the service counter. "I want to hear everything."

I unwrapped my scarf and tucked mittens into my pockets as I followed.

The café was my favorite place on the farm, a life-sized gingerbread house serving Mom's most delicious treats. The sights and scents alone made the Hearth a delight to the senses. Add in the cheerful holiday tunes and a single bite of anything from the kitchen, and I wasn't sure why anyone ever wanted to leave.

My dad's parents and grandparents had decorated the place years ago. My parents had added their touches over the years. These days, red and green gumdrop chandeliers hung throughout the space, often above wooden tables created by my ancestors from trees on the property. The tabletops resembled chocolate bars seated on black licorice stick legs. Candy cane striped booths lined the side walls, and a service counter faced the front door, separating the dining area from the kitchen. Each detail was more delightful than the next, right down to the white eyelet lace curtains on the windows and drifts of cotton snow on the sills.

Mom poured two mugs of coffee and set them before a pair of empty lollipop-shaped barstools. Worry creased her brow.

I looked like my mom, though she had a couple dozen pounds and years on me. I had a half-dozen inches on her, so it all seemed fair. Our once matching dark hair grew a little more different each year. Mine got longer, hers shorter and more flecked with gray.

Dad rang up a customer at the old-fashioned register. "Hey, sweetie," he said, glancing in our direction. "Holly."

Evan cracked up at Dad's goofy joke. "Hey, Mr. White. You're working double duty today."

Dad was a lumberjack by trade and preferred outdoor activities to anything done indoors, but his preference for my mother topped everything else. Based on how busy the café was, and the speed her friends moved around the tables serving guests, this was an all-hands-on-deck moment.

Mom tented her brows, waiting. Each knitted holiday light on her sweater held a letter. Strung together across her chest, they spelled the words *Merry and Bright*. A hidden battery pack caused the lights to blink, making it hard to accept her grouchy expression. "Sit. Tell us all what the doctor said." Her gaze slid to my bandaged hand, then to Evan.

I don't know what she saw on my husband's face, but when her eyes returned to mine, a tear slid over my cheek.

"Holly?"

Dad stepped away from the register, finished with the sale. He set a hand on Mom's back. "Evan?" Dad asked when I didn't speak.

My husband cleared his throat, then relayed the story of how we received our news. I watched as my parents experienced the same series of emotions I had. Confusion. Shock. Disbelief. Then joy.

"Oh!" Mom leaped and covered her mouth. She hugged my dad, then nearly dove across the counter to embrace me.

A burst of cold air whipped inside, and Mom released me to check the door.

I turned with her, noting the pride on Evan's face as Dad passed him a cut-out cookie in the shape of a golden star.

Cookie hustled in our direction, a flyer clutched in one hand. "I can't believe the Antiques Showcase is coming to Mistletoe! I'm going to make a mint!"

Cookie was at least my grandmother's age, though no one knew the exact number. She had a crown of white hair and enough energy to run circles around me any day of the week. Her given name was Delores Cutter, but her late husband gave her the nickname for her love of baking. There was something about the name Cookie Cutter that encapsulated her to a tee.

"Being this old has its perks. Half my stuff is antique!" She stopped at the barstool beside me, excitement dying as she took in the scene. "Whoa. Who died?"

I burst into laughter and pulled her into a hug. She went willingly, and my parents joined us, engulfing her tiny frame.

"Am I dying?" she asked. Her muffled words sent me into hysterics.

When we broke apart, Evan shared the news again.

"Oh," she said, visibly relieved. "You should've led with that. I thought I had to go home and get my affairs in order. I didn't know what I'd tell Theodore."

Mom patted her shoulder. "At least he's married now. When the time comes, you'll know he's in good hands."

Cookie nodded soberly.

Theodore was a black and white pygmy goat she'd named after her late husband, because they both wore a nice salt and pepper beard. Theodore the second had been her world for a while, but slowly, especially over the last few years, she'd become less *family-friend* to us and more *family*. She'd worried he might be lonely when she opened a cupcake shop with Caroline and joined a dozen groups around town, so she'd decided to find him a wife. She'd even gotten her license to officiate weddings, so she could handle the ceremony. Cookie took very little more seriously in life than the happiness of her loved ones.

"Well," Cookie said, climbing onto the stool at my side. "When will we meet it?"

I frowned at her choice of words when referencing my child. "Next summer. Let's not call the baby It."

"What should I call it?" she asked.

Mom perked at the question. "Do you have any names in mind?"

"Do you want a boy or girl?" Cookie asked. "Or both? Triplets? How soon will you know? Do you want to know?"

Evan made a strangled sound behind me. I didn't have to look to know we'd lost him at triplets. I'd had a similar, though more silent, response.

"I think we should talk about something else," I said. "We just found out an hour ago."

Cookie shrugged.

Mom leaned in her direction. "We should have a luncheon at the inn to celebrate. Something cozy and festive."

"I'll check the inn's calendar and get it on the books," Cookie said. "I love a good luncheon."

Cookie took my role as innkeeper after I moved in with Evan full time. Theodore and his goat wife, Clementine, lived in a fancied-up stall at the stables with the horses. Cookie made Dad promise to keep the stall beside theirs available in case the goat couple had kids.

Mom narrowed her eyes, and I followed her gaze to Evan. "There's something else." Her attention flickered to me, then back to my husband.

He glanced in my direction, then nodded.

"What?" we all said in near unison.

My heartrate doubled with concern.

We'd told them everything about my doctor's appointment. Was there something he needed to tell me?

"Dr. Bright is worried about Holly's blood pressure," he began.

Everyone gasped.

I shoved his arm. *Jeez. Tattletale.* In light of the pregnancy news, I'd completely forgotten. "It's not that serious," I said, comforting the sets of wide eyes staring back.

Mom pressed a palm to her chest.

"I am fine," I said.

Dad groaned. "Doesn't sound fine."

"Sounds serious," Mom agreed.

Cookie helped herself to a whoopie pie under a glass dome on the counter. "High blood pressure is no joke. That's why I work so hard to eat right and get exercise."

I rolled my eyes, knowing she likely planned to wash her lunchtime dessert down with some of her special Earl Gray tea, which was heavily laced with peppermint schnaps. She rarely left home without a thermos full of the concoction from fall to spring.

"I'll be on my best behavior," I said. "Pinky promise."

Evan shifted beside me. "We should probably stop having breakfast at the pie shop five days a week."

I guffawed, spinning on my lollipop to face him. "It's the Twelve Pies of Christmas right now. You said we could try them all."

His lips quirked up on one side. "I did. Maybe we can share a slice instead of buying two."

I pursed my lips and turned back to the counter. "Fine." I made a mental note to research ways to quickly lower my blood pressure so I wouldn't miss out on all the holiday foods I loved this year.

"Well," Mom said. "Speaking of pies, and before you run off to work, I want to tell you how impressed I am that you were able to get tickets to the progressive dinner, Evan." She smiled. "That was quite a feat. Every other person I've spoken to has said what a hit this year's event will be. Apparently, tickets sold out the same day they went on sale."

Evan puffed with pride. "Pays to be the sheriff some days."

The mayor and his team had arranged a town-wide progressive dinner that included the vast majority of cafés and restaurants in Mistletoe. Ticket holders were entitled to a seven-course meal, including drinks and desserts, scattered all across town. Each ticket came with a list of participating locations and the courses they'd serve. On the night of the dinner, participants would take their tickets door to door and get a hole punch on that course from the host where they stopped. Each course lasted half an hour with fifteen minutes in between for travel. The massive event would take five hours.

"I'm sorry I can't join you," Mom said, pressing her bottom lip forward in a mini pout. "When I was young, the progressive dinner was an annual event. My parents and I never missed. The whole town got all gussied up. It was a very big deal. A chance to see everyone who was otherwise too busy for a visit this time of year."

"It's not too late to change your mind," Evan said. "You still have that ticket."

"It was a tough choice," she said, "but I think it's more important for me to be here that night. It was quite an honor for the Hearth to be chosen as one of the stops. I'll still get to see a good portion of the town this way. And I've already passed my ticket on to Libby."

Dad kissed the top of her head and grinned.

We all knew she'd rather serve than be served, and being a dessert stop on a town-wide dining event was her absolute dream come true.

Cookie pulled a thermos from her bag and poured her special tea into the lid that doubled as a cup. "I can't wait," she said, lifting the drink in Evan's direction. "To the sheriff!"

"Don't mention it," Evan said.

"I love to mention it," Cookie countered. "I've been bragging to the ladies at the goat yoga studio before every class. They're all jealous. I love it."

I raised my mug to my lips, enjoying the moment.

Evan rose and kissed my head. "I've got to get going. My shift started ten minutes ago. Call me if you need anything," he told me.

"Will do."

"She's in good hands," Dad promised.

The look exchanged between the men made me think they'd agreed to roll me in bubble wrap for the next several months with my arms pinned to my sides.

I watched Evan leave. When I turned back to my coffee, the mug had been swapped for cinnamon tea.

"This is better for the baby," Mom said. "Too much caffeine isn't good for anyone."

I looked from the snowman shaped mug with a cinnamon stick stirrer to the coffee I'd barely touched, now being sipped by my dad.

"I'll get you a bowl of soup and a sandwich," Mom said. "I'm guessing all you've had today is pie and coffee."

She wasn't wrong.

Cookie swigged her tea and grinned. "They took your coffee."

Mom pressed a hip against the swinging kitchen door, then paused. "When I come back, I want to hear every word Dr. Bright said. Don't leave anything out."

I thought of the paperwork in my pocket, instructing me to watch my diet, and I had no doubt the author of that pamphlet had never spent Christmas in Mistletoe.

Chapter Three

I decided to visit the farm on my own the next day after breakfast. Evan's shift started before dawn, and while I was a morning person, generally, that didn't kick in until after the sun rose.

I'd had a mug of half-caff coffee with oatmeal and fruit for breakfast, then tidied our already immaculate home and fluffed the Christmas tree before getting dressed to leave. I wasn't good at being still, especially when there was so much to do on the farm, and if I stayed home alone too long, I'd undoubtedly help myself to pie.

I called Mom first, but she insisted things were under control at the Hearth, and she encouraged me to soak in a bath or go back to bed.

It was as if she didn't know me at all.

I dialed Cookie next. She was thrilled to hear I had time on my hands.

So I dressed in my softest jeans and a navy blue Mistletoe Sheriff's Department hoodie, then paired my puffy down parka with my favorite snow boots and headed for the door.

Reindeer Games sent more than three hundred holiday cards every Christmas, each with a personalized message inside.

Anyone who stayed at the inn on the farm became family, and we took that very seriously. Guests were given a stocking from the fireplace, embroidered with their name before arrival, and if we did things right, they left with wonderful memories to last a lifetime as well. The holiday cards were a nice reminder that they weren't forgotten.

The innkeeper sent the cards as part of her duties. I'd handled the mailing when I played that role. Now Cookie was in charge, and she wasn't a fan of all the stamps and signing. I promised to be there inside the hour. Even with a bandaged hand, I could stuff envelopes, add mailing labels and stamps.

I parked my big red Reindeer Games pickup outside the inn and stepped carefully onto the salted pavement.

Dozens of visitors in brightly colored coats, hats, and gloves sprinkled the field across the way. They rolled snow into massive spheres and stacked them into snowmen, each vying to win the annual Build a Big Frosty competition. It was the oldest of our farm's Reindeer Games and always a huge hit.

People came from across the country and throughout the world to experience the magic of Mistletoe at Christmas. For many, a visit to the farm was an annual tradition held for generations. I loved being a part of so many lives.

My gaze caught on a trio of children pulling a baby on a little sled, and my new mama's heart swelled with anticipation. I couldn't wait to meet my little snowflake. Was it too soon to feel that way? Was Snowflake a good name?

A year from now, Evan and I would have our own baby and little sled.

I covered my mouth with one mitten, beyond delighted by the thought.

The low whirr of an approaching engine drew my attention to an arriving four-wheeler. Gage, one of the farmhands, nodded at me in recognition, then carried on, driving a painfully slow path over the walkway to the inn, a little deicing apparatus attached to the rear, dispersed masses of blue granules across already dry cement.

I tucked a box of my jewelry-making materials under one crooked arm as I followed the ATV to the inn's porch.

Melting old bottles into the shapes of holiday candies and treats was a hobby of mine until enough people asked to buy the pieces right off my person. Now it was a full-time business, selling both online and in local shops and stores. I earned nearly as much as Evan last year, and I was on my way to doubling that before the new year. I couldn't wait to buy Evan an epic Christmas gift, now that I could afford one. The thought elated me as long as I didn't think too long or hard about the reason for my recent popularity.

My gumdrop earrings and charms sold faster than I could make them, creating a back-order log as long as Santa's toy list, all thanks to an obnoxious podcasting duo who'd featured me on their show last Christmas.

My knack for stumbling into a killer's clutches while attempting to find the truth was a bit of an embarrassment for me, good fun for them, and they'd nicknamed me the Gumdrop Gumshoe for my effort. Hence the wild uptick in these particular jewelry sales.

I walked a fine line between irritation and gratitude.

Currently, however, I walked the driest, clearest path in town.

Gage parked the four-wheeler and darted ahead of me on foot to the inn's porch steps.

I eyeballed him as I passed.

He waited, without speaking, presumably assigned by Dad to keep me from slipping on slick ground or rolling down the short flight of wooden steps.

"Thank you," I said, when I reached the door and rang the bell. "I've got it from here."

Cookie greeted me with a grin. "You look pretty."

"Thanks," I said. "So do you."

She bobbed a curtsy, pulling the skirt of her red velvet dress out a bit on each side. She wore black tights and Mary Janes with a white cashmere shawl.

"You've got a real Mrs. Claus vibe going."

Her blue eyes widened. "You think so? That's what I was aiming for, because folks seem to like that so much. Adds to the whole appeal of staying at an inn that Santa built. Don't you think?"

I tried not to smile. My parents befriended a man named Christopher, with a white beard and a crew of relatively *not tall* men, who designed, erected, and finished the inn in record time. Christopher did a miraculous job and regularly got tongues wagging about the possibility he was Santa Claus. I did my best to just enjoy the force of nature he inarguably was.

"He's collecting toys again for the annual toy drive," she said. "The whole office is filled with donations. We need to schedule another wrapping party, or I'll never get them ready in time for the Christmas Eve pickup."

"I can help with that," I said. I loved our newest tradition of wrapping toy donations while chatting and snacking with my closest family members and friends.

"Appreciated!" Cookie said. "What do you think about the decorations? I tried to remember the way you set it up last year. Did I miss anything?"

I shucked off my coat, hat, and gloves, then hung them from the pegs in the foyer.

The inn stayed dressed for the season all year round, but we kicked things up a notch from the day after Halloween through the first week of January. The office stood just inside the front door, and to the right a parlor sat opposite. In between, the foyer stretched into a broad hallway on the first floor, showcasing a winding staircase, bookended by life-sized nutcrackers. The décor was traditional, in shades of scarlet, green, and gold. A fire crackled on the parlor's hearth. And a fully adorned, cheerfully lit Christmas tree twinkled merrily in every room, nook, and cranny.

Additional spaces on this floor included a formal dining room, massive eat-in kitchen with breakfast nook and walk-in pantry, a laundry room, mudroom, gathering space, and library. The innkeeper's suite stood near the back door, beyond the kitchen, giving Cookie a place of respite and privacy from her duties and guests. The spacious bedroom and bath were magazine worthy, and her sitting area included yet another Christmas tree.

Upstairs, six well-appointed guest rooms remained perpetually decked out for the season as well, each with a little fireplace and, yes, a tree.

I smiled as I thought of my days as innkeeper. It wasn't a job for the impatient or weak spirited.

"I think everything looks marvelous," I told her, speaking from the heart. "You did an incredible job."

Her cheeks flushed and her smile spread.

"Let me fix you some tea," she said, leading me to the kitchen. "I've been in here all morning, working on some new recipes for the kids."

"Your guests have children?" I asked.

She frowned, visibly confused, as she moved into position behind the island. "No."

We stared, awkwardly frozen, for a long beat before she snapped back to life.

"Oh!" She chuckled. "No, for Theodore and Clementine's babies. She's not pregnant, but I like to plan ahead. I was thinking about making a baby goat calendar next year. The last few did pretty well, but maybe it's time to switch things up."

I nodded. Each year, Cookie commissioned a calendar she called "A Goat for All Seasons," and Libby's husband, Ray, mocked up pictures of Theodore doing different things for every month. Snowboarding. Jet skiing. Salsa dancing. The whole thing was a hoot and raised thousands for local charities. "Sounds adorable."

"Thanks! Maybe your kid can be in next year's calendar."

I frowned, imagining my baby as a little goat.

"Hey," Cookie said. "Have you told Caroline your news?"

"Yeah, last night. She came over the minute I uttered the words," I said, taking a seat on a stool across the island. I set my box of jewelry-making materials on the chair beside mine. "Literally. She got in her car and drove while we continued the conversation. She didn't hang up until I let her in the house."

Cookie set a kettle of water on the stove. "Libby?"

"Has been sending me pictures of Evan as a baby all day. Ray volunteered a free pregnancy shoot for me and Evan in the spring." My husband generally avoided having his picture taken, and I wasn't keen on being the center of attention, but I didn't hate the idea of commemorating the experience. I didn't plan to do this again. I'd liked being the only child, and I loved the idea of giving all of myself to only one offspring.

Evan made it clear we could have zero children or twelve and he'd be equally as happy, because I was happy. I really had picked a winner with him.

"Fun!" She set two mugs on the counter, then produced a tray with sugar cubes, honey, cinnamon sticks, and cream. "Are you hungry?"

"I could eat," I said.

Cookie went to work in the refrigerator and returned with vanilla yogurt and fruit, then added granola and a stack of graham crackers.

"Where are the cinnamon rolls and bacon?" I asked. Cookie hooked me on the combo early this year. Now it was the only thing I wanted when I came to the inn before noon.

She hiked a thin white brow. "Has your blood pressure come down since yesterday?"

"Maybe."

"Hmph." She scooped fruit and yogurt into a white parfait dish, creating pretty layers, before topping them with granola and a whole strawberry. "There you are."

The kettle whistled and she turned to make the tea.

"Did you say you were working on a recipe for Theodore's future kids?" I asked, sinking a spoon into my parfait.

"I'm trying," she said, "but I can't quite get it right."

"Won't goats eat anything?" I asked.

Cookie pulled her chin back in offense. "Theodore is a very picky eater. I can only assume his kids will be as well."

"Right," I said, recalling all the things I had seen him eat, including the bottom half of my favorite jacket when I left it on a fence post last spring. "Sorry."

"It's okay," she said. "Goats get a bad rep. They're just misunderstood."

I sipped the tea she set before me, then sweetened it with sugar cubes and honey.

"Is that what you're wearing tonight?" she asked. "It's supposed to snow, but I picked this outfit for the progressive dinner. Plus, Caroline's coming, and I always feel like a potato next to her."

I smiled. "You and everyone on earth."

Caroline was my best friend and Cookie's business partner. She was also a leggy blonde, raised by the mayor in the spotlight. She had grace, poise, and naturally unblemished skin no amount of product could ever achieve.

"I'm glad she can come along," I said. "She never gets a break from your cupcake shop this time of year, and we all need a little time to enjoy the season."

Cookie nodded. "She's a bake-a-holic. We have enough help, but she's a perfectionist, and her name's on the logo, so she feels the product quality and customer experience reflect directly back to her."

"Yeah," I said. "Last night she warned she might run late picking us up, because she's baking all day for the event. Then she's taking the cupcakes to one of the dessert locations as a contribution to the cause." She'd hated that her shop wasn't big enough to be chosen for the dinner, but it didn't stop her from finding a way to get her products into the mix.

"So, what about the outfit?" Cookie pressed, returning me to her original question.

I looked at my hoodie and jeans. "I'll put on a holiday sweater."

She bobbed her head in approval. "You always look cute in those. Since you were a little girl."

"Mom got me hooked early," I said. I think I came home from the hospital in a holiday-themed onesie.

"Now we just have to agree on where to go for all seven courses," Cookie said. "Have you reviewed the options?"

"Not really." I had a ticket to five hours of free food, and there was a vetting process for businesses who wanted in on the action. Everything served tonight would be top tier. I only wished I could visit every spot on the roster. "I'm just excited for the girls' night out."

"Me too," Cookie agreed. "But I have definite favorites for every course." She whipped the flyer with a list of participating locations off the refrigerator and smoothed it on the island before me. "I marked them with a little red star. You look at this. I'll be right back."

"Where are you going?"

"To my office. I almost forgot, another package came for you."

I pinched my lips and focused on the flyer, about 90 percent certain I knew what she'd bring with her when she returned.

The options for each course were plentiful, providing three to five places to choose from for every section of the meal. With seven courses—hors d'oeuvre, soup, appetizer, salad, main course, desserts, and drinks—the number of possible combinations were immense. I wondered how many people, aside from my party, I'd see more than once throughout the night. We likely wouldn't see some people at all.

I skimmed Cookie's choices, and my mouth watered.

She returned a moment later and set an open box on the island beside me. "There you go. Another load of fan mail for the Gumdrop Gumshoe."

I sighed.

"I'll bet there're a lot more requests for autographs in that box. You must be making a killing on that racket," she said, sounding far more excited than I felt.

The Dead and Berried podcast was ridiculous, pairing true crimes with foods, like some kind of macabre sommeliers. The duo behind the show, goofily known as Tate the Great and Harvey from the Harvest, were a couple of amateur sleuths, perpetually chasing a story.

The guys weren't all bad, but they were highly annoying, and while I didn't agree with what they and their fans considered entertainment, they all seemed to think I was fantastic. And Cookie was right, I'd made a nice side hustle of signing the show's propaganda for fans. It was hard to be mad about that part when the money would go to doing something impressive for Evan this year. He always beat me at finding the perfect present, and for once, I planned to win.

He insisted gift giving wasn't a competition, but that was probably because he won.

I stayed at the inn as long as I could, chatting with Cookie and helping with holiday cards, then catching up on jewelry orders. I took the box of Dead and Berried fan mail with me when I left. That was a job for another day.

For now, it was time to go home and change my sweatshirt. I had a seven-course dinner awaiting me.

Chapter Four

I packed the last of my jewelry orders for shipment that afternoon and stacked them in the carrier for Evan to take to the post office tomorrow, a routine we'd begun earlier this year. I appreciated him and his ready-to-help nature beyond measure. Especially as I looked around the spare bedroom I'd converted into my business office. We'd barely finished the transition, and it was time to change everything again. This time to a nursery.

I saw the process taking shape the moment the thought entered my mind. First the room needed emptying, then Evan would paint a neutral shade of green on the walls and refresh the white trim. I'd add murals of the tree farm as a focal point on the longest wall, perfecting the details throughout the spring. Ray would gift us photos of the town, taken by him, and placed inside brushed gold frames by Libby. Cookie would surprise us with a Red Sox mobile made with felt and love, which we'd hang over a crib at the room's center. A wardrobe of next year's hottest baby trends would fill the closet, all courtesy of Auntie Caroline, and perhaps an infant-sized barn coat would hang on a wooden peg, thanks to my dad.

My imagination took the vision farther into the future, until I saw it all dimly lit, with a baby in Evan's protective arms. He'd rock and soothe our child without hesitation, especially those first few nights, while Mom kept vigilant care over me.

Tears blurred my eyes, unbidden, and I laughed at the way a human the size of an apple seed had already hijacked my emotions. "Get your head in the game, Gray," I told myself. "We've got five hours of fun with friends and food ahead of us. Tighten up!"

I spun for a look in the nearby mirror at my long red sweater and black leggings. A simple outfit with big purpose. Now I wouldn't have to unbutton my jeans before course three.

My phone buzzed with the message I'd been waiting for all afternoon. Caroline was in my driveway.

I bundled up and grabbed my bag, then locked the front door as I left home. I climbed into the back seat of Caroline's new high-end SUV and hugged Libby, my seatmate, immediately.

Cookie and Caroline called out their hellos from the front.

"Ready?" Caroline asked.

We whooped like teens on their way to a concert, and she reversed out of the drive.

The interior of Caroline's car always smelled of leather and spun sugar. I supposed the latter was a result of baking the world's best cupcakes for a living. Her long blonde hair hung in waves over her shoulders, a dramatic contrast to her elegant black dress coat.

Cookie wore a red cloak trimmed in fur.

Libby stared at me, and my smile drooped.

"What?" I asked, giving her a once-over.

She'd worn black leather pants with a shimmery gold tunic beneath a leather coat. Her matching hoop earrings and signature red lipstick complemented her thick auburn hair. Very sassy Boston native of her.

I loved it.

Something flashed in her green eyes before she spoke. "How are you feeling?"

"Fine." I tried not to envy her thick black lashes as they curved up toward neatly sculpted brows. Or the perfect application of liquid eyeliner, forming razor-sharp points on the outside corner of each eye.

I struggled finding the patience for basic mascara and lip gloss.

"You're not stressed out?" she asked. "This time of year always sends you into a tailspin."

I got comfortable in my seat and ignored the comment. "Not this time. Cookie's running the inn now. I just make jewelry and help around the farm as needed. Plus, your brother spoils me pretty severely. It's a cushy life."

"When do you see the doctor again?"

I rolled my head against the seat back to meet her gaze. "Next month."

Her eyes narrowed. "Why so long?"

"Why not?" I asked.

"Uh, your blood pressure," she said smartly, as if I was completely daft.

"She's eating healthier," Cookie chimed in from the front. "And giving up caffeine."

The promises weren't completely true, but I let it go, so I could have a good night.

Libby crossed her arms. "Good. I'm not trying to be a pill. I just worry. Historically, this is a bad month for you, and now there are two of you—one of which is my niece or nephew. So, you can understand my apprehension."

Understanding didn't make her pestering any less annoying. "December is a great month for me," I said, determined to nip this in the bud. "Arguably, my favorite of all the months."

"You sure about that, Gumshoe?" she challenged.

I blew out a long breath.

Outside my window, the sun hung low in the sky, thanks to daylight saving. Porch and landscape lighting flashed on as we motored past. Inflatable Santas, grinches, and elves rose to life on lawns and roofs.

Chuck Berry sang "Run, Rudolph, Run" on the local radio station, playing only Christmas music until the new year.

I let my eyelids sink shut, enjoying the moment and letting my heart swell with joy. I had a perfect night ahead of me, with three of my favorite humans, townsfolk I barely had time to chat with these days, and the equivalent of a walking tour of downtown Mistletoe at Christmas. I wouldn't let anything spoil this night. Certainly not my blood pressure or a sister-in-law who cared. I opened my eyes and smiled at Libby, then squeezed her hand. "This year is different."

"Where to first?" Caroline asked, as rows of festive homes gave way to the bright lights of the town square.

"Cup of Cheer," Cookie said. "They have something I want to see."

"Anyone else?" Caroline asked.

Cup of Cheer was off the beaten path a bit, situated away from the town square, in a mostly residential neighborhood, but it had become one of my favorite lunch spots. I'd met the owner, Alice, last Christmas and immediately loved her. She was a recent transplant from Sweden, a delight to speak with, and our energies matched incredibly well. Her enthusiasm for her home and family, not to mention her passion for this business, were all things to which I easily related.

Libby and I gave nods and statements of acquiescence.

"All right," Caroline said. "Oh, hey." She stopped at the light on the square and fished something from beneath her seat. "This is for you." She passed a neatly wrapped box between the seats to my hands.

"Christmas isn't for another week and a half," I said.

"It's a blood pressure cuff. You can test yourself every day."

My smile failed.

Libby grinned.

"Thank you," I said. It was the thought that counted.

Caroline smiled, catching my eyes in the rearview mirror. "Did you see your name in the crossword puzzle yesterday?" she asked. "I thought of you immediately. Are you and Evan still doing those?"

I perked, thankful for the change of subject. "Yes! I saw that! I loved it."

"Very cool," she agreed.

"Did you do the puzzle today?" I asked.

She shook her head. "Today was nuts. No time."

"My last name was in there today," I said. "Well, my old last name. White. I'll be dreaming of a blank Christmas."

"Cool!"

Cookie harrumphed. "Must be nice to have such a festive name."

Caroline glanced at the woman in her passenger seat. "You're Cookie Cutter. That's a very festive name!"

Cookie offered a bland expression. "Well, I don't see it showing up in the paper."

I looked to Libby. Time for another subject change. "How's the new private investigations business coming along?"

She scrunched her freckle-covered nose. "There's a shocking amount of infidelity in this town, but Zane takes most of the cases where one spouse suspects another of cheating. Spoiler alert, if you think they might be stepping out on you, they probably are."

I cringed, thankful yet again for Evan as my husband.

Caroline met my eyes in the mirror. "Zane's loving it," she said. "He feels like a vigilante, busting middle-aged cheaters and stopping their lives of civil crime. He's stumped by the snowmen thief, though."

"Snowman thief?" Cookie asked, at the same time I said, "How do you steal a snowman?"

"Inflatables," Libby clarified. "Twelve-foot Frostys are disappearing all over town. It's probably just kids, but we can't find them or the snowmen."

I considered the dilemma for a long beat. Then an idea came to mind. "Why don't I buy a couple and set them up on my lawn? You can come over for a stakeout, maybe catch the thieves in action?"

Libby looked pensively in my direction. "I can't just stay there around the clock."

"They probably don't work by light of day," I said. "You and Ray can come for dinner every night. Or we can buy one of those teddy bears with the nanny cameras and set it in my front window."

Libby stilled, eyes fixed on me.

I braced for her warning to leave the petty theft alone.

"I'll bring the bear and the snowmen this week," she said. "Warn your husband. He won't like it."

"I don't know why he'd care," I said.

The SUV slowed, and Caroline initiated the turn signal before pulling carefully into the alleyway beside Cup of Cheer.

Cookie shifted forward on her seat. "I've been waiting for this," she said. "The café is full of goats, and there's supposed to be a big one out back now!"

The SUV cruised slowly around the side of the building to the rear parking lot, and the passengers of our vehicle collectively gasped.

"Whoa," Libby said. "You weren't kidding."

A massive twelve-foot straw goat stood outside the door, wrapped with wide red ribbons on its legs, neck, and snout. Tufts of hay stretched down from its chin, forming a giant goat beard. Two tightly bundled horns curled back from its crown.

People took photos in front of the structure on their way into the café.

Cookie's breath steamed up her window as she stared through the glass.

She was the first to climb out after Caroline parked. She raised her camera for a photograph, then approached the giant goat slowly and with reverence. "Holy cow. This thing is really made of straw! I thought it was an optical illusion."

We followed her along the cobblestone path for a closer look.

"How much hay do you think this took?" Caroline asked.

I craned my neck to take in the goat's full height then reached out on instinct and grazed my fingertips along one leg. "Good question. And how long did it take to create this?"

"Also why?" Libby asked, passing us on her way to the café door.

Caroline's fair brows tented as she examined the strangest thing I'd ever seen. "I knew goats were a big part of Alice's traditions, but this is wild. I can't believe I didn't notice something this big being built. I don't normally get back here, but I'm downtown every day at the cupcake shop. You'd think I might've noticed all the materials being delivered. A parade of trucks filled with hay should've gotten my attention."

"Why don't we go inside and ask?" Libby called from the small porch. Her petite frame shivered in the frigid air. "I'm too cold to speculate out here."

"Spoken like a true private eye," I said, following for my own reason. I was starving!

We filed through the front door and took a moment to marvel at the décor. Alice had added thousands of additional white twinkle lights to the already pretty interior. The overall color scheme was white on white with pale blue and golden accents, an homage to the Swedish flag. She'd hung paper snowflakes from rafters, and white Christmas trees stood jauntily in corners and alcoves. Dozens of little goats hung from their branches.

"Holly!" Alice cut through the crowd, moving quickly in our direction. "Caroline, Cookie, Libby!" Her arms opened, and she pulled us into a quick group hug before jumping back. "I hoped you'd choose this spot for appetizers. I'm so excited to be part of this. Can you believe Cup of Cheer was selected? Your town just keeps making me feel as if I've been here all my life instead of the five minutes that is more accurate."

I grinned. "It's all part of the grand plan to never let you leave."

She laughed, and her fair cheeks pinked. She'd plaited her long blonde hair into an updo and paired black flats with an ice blue sweater dress for the event. I envied her fresh-faced look and could never quite guess her age. If she was an actress, instead of an incredible restauranteur, she could easily play characters from thirteen to thirty. Based on the many conversations we'd had this year, I guessed her at roughly the latter.

"I think we have to get started," she said. "Grab a seat."

My group and I found a table for four and waited while Alice got the room's attention.

"Welcome," she called. "I'm so glad you're here. I'm honored to kick off this night's feast for you and share some of my family's favorite holiday recipes. Many of you know I am originally from Sweden. Specifically, the town of Gävle."

My smile grew as I watched and listened. Alice's pride and joy when speaking of her roots resonated deeply with me, and I instantly loved her all the more.

"Some of the more perceptive of you might've noticed the newly erected goat sculpture out front." She paused while the crowd laughed. "That is also part of our Christmas traditions. In Gävle, a giant straw goat is erected on the square every year in honor of our traditional Yule Goat. I've gotten a lot of varied explanations about the origin over the years. Some say it has to do with Norse mythology, others say it has to do with the magic of the fall harvest. My family just enjoys the tradition for what it is. Deeply, deeply Swedish." She clasped her hands before her and glanced pointedly around the room. "My grandmother was especially fond of the Yule Goat, and after her passing last year, extended family members helped ship her entire collection of related baubles, ornaments, and treasures to me, as that was her wish. I've displayed them all here tonight for you to enjoy. I want to share my traditions as warmly and openly with you as you have all shared yours with me."

Alice checked her watch. "I'd better stop talking and bring on the appetizers, or you'll all be late for your next course!"

"Oh, boy," Cookie said, fizzing with energy at my side. "I knew I loved this place. Now I need to visit Sweden at Christmas. Maybe I can sneak away after Thanksgiving next year."

"That sounds wonderful," I said. "You'll have an amazing time."

"Theodore probably won't want to go, now that he's married," she said. "Makes me miss Theodore the first. He did whatever I wanted, and we had the best of times."

I set a palm over Cookie's hand on the table and gave her fingers a gentle squeeze. She didn't often talk about her late husband, but I knew she missed him most around the holidays. I guessed that was one reason she stayed so busy this time of year. Working at the inn and cupcake shop, caroling, dancing, and apparently taking goat yoga, among other things.

"We're bringing a mini julbord, or smorgasbord, to each table with a sampling of popular appetizers," Alice said. "Most are served all year round. Usually this would be served buffet-style, but we're on a timeline, and every delicious moment counts. I hope you'll find a new favorite among the offering tonight."

The Cup of Cheer staff descended on the tables, delivering wooden trays with matching bowls and platters on top. Rectangles of white linen cardstock lay before each food, a Swedish word written in neat calligraphy.

"The julskinka is a traditional Christmas ham," Alice explained. "The seasoning process takes nearly two weeks to complete. You'll also find cured salmon, saffron buns, and beetroot salad. We'll be around with pitchers and cups for glogg or julmust while you make your plates."

Alice moved into the mix with a pitcher in each hand, assisting her staff with the work. "Glogg is a delicious warm, spiced wine, and for those who aren't partaking in spirits tonight, julmust is our version of a holiday cola."

I was a little disappointed to miss out on the glogg, but simply recalling the reason brought a smile to my face.

Cookie passed out the stacks of plates and silverware rolled in napkins while the drinks were delivered. Then we all dug in.

Caroline sipped the glogg, then dotted her lips with a napkin. "Is anyone planning to attend the antiques show?"

"Me," Cookie said. "I wouldn't miss it."

"Meh," Libby said. "I can't imagine finding free time for anything before the end of the month. If you're organizing another outing, you'll have to send me pictures and tell me about it afterward."

Caroline tipped her head and pulled her lips into a frown. "I'm going to try to get there. It's kind of a big deal. The last stop after thirty years of travel. Apparently, the show's lost funding as a result of diminishing interest. Dad really worked to convince the producers to choose Mistletoe for their big goodbye."

"I'll go," I said, glancing from Caroline to Cookie, then back. "Sounds like fun." I didn't know much about antiques, but another day out with friends sounded like an excellent use of time.

Something crashed nearby, and we turned collectively toward the sound.

"What was—" Before I finished the question, I spotted Alice, tussling with a woman I didn't recognize. Both struggled for claim of a small metal goat.

Libby jerked to her feet. "What's going on?" she called, her naturally sassy voice suddenly an octave lower and wholly authoritative. Her smooth Boston accent clung to the words, reminding me so much of her brother, I smiled.

The room went silent.

The stranger stilled, looking toward the gaping crowd. Alice took the opportunity to knock her opponent down.

A gasp rolled through the room, and the woman released a sound like *oomph* as she slid backward on the slick marble floor.

I set my napkin aside and rose, unsure what to do next.

The woman jolted upright and ran out the door, leaving us all to stare in her wake.

"What on earth?" Cookie exclaimed. "Are you okay?"

I followed her gaze to Alice, who smoothed a palm over her falling updo, nodded woodenly, then walked quickly into the kitchen.

My friends, and the rest of the guests, returned to their seats, exchanging confused looks and fervent whispers.

Cookie refilled her wine and selected a saffron bun. "The night's getting interesting and we're only at the appetizer course."

"Should I check on her?" I asked.

"Nah," Cookie said. "But you might want to open Caroline's gift and check your blood pressure."

I gave her some heavy side-eye as my heart pumped wildly in my chest, then I fixed my gaze on the kitchen door where Alice disappeared.

Chapter Five

I slipped away from the table and made my way to Alice when she returned from the kitchen.

Others took notice but continued with their appetizers and discussions, though most, no doubt, still spoke of her and the recent kerfuffle.

She'd fixed her hair and straightened her dress, but her cheeks remained flushed. A small metal goat was still clutched to her chest.

She cringed as I approached. "I'm so sorry about that," she whispered. "I shouldn't have shoved her. I didn't expect her to fall."

"I don't think she expected to get shoved," I said, offering a small smile. "You did what was necessary to end the dispute. Do you know her?"

I glanced at the object in her hands and waited, hoping she'd volunteer the details I wanted to hear.

She swept the room with her gaze, then returned her attention to me with a sigh. "No. Not really," she said. "She had lunch here yesterday and seemed nice enough. So when I saw her examining Grandmother's baubles, I approached to tell her about their history. She seemed spooked, so I asked about her instead. Then she tried to leave, but she still had this goat in her hands. I told her to return the figurine, but she kept moving, so I grabbed her wrist. She tried to get free, and I reached for the goat with my other hand, afraid it would fall."

Her voice shook as she spoke, and her breaths, though deep, were ragged. "It doesn't make any sense," she said. "If she'd attempted to take anything else, I probably would've just let her go, but I couldn't—" Despair crept over her features. "These are part of my heritage. Grandmother wanted them with me."

I stepped closer and set a hand on her arm. "I understand. No one can fault you for your reaction."

"Should we call the sheriff's department?" she asked.

"Probably," I said. "At least to file a report. Do you want me to keep an eye on the time before the next course and escort everyone out while you make the call?"

She shook her head. "No. Nothing was stolen, and no one was hurt. I think it will be okay to call after you all move on to the soup portion of the night."

"Okay," I said. That seemed reasonable enough to me as well. "Do you mind if we come back when the dinner ends and check on you?"

Alice smiled. "I'd appreciate that."

I considered returning to my seat, but a question wrestled into mind. "Has anyone else shown an interest that strong in the goats?"

She puzzled for a moment, giving my question real thought. "Now that you mention it, a lot of people have. I get questions all day about their age and origin. I had no idea Americans would love them so much."

"Neither did I," I muttered, scanning the dining area and noticing the sheer volume of goats. "They are pretty cool."

Many were made of straw. Some were blown glass or ceramic. Others, like the one in her hands, seemed to be made of metal. And this one was a mix of brown and green. Copper, I realized, like the Statue of Liberty.

"I think so," she agreed, "but I'm clearly biased."

I turned to go back to my seat when something else popped into mind. "Have those people shown interest in your grandma's collection, specifically? Or the Yule Goats in general?"

Alice frowned. "Both, I suppose." Her gaze slid away for a long beat, and I waited, certain she wasn't finished with her answer. "I guess most of their questions were specific to Grandmother's pieces. Why?"

"I'm not sure," I said. But the Antiques Showcase was in town, which meant a lot of collectors were here as well. I couldn't help wondering if Alice's grandmother's collection held a higher monetary value than she realized, and if the woman had hoped to steal, then sell the piece Alice still held tight. "You might want to hang on to that one," I said, flicking my gaze to the item in question. "Maybe take it upstairs for safekeeping, at least until you've filed your report."

Alice lived in the space above her café, which made commuting a breeze. I'd had a similarly cakey setup when I lived at the inn where I'd worked.

Her expression shifted, and I recognized the moment she saw through the words I'd spoken to the intention underneath. "You think Grandmother's collection might be valuable."

I dipped my chin once in confirmation, not wanting to talk too long about the subject in a room full of lookie-loos and eavesdroppers.

She cast her gaze across the faces no longer pretending not to listen. "I'll try to find out, then get them insured, if that's the case." When her attention returned to me, her jaw set. "Holly, I won't ever sell them."

I nodded. "I understand."

As if summonsed, a man I'd never seen strode to our sides, hand extended in greeting. "I'm sorry to interrupt," he said. "I'm Kent George. My friends and I are on our way out, but I've enjoyed all the appetizers this afternoon. Thank you so much. What a great way to kick off this event."

"You're welcome," Alice said. "I'm deeply sorry about the disturbance."

The other members of his party waited a few feet away, ready to move on to their next course.

Kent lifted a palm to Alice. "Don't worry about it. I would've done the same thing to defend my family heirlooms. Legacy is important. So is history. Some things simply can't be replaced. Like the Copper Goat of Gävle." He stared at the figure in her hands. "Hold tight to that. Very few were ever made. You're incredibly lucky to have one."

A woman with white pixie-cut hair and a red wool coat touched his sleeve, and he turned to her with a smile.

"We aren't the only ones admiring the Yule Goats," he said.

"Certainly not," she agreed. Her gaze roamed over the displays throughout the café, then back to Alice. "You have an exquisite collection. How many are there?"

Alice's fair brow furrowed. "I'm not sure."

The woman nodded, then looked to the man. "We should get going so we aren't late for our next course."

They said their goodbyes then departed with their group.

Alice hugged the little goat to her chest as we watched them leave.

"I'll be back in a few hours," I promised. "Or I can stay if you'd like. I don't mind."

She shook her head and refreshed her smile, but it didn't reach her eyes.

"Okay," I allowed, not wanting to overstep, even if my offer was well-intended. *Like the blood pressure cuff*, I thought. "Lock up and try to rest after you give the sheriff's department a call."

* * *

Caroline hurried to unlock her car outside the pie shop, where we'd eaten dessert. I was with her in spirit but feeling so full I had to waddle. The rapidly dropping temperature and increasing snowfall changed our minds about walking to our final destination for nightcaps and coffees. Instead, we were riding in style.

I wasn't supposed to have nightcaps or coffees, so I hoped to be still and digest while the others partook and enjoyed.

Thankfully, our evening had passed without incident after leaving Cup of Cheer. I thought of Alice at least a dozen times but did my best to stay present in the moment. Getting a night out with my friends so close to Christmas was rare, and the progressive dinner was something I'd only heard about until this year. I couldn't let a would-be thief ruin any of it.

"I hope the town brings this back every Christmas," I said, especially thankful I'd had the forethought to wear my stretchy pants.

"Me too," Cookie agreed. "But this Santa dress isn't working anymore. I feel more like a stuffed Thanksgiving turkey."

"Tell me about it," Libby said. "I wanted to live in that Italian wedding soup. If I could cook, I'd never stop making it."

Caroline climbed behind the steering wheel while the rest of us piled into the SUV. "What did you think of the Christmas salad? How did I not know that was a thing?"

I'd been surprised by the Christmas salad too. No one I knew ever served it, and I couldn't wait to ask Mom if she had the recipe. I racked my brain for the ingredients and typed them into my notes app. There were walnuts and honey, chili powder and pears, avocado, and pomegranate—I groaned. If I wasn't so full, I'd be hungry again just thinking about it.

Caroline started the engine and cranked the heater.

I puffed hot breath against my mitten-covered hands, then buckled up while the defrosters did their job.

Libby leaned forward, speaking to Caroline from between the front bucket seats. "Your cupcakes and pie were the perfect ending to the night. I know there's another stop, but I don't need a nightcap or coffee. I need to digest and sleep."

"Same." We all groaned, then laughed at our united responses.

Cookie twisted in her seat when Libby sat back. "I really liked those little individual butter sculptures at the bread station. We should have those at the inn. It was a hoot lopping off the snowman parts to spread across my buns."

"Things you never expect to hear anyone say," Libby muttered, and we all laughed again.

I wiped my eyes and gazed through the windows at my passing town. The shops were closed, or closing, at this hour, but the streets were alive with folks making their ways to and from cafés and other final stops on the progressive dinner tour.

I was glad we'd decided to skip the coffees and drinks in favor of checking on Alice a little sooner.

Caroline piloted us away from the square and in the direction of Cup of Cheer.

Cookie adjusted the vents on the dashboard. "I hope a deputy came out to take a proper report about that would-be thief," she said. "I think seeing someone in person would be more comforting than just a chat by phone."

"Agreed," Libby said. "I like to think one of the deputies would take the time to check on her. I usually enjoy dinner and a show, but I'm sorry Alice had to be part of the latter."

"Yeah," we all said softly.

I warmed at the fact Alice had remained on all our minds.

Caroline slowed to navigate the residential neighborhood. "But I'll take a failed robbery attempt over the annual holiday homicide any night of the month."

My stomach twisted, and I pulled my phone from my pocket. "I'll text her and let her know we're almost there," I said. "She won't be expecting us to skip the final hour of the dinner, and I don't want to give her another scare."

"Good idea," Cookie said. "If I was her, I'd be especially cautious tonight."

I watched the screen. My message was delivered, but it wasn't opened.

"She hasn't responded," I said as Caroline made the final turn toward the large, empty lot outside Alice's café.

"Maybe she fell asleep," Libby suggested. "The trauma could've knocked her out."

Caroline made a disbelieving sound. "If it was me, I wouldn't sleep for a week. I wasn't even involved, and that whole thing has me rattled. I mean, who does that? Who tries to steal something in front of a room full of people?"

"I'll try calling," I said.

I dialed Alice's number as we parked and climbed out into the night.

Caroline, Cookie, Libby, and I gathered at the front of her SUV. The headlights illuminated a path toward the darkened café doors.

We made our way in that direction while I waited for Alice to pick up.

"Voicemail," I said a moment later, when the call rang through without answer.

Libby's strides lengthened until she took the lead. A moment later, her arm swung out to stop us. "Hold up." She crept forward, and I scanned the scene for whatever had put her on alert.

Then I saw it. The glass on the door was broken.

Caroline and Cookie moved in close, bookending me on each side.

Libby crept forward, igniting the flashlight app on her cell phone and pointing it at the shattered glass.

Caroline gripped my arm as tension ratcheted in the icy air. The SUV's headlights shut off, and Caroline gasped as we were thrown into darkness.

I wrapped my fingers around her hand, feeling suddenly unsteady on my feet.

"Um, Holly," Cookie said, tugging my opposite elbow. "I don't want to alarm anyone but—"

Libby spun and jogged back to us. "What's wrong?"

Cookie extended a finger in the direction of the enormous straw goat. "I think there's something on the ground over there, but I'm hoping you'll say it's only a shadow."

My gaze spotted the form immediately, and I willed myself to stay upright as my knees grew weak. "Oh no," I whispered. "Not again."

"Please don't let that be Alice," Caroline said, voicing the rest of my thought.

My feet rooted, and my heart broke at the possibility.

A quiet sob reached my ears, and the figure stretched slowly upright.

"Alice!" I called, racing to her side. "Oh! Thank goodness. Are you okay? Why are you out here?" I asked, confused as I watched her shiver. "Where's your coat?"

"And what happened to your window?" Libby asked.

The beam of light from Libby's phone hit the ground at our feet, and Caroline released a bloodcurdling scream. Alice hadn't been the only thing creating the strange shadow.

The café's attempted robber lay curled on the ground, slack faced and eyes unseeing.

Before me, a silent, trembling Alice clutched a bloody metal goat with blood-stained hands.

Chapter Six

An hour later, I stared in shock at evidence of the night's gruesome end.

Emergency responders surrounded the space outside Cup of Cheer. Heavy-duty orange extension cords lined the crime scene perimeter, powering a collection of strategically placed, freestanding spotlights and acting as a barrier to all who didn't belong.

The coroner and his team crouched beside the deceased.

Evan spoke with Alice inside the café. A pair of deputies stood guard at the door.

Caroline sat on the open tailgate of an ambulance. She'd been examined and treated for shock, then wrapped in a blanket and left to her boyfriend, Zane, for comfort.

Cookie, Libby, and I huddled near a freestanding heater ten feet from the giant goat, inside the line of crime scene tape but outside the ring of power cords.

Blowing snow and wind had cleared my head and pushed me into observer mode. Maybe, I thought, this was my brain's reaction to extreme stress. Maybe if I couldn't save the victim, and I didn't want to suffer the symptoms of extreme shock, I could concentrate on finding answers instead.

I strained to hear what first responders said as they moved around the scene, but whistling winds and low voices made that impossible.

"You think she did it?" Cookie asked.

"Cookie!" Libby scolded.

"No," I said. "Of course not."

"I was only asking," Cookie said. "They're definitely going to arrest her. Remember when I was caught with that nutcracker?"

I wrapped an arm around her narrow shoulders. I'd never forget the stress her situation had caused me. And she was right, this looked bad.

"The evidence isn't doing Alice any favors," Libby said. "I want a chance to talk to her, before they haul her in."

Libby had tried to get details from Alice before Evan arrived, but she wasn't talking then. The shock of finding a dead body had been more than she could process.

"Maybe that lady fell and whacked her head on the cobblestones," Cookie said. "It's not a murder site until we know it was murder." She sipped tea from the thermos kept in her purse, then tucked it away.

"I doubt she fell," Libby said.

"What do you think happened?" I asked.

Libby took a moment before answering. "It looks like someone broke into the café. The glass shards fell inside not out. I'm guessing she was responsible for that." She pointed to the victim, finally being covered by the coroner.

Cookie bobbed her head. "You think she went inside to take another stab at getting her hands on that goat?"

Libby shifted her gaze to the object in question, now bagged as evidence and clutched in a deputy's hand. "It was the only thing out here with them when we arrived."

"How much do you think it's worth?" Cookie asked.

I sighed. "Doesn't matter, because it's priceless to Alice, and she said as much to that guy during appetizers. His whole party heard her, if not the whole room."

"The entire café saw her knock that lady down too," Cookie said.

I cringed. That was also true.

The café door opened, and Evan strode outside. He pushed a hand through tussled hair, then stuffed his sheriff's hat back onto his head. His eyes met mine, and his exasperated expression went soft.

He hurried in my direction, then pulled me into his arms. Trademark scents of gingerbread and cologne wafted off of him as my cheek slid against the cool material of his coat. "How are you?"

"I'm okay. Shaken," I said. "I'm worried about Alice, and I'm so sorry for that woman."

He tightened his grip on me briefly before setting me free. "Maybe we should let the EMTs check your blood pressure." His gaze swept over my shoulder to the ambulance.

"I'm okay," I repeated. "I was never in danger."

Behind him, Libby darted into the café and waved her arms around as she spoke to the deputies.

Evan turned to follow my gaze, but instinct told me Libby had her hands full without her brother's interference.

I made a loud whimpering sound and wrapped my arms around him again, drawing his attention back to me. "Who was she?" I asked. "Is her family in town? Do they know?"

"We're working on that," Evan said. "Don't worry about any of this. I've got things under control. Why don't you let Zane give you all a ride home?"

I released him and stole a look in Zane and Caroline's direction. They'd walked away from the ambulance and were headed back to us. He held her protectively against his side, one arm curved to hold her against him.

"I can't believe this is happening again," Evan said, softly.

Cookie patted his sleeve with one small mitten-clad hand. "We're okay. Don't worry."

He released a long, laborious breath, and it rose into a white cloud above our heads. "Every year," he continued. "It's confounding. And finding you at the scene—Every. Single. Time—" He scraped a big hand down his face. "I hate it."

"Sorry, hon," I said, meaning it to my core.

"When I planned this night out for you, I thought it would be the highlight of your season. A chance to get away from all the busyness and work. A time to just enjoy yourself. How did it become the worst night of the month?"

"Don't speak so soon," I teased. "Things might get much worse."

Evan's brows knitted together. His lips pressed into a thin white line, and his cheeks went red.

"Too soon?"

"Not funny," he said.

Cookie refilled the cap-cup from her thermos. "It's kind of funny, because it's true."

Zane and Caroline reached our group, and Cookie offered Zane the thermos.

He accepted and took a generous swig.

"Impressive," I said, when he didn't burst into a fit of coughing or begin shedding tears.

Caroline took my hand. "Are you ready to go? I really want out of here." Her gaze slid in the direction of the coroner and his team, now lifting a bagged body onto a gurney for transport.

"Of course. Just one more minute, okay?" I attempted to tell her about Libby's meeting with Alice inside the café using only my eyes.

Caroline stepped closer, her emotion-filled gaze sliding over me. "You should go home and rest after all this," she said. "It's been a lot, and probably also check your blood pressure."

I bit my tongue against a building scream. I could not spend the next six or seven months under everyone's constant, evaluating gaze. "I am fine. I had a nice dinner with friends, then stood outside this café for an hour. Nothing has happened to me."

"Yes, but the shock," she said, pleading.

I rubbed my forehead and made a mental note to teach my friend group some secret message hand signals. Two fingers pressed against my right temple means I'm stalling for time while Libby questions a murder suspect. One finger waved between us means stop telling me to check my blood pressure.

"Where's Libby?" Caroline asked, finally noticing we were missing one party member.

"Talking to Alice," Zane said, having already clocked her position.

I dropped my hand back to my side and watched steam plume from Evan's head.

"What in the hell is she doing in there?" he asked, spinning to glare through the café's broken glass.

"She's comforting Alice," I said. "She's our friend, and she's terrified. Alice doesn't have any family here. They're all overseas. I can't even imagine what she's feeling." The thought stopped me. "Goodness. I hope she called someone. She shouldn't be alone through this." Alice and I were great friends, but we weren't family, and it would mean everything to her if someone could make the trip from Sweden.

Cookie inched closer to the giant Yule Goat, seemingly mesmerized. The long red ribbons at its legs, neck, and snout whipped and snapped in the growing wind. "I wish Theodore was here," she said softly. "This big statue would blow his mind. He's never seen this much straw in his life." She turned to Evan. "If Alice needs help taking this down, give me a call."

Evan blinked. "I don't—"

"You can let her know," I told Cookie. "She's not under arrest. Right?"

We looked at Evan.

He scowled. "Not yet."

"Not at all," Libby called, marching swiftly back in our direction. "I hate to make your night a little worse, big brother," she said. "But my client is innocent, and I'm going to prove it."

My jaw dropped, and my heart leapt. A giddy laugh slipped through my lips.

Evan shot me a warning look, and I did my best to appear less delighted. "You're what? An attorney now?" he asked. Evan played cool most days, but he wasn't over the fact that his sister had announced her intention to open a private investigation firm last year, or that she'd been overwhelmed with business since hanging out her sign.

In truth, he probably wished she'd go to law school and give up her current career.

"What did Alice say?" I asked.

Libby squared her shoulders, then bounced her attention around our friend group while she relayed the facts. "According to Alice, someone broke into the café. She heard the sound of shattering glass and ran downstairs, but no one was there. She thought a tree with too many glass baubles had tipped over or something equally irritating, but commonplace, had occurred. Then she saw the broken door and looked outside. Someone was on the ground, and she went to help. When she got out here, she recognized the woman who tried to steal the goat earlier. Then she saw the wound and tried to stop the bleeding, but it was too late."

"Was the copper goat the murder weapon?" Cookie asked.

"No," Libby said. "She carried it downstairs with her when she heard the glass break, determined not to let it out of her sight."

"The victim was stabbed," Evan added. He set his hands on his hips, looking as if he might explode.

"Oh." Cookie glanced at Libby, then me, before turning her eyes to Evan. "That's that then. I was afraid Alice's prints were on the murder weapon."

"They probably are," Evan said.

Libby rolled her eyes. "The victim was stabbed with a knife from the café kitchen, but clearly it was stolen during the break-in, along with a bunch of her grandmother's heirlooms."

"The knife, which Alice confirmed as one of hers," Evan added, "was located in a nearby dumpster by one of my deputies. Thankfully this was trash day for the neighborhood, so there wasn't much else in there yet."

I weighed Evan's and Libby's words against the crime scene and the facts of the night. "Did Alice tell you the victim tried to steal from her during the appetizers?" I asked Evan. "The whole café saw it happen."

"I heard," he said. "And that's not helping her case."

His tone irritated me, though I understood his frustration. Probably, in other towns, a group of locals wouldn't butt into his investigations.

But he lived here.

And married me.

"A guy talked to her on his way out," I went on. "He said those Yule Goats were worth a lot of money."

"Also aware," Evan said. "I've asked Alice for a list of attendees, and she's walked the café with my deputy, noting the missing items. All Yule Goats."

The fact her heirloom goats were the target didn't surprise me. "The man's name was Kent George," I reported. Or at least that was the name he'd given us.

Thinking of the appetizer participants reminded me that some killers like to come back to the crime scene. I turned in a small circle, scanning the greater area while the group continued to talk.

Being in a mostly residential neighborhood, versus closer to the town square, meant significantly fewer spectators on the street, taking amateur footage with their phones, and speculating about what happened. But every porch in sight had at least one person on it, bundled up and watching closely.

I didn't blame them, but I wished they'd go inside.

A familiar pickup pulled onto the grass at the edge of the barricaded lot, and Ray jumped out, immediately in a sprint.

Libby broke away and met him at the crime scene tape, lifting it to guide him underneath.

"Looks like the gang's all here," Evan grumped.

Ray extended his hand to Evan for a shake, then offered the same to Zane. "I got here as soon as I could," he told us. "I was taking pictures of the event tonight for the paper and trying to make it to three or four stops every hour." He set his hands on his hips and worked to catch his breath. "Turns out that was—ambitious. Anyway. What'd I miss?" He kissed Libby on her cheek and pulled her close.

"All these couples," Cookie complained. "Can a single lady get a break?"

Libby recapped what we knew so far, and I offered Cookie a supportive smile. I supposed it would get annoying to be single and surrounded by couples all the time. Even my parents were the kissiest pair on earth, and they'd been together more than thirty years. They'd behaved as if it was their honeymoon at Ray and Libby's destination wedding last summer. Mom hadn't been to a beach in so long, she said it felt like seeing the ocean for the first time again. I'd enjoyed witnessing her so carefree and at peace. Dad too. They rarely left the farm for more than the day. I'd assumed that was by choice, but maybe not. Maybe they'd just needed a reason to change their routine.

"What should we do about Alice?" Libby asked, pulling me back to the moment.

Evan glanced at the weeping blonde beyond the shattered café doors.

"She can't stay here," Libby pressed. "Whoever hurt that woman might come back. Plus, she shouldn't be left alone like this. And what about her broken door? Anyone can walk in and do whatever they want in there now."

Evan rubbed his temple. "I'll board up the door, but I can't take her home with Holly and me for a whole host of reasons, if that's what you're suggesting," he said. "It'll be safe to stay here after I finish working on the door, but she's free to go elsewhere if she prefers. She can do whatever she wants until I have enough evidence to arrest her."

"Or exclude her as a suspect," Libby said, taking the words from my mouth.

I grinned, and her gaze fixed on me.

"How are you feeling?" she asked.

I scanned the circle of well-intended friends around me, needing to say something before their desire to care for me got completely out of hand. "Not well."

Caroline gasped. Evan moved closer, as if I might collapse.

"I know we're in the middle of something else right now," I said. "But before you worry any more than necessary about me, please keep in mind that I'm seeing Dr. Bright regularly. I get plenty of steps for exercise every day on the farm. I drink lots of water, and while I eat plenty of sweets this time of year, I also eat a lot of fruits, veggies, lean meats, and whole grains. If the issue with my blood pressure persists, Dr. Bright will put me on a medication that's safe for me and the baby. Also, I'm a grown, capable, intelligent adult."

Libby barked a laugh, then sucked her teeth. "That sounded like a really long, very nice way to tell us to mind our own business, 'cause you've got this handled."

The others nodded apologetically.

I smiled serenely, thankful we had an understanding.

Cookie raised a hand. "I can take Alice," she said. "I don't have a full house at the inn until early next week. She can take the last available room for a few days."

"That's a great idea," I said. "I'll bet my folks won't charge her, given the situation."

Evan huffed. "Of course not."

Cookie beamed. "I'll go make the offer!"

Libby moved into the space where Cookie had stood. "I'd like to collect and remove the rest of her grandmother's Yule Goats in case someone sees the empty café as an invitation to help themselves. Boarded up door or not. Someone was brave enough to bust in once already tonight."

He nodded. "That's fine. Just talk to Alice first."

She looked at him as if she might give him a wedgie. "Duh," she said, then strode confidently behind Cookie to the café.

Evan dragged his gaze to me, as a fresh rush of excitement zipped through my limbs. With Alice staying on the farm, I could talk to her every day while I gathered information online about her grandmother's Yule Goats. Alice would be safe at the inn, and I could help Libby and Zane get to the bottom of what really happened here tonight. All without putting myself in harm's way.

"Holly," Evan warned, his voice low and thick. "No."

I opened my mouth to feign offense, but my husband cut me off with another sharp look.

"No," he repeated.

Well, we would see about that.

Chapter Seven

I drove to the inn again the next morning, eager to check on Alice after such a traumatic night. If she'd thought of any useful details from the break-in, I hoped to hear those while I visited as well.

Cookie answered the door in a festive dress and frilly apron. "Right on time," she said. "We're in the kitchen."

I followed her down the hallway, inhaling delectable scents of cinnamon and nutmeg. "What are you making?"

"Applesauce ornaments and oatmeal," she said. "Make yourself comfortable."

I waved to Libby and Alice as they came into view, already seated at the massive marble island. "Hey. How are you?" I asked, pulling Alice into a hug.

"I'm okay," she said. "Better than last night." She wore jeans and a dark purple sweater that made her ivory skin seem strangely bruised. Her pale blue eyes were puffy and a little red, presumably from fatigue and a morning round of tears.

"Were you able to sleep?"

She shook her head. "Not without seeing her—"

I squeezed Alice's arm, not needing to ask who she meant. I'd seen the victim's face a thousand times since returning home last night as well.

I took a seat beside Alice at the counter.

Cookie set a cup of herbal tea in front of me. Then she dished out bowls of oatmeal with chunks of apple and fresh ground cinnamon sprinkled on top.

She put the pastry tray away.

"What have I missed?" I asked, digging into my oatmeal.

"Not much," Libby said. "I just got here. We knew you wouldn't be far behind."

I grinned and looked to Cookie as I bit into a piece of pecan. "This is delicious. Thank you."

"Don't mention it," she said. "Looking after you has been a group effort for as long as I've known you. This year it's just a little more multifaceted."

I offered her a pointedly bland expression, then turned back to Libby.

She lifted her phone from the counter and navigated to her photographs. "Alice sent me these images. This is everything that went missing after the break-in."

I watched carefully as she swiped through several photos, memorizing as many details as possible. The Yule Goats were small enough to fit into the pockets of an average winter coat. Each piece was unique, clearly handmade and not mass produced. The attention to detail was incredible; even their small faces had individual character.

"You like them," Libby said.

I pulled my eyes from the screen, realizing belatedly how intently I'd been staring. "The craftsmanship is unparalleled. My melted-glass charms look like a toddler's work in comparison."

Alice smiled. "Grandma named all the goats. She worked them into bedtime stories when I was small. They were a big part of my childhood in Gävle. I hope they can be returned."

"We'll find them," Libby said. "My best guess is someone plans on taking them to the antiques show for a quick sell."

Cookie snorted. "That's silly. Everyone knows they're missing. I'm sure the sheriff has notified the event administrators to be on the lookout."

Libby shrugged. "There are a lot of vendors, and there's no guarantee they'd all listen. Especially if there's a collector who realizes their worth. I still think someone overheard that guy mention the value, and they thought it'd be an easy smash and grab situation after everyone moved on to the next course for dinner. They probably never expected Alice to live above the café and hear the break-in."

"What about the victim?" I asked. "How does she come into play?"

"I'm working on that," Libby said. "All I know is in my experience, books and television give criminals too much credit for brains and forethought. I think those people are the exceptions to the rule, and most just see a chance to make fast cash and they jump."

I considered her words. Libby knew a lot more about criminals than I did. She grew up with Evan and became a private eye. I grew up on a tree farm and only recently ran into a few killers. So far, I hadn't noticed any patterns.

Alice released a shuddered breath and wrapped her palms around her steamy mug. "I can't stop replaying it all. From wrestling with her during appetizers to hearing the glass break. I was so scared when I walked downstairs," she whispered. Her unfocused eyes stared past us, through the glass doors where snow fell on the rear patio. "I turned on all the lights, so I'd see if anyone was hiding but hoping to find a fallen Christmas tree. I thought maybe people fussing with the ornaments had made a tree unbalanced and it just gave way. Then I saw the door. And her." Alice cleared her throat, struggling to speak. "I ran to help when I saw someone on the ground. I wondered if they were ill or injured and pounded on my door for help until it broke, then gave up and tried to go elsewhere but couldn't. Anything other than what I found. I recognized her after I got close. She'd been so aggressive earlier, but she was still then. There was blood on the walkway. She didn't answer when I called. Then I noticed her chest didn't rise and fall, that only my breaths made clouds in the night air."

"I'm so sorry," I told her. I'd been in Alice's position enough to understand the shock and pain. "It's not easy to process something like this. It takes time. Probably a significant amount of counseling too. For now, you have us, my parents, and Caroline. We're here for you while you get through this."

"And Ray," Libby said. "He's got your back too, if you need anything."

I nodded. "Even though Evan is the sheriff, and there might come a point when it seems as if he's not on your side, he is," I added. "Trust him to figure this out while we help keep your chin up."

Cookie refreshed her coffee. "Being arrested isn't so bad. I got hauled down to the pokey once. They let me take a weapons training course. That was kind of fun!"

Libby's brow furrowed. "What?"

I let Cookie tell her all about the experience from her perspective while I worked on my oatmeal. I'd visited Cookie at the sheriff's office when she was the main suspect in a previous murder. Evan hadn't given her weapons training as much as he'd let her play a target practice video game in the conference room using a plastic gun. But her version made a better story.

"He said I was a crack shot," Cookie continued.

"Do we know anything about the victim yet?" I asked, after the conversation lulled. "I can't help wondering if there's any chance the murder was about the woman, not the baubles."

"Then why take the figurines?" Alice asked.

"Misdirect," Libby guessed, as I offered, "Maybe as a coverup?"

Alice nodded. "That would make this more complicated," she said. "If things aren't what they seem."

"Yeah," Cookie, Libby, and I agreed.

Libby sat back on her stool, pulling long auburn locks over one shoulder. "So far, all I have on the victim is a name. Evan isn't releasing it to the press until her family can be notified. They might've accomplished that overnight. I haven't spoken to him yet today."

"Me neither," I said. "He was up and out the door by dawn."

"Avoiding your questions, probably," Libby said. Her grin widened. "I love that you make him nuts. It keeps him on his toes."

"I don't intend to make him nuts," I argued.

"Could've fooled us," Cookie said. "That's been kind of your schtick since you met."

I wanted to argue, but recalled being locked in the back of Evan's cruiser following our first conversation, which happened over a dead body on the Reindeer Games property. We hadn't exactly hit it off. "Why did Evan tell you the victim's name?" I asked instead.

Libby frowned. "He didn't. I caught sight of her keychain when the coroner was performing his preliminary examination. There was a BMW logo. So I made note of BMWs within a four-block radius of Cup of Cheer. I assumed the temperature last night would make more than two blocks an unreasonable walk, but I doubled it for due diligence. Then I checked back on my way over here this morning to see if any remained."

My eyes widened. "That's brilliant," I said. "And?"

"One didn't move all night. There was a rental company sticker in the window, so I took the plate number and called to get the woman's name by pretending to be her since Evan wouldn't release it."

My jaw dropped.

"The car was leased by Hannah Ford," Libby said. "Age thirty-five. An antique collector from Rockland, Maine, a small town on the coast. I looked up her name online and matched the photos to the victim and confirmed I had the right person."

I released a shaky breath. Hearing about the victims made them less surreal and more like someone I knew. I sent up a mass of silent prayers for Hannah's loved ones.

"She came a long way to steal some trinkets," Cookie said. "Even if one was brass."

"Copper," Alice corrected. "Hand molded in the late nineteenth century by my great-great-grandpa, who was a renowned blacksmith in Sweden."

We turned to look at her.

She offered a small smile. "He was kind of a big deal at the time, to hear Grandmother tell it at least," she said. "He made a single run of those goats for our family and his friends."

"They became collectors' items," Libby said.

Alice didn't look as if she cared. "I had no idea Americans, or anyone outside my hometown had ever heard of them. To me they're just part of my family's memories."

I mulled that over for a moment. "Did you know the man who spoke to you about the Yule Goats during appetizers?" I asked.

"No," she said. "His face was new too."

Libby waved a hand. "I looked into Kent George. He's visiting town with his family from New Hampshire. He has a booth at the antiques show."

"You think he decided to steal one of those goats?" Cookie asked. "We heard him say how valuable they were. He obviously knew exactly what they were."

My eyes lit as I imagined taking a trip to the antiques show to ask Kent if he'd heard about the crime. "That's true. Maybe—"

"No," Libby said. She pushed a finger in my direction. "Absolutely not. Not with my niece or nephew onboard."

I guffawed. "I haven't even said anything."

"Yeah, but you were thinking something," she said. "I saw it in your eyes. They get wild when you're making plans to put yourself in danger."

"I don't make—"

"Nope," she repeated, cutting me off again. "I will look into Kent George. Not you."

She sounded exactly like her brother when she got bossy. Mistletoe voters gave Evan a certain amount of authority. Libby didn't require anyone's approval.

Libby crossed her legs and drummed her thumbs against the counter. "The antiques show is drawing a bigger crowd than anyone expected, and they aren't a bunch of little old ladies as I anticipated."

"I wish there were more little old men," Cookie said. "You try getting a date when most of the guys from your generation have moved on to the big castle in the sky."

I frowned. "Jeez."

She lifted and dropped a palm. "I'm just saying. Everyone asks why I don't remarry. Who am I supposed to marry?"

"I didn't know you were interested," I said, pulled completely off track by her unexpected statement. Maybe setting up Cookie with a nice fellow was something I could manage this year. I wasn't sure it beat my usual gift of cherry cordial fudge for her, but I was willing to try something new.

Libby hoisted the laptop bag, hanging on the back of her chair, and unzipped it on the counter, then liberated her computer. She typed on the keyboard as the rest of us sipped our drinks, and I finished my oatmeal.

"What are you doing?" Alice asked.

"Trying to learn what the missing pieces are worth," she said. "I should've done this last night."

"They're priceless to me," Alice said. "I just want them back."

"It's still worth a look," Libby said. Several moments later, she made a sharp choking sound, then turned the laptop to face us. "Found them."

Cookie, Alice, and I leaned forward, scanning the information below images of the goats onscreen.

According to the site, offering valuations of international heirlooms and vintage pieces, the copper goat Hannah and Alice fought over was worth more than forty-thousand dollars! The smaller glass pieces were worth upwards of one to five grand each.

Alice shouted an unfamiliar word that I assumed was a Swedish curse.

"I guess we have a clear motive," I said. "And with the antiques show in Mistletoe, we have a good chance of catching the thief and killer before they leave town."

"Assuming they haven't gone already," Alice said. "If I was them, I'd find somewhere else to sell."

Libby shut her laptop and caught my eye with a grin. "My bet is on the money. I don't think they'll leave town without making an attempt to cash out."

I certainly hoped she was right.

Chapter Eight

When Cookie's other inn guests made their ways downstairs for the afternoon, following their leisurely morning in bed, I grabbed my laptop from the truck and trudged across the field to the Hearth. I took up residence at my favorite booth and opened the computer. Then I helped myself to hot chocolate and a little snack while Mom greeted new guests.

She hiked a curious brow as she passed me, carrying a tray of steaming mugs.

I smiled as I logged in and opened an internet browser. I'd finished my homework in this same booth more times than I could count, and Mom had mended my broken hearts here with her hot chocolate cure. Never once had I imagined I'd sit here in my thirties, researching Swedish goat figurines and their connection to a local murder.

Funny how time could change both everything and nothing at all.

I opened several windows on the laptop and typed "Hannah Ford" into the search engine on one, "antique Yule Goats" in another, and "the Antiques Showcase" into a third. Learning as much as I could about all three topics seemed the best course of action if I wanted to offer assistance to Evan and Libby. They could go out and pound the pavement, question locals and visitors, to find answers. I had slightly elevated blood pressure and a tiny human on board, so this was my best chance to help. I planned to make the most of it.

I hit the jackpot on Hannah. Her social media profiles were updated regularly with lots of selfies and candid shots with friends and family members. Posts about random antiques for sale interspersed the feed. She had a lot of followers and interactions. Even today, a handful of clueless people posted on her wall and tagged her in holiday well wishes. So far, there wasn't any indication of her passing.

Her husband appeared to be a bit of a Poindexter and in London on business until next week. That seemed easy enough for authorities to confirm, so she probably beat the statistic of being another woman killed by her spouse or lover.

Now what?

"Shoot," I muttered. I'd never had to rely solely on the internet for my investigations before. This was a lot slower than talking to people in person, and I wasn't known for my patience.

I turned longing eyes toward the door.

Mom stepped into view, effectively changing my plan for escape. "Hello, sweetie," she said. "How are you feeling? What can I get you?" She eyeballed the empty mug and napkin full of cookie crumbs before me.

"I'm okay for now," I said. "I'm just going to hang out for a while. Can I help you with anything?"

She smiled warmly and shook her head. "Nope, but I love that you want to stick around. Please do! What are you working on?"

I closed the laptop. "Just scrolling social media," I said. At least that was partially true. I didn't like fibbing to my mom, but I hated worrying her even more.

"You're feeling all right?"

I nodded, and she beamed.

The door opened, letting in a few new customers and a cloud of swirling snow.

"Welcome," Mom called, then drifted away to seat the newcomers.

I reopened my laptop and turned my focus to the Antiques Showcase tab. According to the website, the traveling event began thirty years ago as a small way to share the love of history and its items of significance. Back then, the creators only hoped to spread their love of the past with those who shared the passion and maybe create some converts along the way.

The show became an unexpected hit by tapping into the public desire to find something in Grandma's attic or purchased at a yard sale that was actually worth a fortune. From there, the audience grew by leaps and bounds. Soon the annual event became a quarterly occurrence and earned a spot on national television, inviting people from all over the country to appear with their most unique treasures and finds.

I nearly rolled my eyes as I realized how many of the visiting enthusiasts likely came for the money and had little or no interest in history. *Why does everything revolve around cash?* I mentally slapped the rhetorical question away, because I knew the answer. Money bought more than things. It bought safety, security, and options. A lot of people didn't have those, and everyone needed them. Those who had them often wanted more.

I looked at the café around me. At my special booth, overflowing with nostalgia, and my mom laughing with guests across the room. The magnitude of my blessings was never lost on me, and each year seemed to bring bigger, better things. And in the case of the coming year, my best gift of all.

I couldn't wait to share this incredible life with my child. The months until that day were sure to pass like molasses, which meant it made sense to stay busy in the meantime.

I also needed to start a list of possible names and stop thinking about my child as Baby. Unless I planned on birthing a *Dirty Dancing* character.

I couldn't think of any good ideas, so I pulled my attention back to the screen and scanned the details about the final show. The Antiques Showcase website featured a massive Christmas tree with a banner and the words:

Join us for a magnificent Christmastime event held in historic Mistletoe, Maine

December 12–December 24

An image of the town square filled with people in Victorian garb centered the section on the page with details, times, and the physical address.

I needed to get to that show. Evan had offered to take me, but would his offer stand now that antiques were tied to a local murder?

If not, I was almost certain I could find a friend or two to go with me.

I clicked the site's main menu in the top corner and saw an option to log in.

"Interesting," I whispered, already entering my email and setting up an account. Was this just for vendors? Would shoppers receive coupons?

A welcome screen appeared, along with links to various forums.

Sweet!

I scrolled through the list, bubbling with excitement. The forums' activities went back for years. I could read all day and still have enough material to keep me busy for the rest of the week. I slid away from the booth and refilled my hot chocolate. I grabbed a whoopie pie on my way back.

Mom caught my eye from across the room and gave me a goofy grin. She'd never stop me from enjoying her treats. Unlike my friends, Mom trusted me to make good choices. Even when I didn't.

I couldn't decide which forum to read first, but the content seemed to be organized chronologically, with newer messages or forums with most recent updates listed first. The farther down the screen I scrolled, the older the content, so I began at the top with a thread called Hot Finds.

Users shared images or details about things they had in their possession, looking for input on the value. In another group, buyers shared descriptions of things they wanted. Each forum read as if it was a small community, where users helped and guided one another by providing feedback. As with all groups, it was easy to spot a few know-it-alls who chimed in on everything, often to correct a previous responder. BeenThereDoneThat14 and HistoryBuff14 were two of the most frequent at pointing out errors. Usually errors made by each other.

I couldn't help wondering why both ended in 14. Was that the year they made their accounts?

The swinging door to the kitchen rattled, and I spun to see Dad knocking his way through, gloved hands full. Snow piled on his hat and the shoulders of his coat. His cheeks were ruddy, but his smile was bright. He tracked Mom with his gaze as he set a stack of mail on the service counter and tugged off his gloves.

She met him there with a chaste kiss. "Coffee?" she asked.

He pulled a thermos from an inside pocket of his thick coat, and she filled it from her pot. After setting the thermos on the counter for later, she poured a little more into a mug and passed it into his hands.

"Holly's here," she said.

His gaze found me immediately, and I lifted my cup in cheers.

"How's she feeling?" he asked Mom.

"Excellent," I answered.

He snorted. "Keep it that way," he said.

My parents spoke softly to one another for a few more minutes before Dad made his exit. He returned the thermos to his inside coat pocket and carried the empty mug into the kitchen with him, presumably to put in the dishwasher on his way out.

Mom checked on me again an hour later. I hadn't finished reading half the entries in the first forum. "How's everything going?" she asked.

"Good." I smiled. "I'm learning about the antiques show. Did you know it started for educational purposes? That's kind of cool, right?"

"It is," she agreed. "I talked to my antiquing friends last summer, after the mayor scheduled the show to stop here. I'd expected to see the town filled with harmless history buffs. I'd hoped to get a break from the annual scandal and crime spree."

I wanted to argue that crime spree was a little dramatic, but she was right. The dead body was never the end of the story around here. Follow-up incidents always ensued, frequently involving me. But not this year.

"Anyway, here we are." Mom pulled an envelope from her apron pocket and refreshed her smile. "Your dad brought the mail, and it reminded me of this." She set the letter before me. "It arrived a few days ago with your name on it. Looks like it's from Christopher."

"Gee, how can you tell?" I asked, grinning as I lifted the ridiculously high-quality envelope and turned the elegant black calligraphy of my name to face her. A crimson wax seal with the initial C held the flap closed. Tiny embossed holly leaves and berries adorned the corners.

Mom laughed. "Just a guess." Her expression sobered as she watched me. "I had it with me the day you told me I'm going to be a grandma. Since then, I've thought of very little else."

I smiled. "Me too."

"I wasn't sure why Christopher left the letter here at first, but I suppose you were on your way over after the doctor's office," she said.

I opened my mouth to say that Christopher didn't know that, but he somehow seemed to know everything.

"What does it say?" she asked. "I wonder what he's up to."

The little seal gave way with some effort, and I slid a trifolded sheet of unnecessarily thick paper from within. The same crest and letter C centered the top of the page, and tidy script matching that on the envelope continued below.

"Dearest Holly," I read aloud. "You do so much for everyone else, I wanted to give you a special gift this year. If I asked, I'm sure you'd say you have everything you want already, but I know how much you enjoy a good puzzle. Do you not?"

"I do," I said, catching Mom's knowing eye.

She frowned. "He's giving you a puzzle?"

"Seems so." I looked back to the letter. "I hope you'll enjoy solving this one as much as I enjoyed making it. Be patient with me if it's too simple, this was my first!" I could nearly hear his deep, vibrant laughter in the space between paragraphs.

My jaw dropped as I took in the final line. "Merry Christmas and congratulations on the news. What a lucky child to be born into your care."

My throat tightened, and my eyes misted.

Mom bent to hug me. "He's absolutely right, you know?"

I blinked through the brimming tears. How did he know? And when had I gotten so emotional?

If I cried at every kind or wonderful thing I saw or heard, I'd be a mess all year round.

"Hormones," Mom said, as if reading my thoughts. "Plus, I'm pretty sure your heart grows ten times its size the moment you become a mother."

"Oh, great," I said, only half joking. I sipped my tepid drink as I contemplated the letter. "So our general contractor made me a puzzle. Did he leave it with you?"

She shook her head. "No. There was only that envelope on the countertop when I came in to work. Maybe he'll deliver your puzzle with the other toys on Christmas Eve."

I pursed my lips and nodded, though that made no sense to me. Why tell me about my gift now, if I didn't get it until Christmas?

Why tell me about it at all?

"Oh! Speaking of puzzles," Mom said. She ducked behind the counter, then returned with the morning paper. "Are you and Evan still doing the crosswords together?"

"Yeah, but he left before I got up today."

"Do you need the paper?" she asked, setting her copy on the table.

"Mine's at home, but I'll take this one if you aren't using it." If I got bored later, I'd get a head start on Evan.

She freed the page with the puzzle, and I took a look at the clues. "Holiday song lyrics seem to be a theme this week," I said, then tucked the paper into my backpack.

"'Tis the season." Mom winked, then tapped my table with her knuckles as a customer approached the counter with their bill. "Let me know if you need anything else."

Then she went to handle business.

* * *

The Hearth was packed as lunchtime rolled around, and I was taking up prime real estate in my booth that easily sat six. So I headed outside to the series of connected wooden stalls that made up Santa's Village, a newish addition to the tree farm. Locals were invited to rent a space and sell their goods during the week or two before Christmas.

Might as well get a jump start on my last-minute holiday shopping, I thought.

Also, why was gift buying so hard? And why was I so bad at it?

Seasonal music piped through speakers on poles throughout the village drew shoppers in as they made their way around the farm. Dad and his crew had handcrafted the wooden faces that made the stalls into a historic street of shops. The faces were repainted last summer, sealed to prevent rot and weather damage, then revived with fresh shades of navy, gold, evergreen, and maroon.

I spotted Ray quickly in the crowd, standing a half-head taller than everyone around him. He held his trusty camera to his cheek, likely snapping photos for the paper. "Hey, you," I said, stopping at his side. "How's it going?"

"Holly!" He released his camera, letting it hang from the strap around his neck, then he drew me into a hug. "How are you feeling? I didn't get to say it when I saw you last, but congratulations!"

"Thank you," I said. "I'm feeling good. Are you working?"

"Yeah. I wanted to get a few shots for the Events section of Saturday's paper. I thought it'd help the tourists decide what to do while they're in Mistletoe."

"Smart," I said. Typically, we were overrun with the kind of visitors who came to see the sights and participate in events they'd already learned about online, from friends, or past experiences. This year, the antiques show brought a new kind of guest, and they might not realize what an incredible place our town was, and just how much they could do here at Christmastime.

"Thanks," he said. "What are you getting up to today?" His tone was light, but the tightness in his gaze made me feel as if I was on camera.

Reporting back to his wife, my sister-in-law, by chance? Or maybe my husband?

Was he even really taking photos for the paper?

A yawn stretched open my mouth mid-thought. Creating a new life made me paranoid. And tired.

"Naptime?" he suggested.

I inhaled, pulling the fresh, clean air into my lungs. "Nope. I just need a little more oxygen to get my blood pumping. Speaking of," I segued poorly. "Any news from Libby on Alice's case?"

He frowned.

I waited.

"Holly," he warned. "You're pregnant."

I glanced at his boots and considered kicking snow on them. "I'm not asking about the murder," I said. "I'm checking on my friend."

Ray rolled his eyes and took his sweet time with the performance. "Please. Don't act as if I just met you. There was another murder, and I know you're going bonkers with a need to drive into town and pester everyone in sight. It's killing you not to get involved."

I crossed my arms and willed myself not to stick out my tongue.

We engaged in a childish staring contest until I won.

"Fine," he said, shoulders drooping slightly. "No. I haven't gotten any updates, but Libby's doing all she can to trace that woman's steps in town and everything she did between her arrival and the night you found her."

"Alice found her," I said. "Cookie, Caroline, Libby and I found Alice."

"Potato. Tomato."

I screwed my features into a knot. "That isn't a saying."

"It is," he argued. "I just said it." Then he matched my expression. "Wow. I'm starting to sound like Cookie."

I cracked up, and Ray rubbed a hand down his face. "Wait until you see this year's charity calendar."

"Trust me," I said. "I'm counting the days."

Chapter Nine

Ray motioned me deeper into the rows of booths. "Walk with me?"

I linked my arm in his as we moved together through the crowd, stopping to check out each vendor and their wares. Ray took enough photos to curb my suspicion that he'd come to babysit me under guise of work. And I found joy in chatting with sellers and guests.

I especially loved all the creative ways people turned the utilitarian stalls into something personal and engaging. Many of the spaces were decked out in holiday attire, complete with garlands, twinkle lights, and wreaths. Others had a general winter theme, featuring snowmen and snowflakes, or my favorite, seasonal baked goods. Every time I thought I'd seen the best-looking display, the next one impressed me even more.

I bought mason jars of homemade hard candies for my dad, and homemade soaps, embedded with dried flowers and honeycombs, then tied with twine, for Caroline. One big bag of kettle corn and a smaller paper pouch of honey-roasted pecans were for Evan and me to share.

I slid the satchel off my shoulder and tucked my purchases inside with my laptop and wallet.

Ray found a sleeve for Libby's e-reader adorned with images of houndstooth caps and magnifying glasses. Then he bought a Sasquatch jacket patch for my dad.

"Bigfoot?" I asked, smiling as he tucked the receipt into his pocket.

"I figure if anyone has a chance at seeing him out here in the forest, it's your dad," he said.

I laughed, and the sound grew as I imagined Dad opening the little gift. "None of us have ever seen Dad and Bigfoot in the same room, you know."

Ray's eyes went comically wide, and my laughter began anew.

The sun shone brightly in the December sky, heating my cheeks and glistening off the brilliant white snow. I tilted my chin upward, savoring the warmth on my skin as we waited for a peek at the next display.

"Hey," Ray said. "Look."

I opened my eyes as he cut through an open path to a booth selling tiny hats and mittens. He pointed at a white velvet set with snowflakes in varying shades of blue. The words "Baby's First Christmas" were stitched along the bottom of the stretchy hat. "They say one size fits zero to two," he said. "How old will Baby be next winter?"

I sighed inwardly at someone other than myself referring to my child as Baby. "About six months."

I really needed to brainstorm some names or at least find a cute placeholder.

Ray purchased the hat and mittens with a look of pride in his eyes. "I will always be the first one to buy Baby a gift."

"Evan and I literally gave this child the gift of life," I argued.

"Doesn't count. Can't wrap it. I win." His smug expression said that was the end of the conversation.

"Gift giving isn't a competition," I told him. "Goof." I shook my head in exasperation, loving that Ray thought enough of my father and baby to buy them gifts at Christmas. My friends were so good to one another, and to me, it was one more thing I never took for granted.

"Hey," Ray said. His voice was soft, his expression pensive. "Your baby is my niece or nephew!"

My heart swelled. "Yeah," I said, feeling my smile widen. "Poor kid."

Ray barked an obnoxious laugh.

We'd grown up in Mistletoe and attended high school together, though I didn't remember him from those days. He was two years younger and not on my teenage radar, but he'd quickly become one of my first adult friends following my return to town a few years back. I never dreamed we'd become family one day.

We stopped walking again a few paces later. A booth with books, magazines, and old newspapers caught his attention and mine. He examined framed articles with sepia images of the railroad being installed throughout the country and men eating lunches on scaffolding high above the burgeoning New York City skyline.

I selected a cloth-covered children's book seated atop a collection of similar tomes.

Copies of classic stories from generations past stood in brightly colored stacks and rows across the counter. *The Black Stallion*, *The Velveteen Rabbit*, *Charlotte's Web*, and *Mother Goose*.

I wanted them all.

"Book lover?" The woman manning the table asked. Her blue eyes flashed behind large, round-framed glasses.

"Yes," I said. "These are amazing. My grandmother gave me her Beatrix Potter collection as a high school graduation gift. I adore them. They're still like brand new."

"Peter Rabbit," she said. "One of my favorites."

I set the book down and offered her a mitten-clad hand. "I'm Holly Gray."

"Peggy King," she said accepting the shake. I guessed her at my age or perhaps a little younger. She wore a pink wool coat with striped gloves, a matching hat and scarf. "Do you live around here?"

"Yeah," I said, chuckling. "Right here, actually, and I also have a place in town. What about you?"

"I'm from Orono."

"Did you come for the antiques show?" I guessed.

She pushed a swatch of windblown hair away from her round cheek. The stick-straight brown lock fell still as the breeze subsided. "I did. How'd you know?"

I motioned to the contents of her booth. "Easy guess. Plus everyone seems to be in town for the same reason this year."

Ray moved closer, smiling congenially until a blush rose on Peggy's cheeks. "Holly's a bit of a gumshoe," he said.

And he was adorably handsome, in a boy-next-door kind of way, which she'd clearly noticed.

Ray nudged me with his shoulder, oblivious to her blush.

I tensed, turned, and glared.

He cracked up. "I'm Ray, by the way."

They spoke casually for a moment, while I let the steam clear from my head. The last thing I needed was for him to announce my unwanted nickname in a crowd full of people. What if someone recognized the name from the podcast? They'd want autographs and pictures. They'd probably have a bunch of questions about all the annual murders. Or worse, the most recent one.

No, thank you.

"I'm excited to be part of Santa's Village," Peggy told him. "I tried to get a space at the antiques show's pavilion, but those spots sold out months before I knew I could participate. The spaces are incredibly expensive there too, so this is the real win," she continued. "There's so much to do on this tree farm. If I was stuck at the show all day, the only thing I could do is shop and eat. Plus, I'm still seeing lots of collectors."

I smiled. She had a point about the farm. There wasn't any shortage of things to do. Horse-drawn sleigh rides. Indoor games. Outdoor games. Ice skating when the lake was frozen solid, pictures with the animals, craft-making, and she could shop and eat here as well.

"How long have you collected children's books?" I asked.

"Forever," she said. "I'm a bit obsessed with history. I have the degree to prove it." She released a puff of air in lieu of laughter. "Not as if I ever actually use it."

"I have one of those too," I said. "Mine's in business, and it's covered in dust, figurative and literal."

She nodded animatedly. "Exactly. Books are my favorite, but I collect everything. Things have meaning and nostalgia to me. My whole family is the same way, especially about books. When my kids were born, we immediately started a library for them. I bought new copies to read and old copies for display. Now I can't seem to stop buying them." She motioned to the copies for sale at her booth.

I laughed. "How old are your kids?"

"I have a toddler, Henry, who just turned three," she said, beaming as brightly as any mother could. "I guess he'll be a preschooler soon. And my baby, Eloise, is eight months old."

I pressed a mitten to my chest. "Precious. It must be hard to be away from them," I said.

Peggy looked briefly away, and her mood fell.

I imagined thumping the heel of one hand against my forehead. "Sorry. I shouldn't have said that." Her life wasn't any of my business. And prodding was just plain rude.

"No, it's okay," she said, returning her gaze to mine. "Being away from home is hard, but we do what we have to do for our kids, right? And sleeping through the night for a few days isn't a hardship." She laughed.

I relaxed a bit, thankful I hadn't offended her. It seemed so strange that Evan and I would soon be sleep deprived and craving time away as well.

"Have you been to the antiques show yet?" she asked. "It's amazing. Absolutely huge. The producers went all out to make the last show a memorable one."

Ray slid his gaze in my direction, probably thinking the same thing I was—this year would be memorable all right, considering someone was recently murdered over an antique goat.

"I plan to check it out this week," I said. "I'm not much of a collector, but I certainly appreciate history." Living in Mistletoe made sure of that. "I spent some time on the website today. I didn't realize what a community they have."

Her expression turned disbelieving. "Sure. As long as you don't mind the jealousy, backbiting, and proverbial claws, it's fantastic. Or you can be like me, stay in your lane, and only show up on the weekends when they host the show within driving distance."

"What do you mean?" I asked, ignoring Ray's crossed arms and bland expression.

Peggy shrugged. "The sellers who travel around the country with the show get really invested in all of it—emotionally, I guess. They're competitive with one another and supremely petty. The full-time seller community can be unbelievably tense. The rest of us, who pull up on weekends, then roll out on Sunday nights, however, get to enjoy the experience without the drama." Her smile returned. "Win-win."

"What do they fight about?" I asked.

She pulled her chin back, apparently surprised by my follow-up. "I don't know. I guess there's a lot of competition in antiques. There are only so many of the world's most valuable things available, so getting your hands on one of them is a bit like winning a treasure hunt, I suppose. Some people buy and sell internationally, which creates a bigger market, and puts more money on the table. Yet another reason I stick to local art, popular books, and things that make me smile. No one cares about my goods, and no one's trying to take them from me."

I looked at Ray. *Internationally*, I said internally, sending the thought to him via my best attempt at telepathy. *As in Sweden.*

He narrowed his eyes. "Are you okay?"

I sighed. Clearly my extrasensory powers hadn't kicked in yet.

"Do you need to sit down?" he pressed.

I made a throaty, disgusted sound. "No. I'm fine. Never mind."

"Never mind what?" he asked, casting his attention from me to Peggy and back.

I raised a hand. "Can we rewind a minute?" I asked, redirecting my gaze to Peggy. "When I was on the antiques show's website, I noticed a few handles that interacted more than others. Do you spend time in the forums?"

"I'm mostly a lurker," she said. "I pop in to see what's going on from time to time, but I rarely interact."

I deflated a little, losing my hope on the new lead.

"I will warn you, though," she said, pulling my eyes back to her. "BeenThereDoneThat14 is a troublemaker, and they always seem to be butting heads with another user. I can't remember the other name."

"HistoryBuff14?" I asked.

She lifted her shoulders and pursed her lips. "I'm not sure. I can check when I get back to the hotel tonight. Will I see you here tomorrow?"

I nodded. "I'll look for you."

Peggy smiled. "Fun. Okay. It's nice to know at least one familiar face."

"Two," Ray said, raising a pair of gloved fingers in a peace sign.

"Two," she agreed.

I stepped aside to let another shopper check out the children's books.

"Hey," Peggy called. "One more thing."

"Yeah?"

"Since the show is in town, if you have any specific questions, you can always ask the founder," she said. "He knows everything about international goods. He even wrote a book on the subject. He's an excellent resource, and he's available in person. How often is that a possibility?"

"Never?" I guessed.

"Exactly!"

Ray tugged me along, and Peggy chatted up her new customers. "Stop that," he said.

I pulled my sleeve from his grip. "Rude. I was making a new friend."

"You were investigating, and you need to knock it o—"

I spotted another familiar face and hurried away before he could finish his complaint.

The man who'd spoken to Alice about the copper goat at Cup of Cheer held a pine door wreath several dozen feet away.

I waited as he paid and poked his arm through the wreath's center, hooking it onto one shoulder like a purse. I smiled brightly when he noticed me.

"Oh, hello," he said. "We met at the dinner. Appetizers, right?" He put his wallet into his pocket and waved goodbye to the vendor, then pulled the wreath back into his hand.

"That's right," I said. "I mean, it wasn't official, but yes. I'm Holly Gray." I offered him my hand.

He easily accepted the shake. "Kent George."

"Hi." I released him and gently massaged my suddenly achy but slowly healing hand. "Have you heard about what happened at the café after we left that night?" I watched his guarded expression carefully for signs of guilt or fear.

We stepped away from the booth, allowing others to shop the beautiful assortment of pine greenery. "I did," he said. "It was absolutely awful. And shocking. Who would do something like that? It was such a joyous night."

My brow puckered. The night had been fantastic if I didn't consider the initial brouhaha, then later a murder.

I couldn't get a read on his tone or discern the reason for the tight set of his features. Did he know something about what had happened that night? Or was he simply surprised by my appearance and line of questions?

"Kent?" a woman called.

He turned and raised a hand.

I recognized her pixie-cut hair and red coat from Cup of Cheer. "Your wife?" I asked. My mental wheels creaked to life as I recalled the woman asking Alice how many Yule Goats were in the collection. Alice hadn't known. Could this woman have helped herself to a few of the collectibles, assuming Alice might not notice they were gone?

"A colleague," he said. "Nancy Grace."

When Kent met my eye again, he chuckled. "You got me," he said. "I couldn't understand where this was coming from, but I see now you're in character."

I frowned, confused by his change in disposition.

"It was nice seeing you again," he said. "Good luck on your case." He strode passed Ray on his way to meet the woman who'd called for him.

I turned in a slow circle to watch him go, then I spotted the booth across from us. And Ray, grinning ear to ear.

A giant picture of my face with a superimposed Santa Claus hat and crime scene tape sweater stared back at me. Additional signage on the booth urged people to fill out a slip of paper with their name and address to receive an autographed postcard from the Gumdrop Gumshoe. A red gift box with thick golden ribbon and a wide slit cut through the lid held a smaller sign encouraging donations. The *Dead and Berried* podcast logo spread across the top of the stall.

Tate the Great and Harvey from the Harvest rented a booth at my family's farm. I wasn't sure who to explode on first. The podcasters or my parents.

Ray slung an arm across my shoulders. "Before you light a match and burn that to the ground, allow me to remind you how many people you make extremely happy by signing things for them. And the money you're making for each of those signatures goes to a great cause," he continued. "You're going to blow Evan's mind with the perfect Christmas gift this year, remember?"

I hummed a low, frustrated sound.

"Are you growling?"

"No," I said, reluctantly. "But you'd growl too if someone publicly posted a picture of your head at ten times its size and assigned you a goofy nickname."

Ray moved to face me. His expression turned compassionate. "You're right. I'm sorry," he said. "If it makes you feel any better, you're all bundled up, so it's highly unlikely anyone will know that's you." He lifted a finger in the direction of the picture.

Something tugged at my sleeve before I could accept his words. A preteen with jet black hair and matching nail polish stepped back when I turned.

"Sorry," they said. "Is that—" Their gaze jumped to the giant Gumdrop Gumshoe sign. "Are you her?"

I shut my eyes so I wouldn't roll them rudely.

"Yes," Ray said. "This is Holly Gray. Formerly Holly White. Currently the Gumdrop Gumshoe."

I raised my most heated glare to him.

He placed a hand beside his mouth and stage-whispered to me. "Guess I was wrong."

"I will barehand murder you."

The tween cracked up. "That's so funny. Can I have your autograph?"

A nearby couple took notice and came closer, watching as I signed the kid's backpack with a marker they had on hand. The couple was next to make a similar request.

Ray enjoyed every minute as I smiled for photos and signed my name on everything from napkins and shopping bags to earmuffs and coat sleeves.

A trio of young women stopped before us as the crowd thinned. The tallest caught my attention with a small wave. "Hi," she said. "I heard about what happened outside the café near town this week. What do you think about it?"

"I think it was a terrible tragedy," I said, imagining a recording device in her pocket.

"Do you think you'll find the killer again this year?" one of her friends asked.

"No."

The third young woman balked. "There's no need to hunt for a culprit. The café owner was obviously responsible."

"No, she wasn't," I said, unable to stop myself from defending a friend. "Alice is a wonderful human. She's another victim in this awful mess." Alice wasn't physically harmed, but she'd been harassed, robbed, and traumatized. Now she was a murder suspect. None of that was deserved or fair.

"Well, I'm never eating at that place again," someone farther back in the group announced.

Others enthusiastically agreed.

"Hey!" I said, raising my voice to get the mob's attention. "Alice is innocent. Her café is wonderful. And she does not deserve any of this."

"What are you going to do about it?" someone called.

"Yeah," a man's voice echoed. "Prove it!"

"I will!" I said firmly.

And the crowd went wild with applause.

Ray made a guttural moan and stepped in front of me, effectively blocking my view of anything else. "Sorry, folks, but it's time for the Gumshoe to move on," he announced. "Enjoy your day."

He spun and grabbed my sleeve, towing me away with long, purposeful strides. "Now you've done it," he grouched. "That is exactly what I came here to prevent happening."

I gasped, craning my neck for a look at his face as we fled the scene. "I knew it!"

Chapter Ten

I made a pot of stuffed pepper soup for dinner that night. It was one of the few things I'd never ruined.

Cindy Lou Who, my calico rescue cat, watched as I prepared the meal and adjusted the heat beneath the pot. "Meow," she lamented, eager for a meal of her own.

"I haven't forgotten you," I said, moving on to fill her dish. "Have you had a good day?" I added kibble to her bowl, then refilled the water in her fountain, which was pumping weakly from lack.

She settled before her rubber mat and worked on her dinner, while I stroked her back gently. "You are a beautiful, sweet kitty," I told her.

Cindy stopped eating and released a low growl.

"I know," I said. "You love me too."

Cindy wasn't an affectionate feline. She'd been feral when I'd caught her eating scraps of fish stuck to the grill on my patio in Portland. I'd catnapped her and kept her forever.

She wasn't over it.

I put my feet up in the living room and admired our Christmas tree while I waited for Evan to finish work. After the harsh words about Alice from the crowd at Santa's Village, I wanted every detail Evan had gleaned about Hannah Ford's murder. I hoped he'd share his progress on the case with me. More than that, I prayed he found something to dismiss Alice as a suspect.

I set my bag on the floor and freed the newspaper from inside, then I turned to today's crossword puzzle. I willed myself not to solve all the clues alone, but I couldn't wait to get started.

Soon my eyelids grew heavy, and I let them slide shut. I tugged a blanket across my body while I listened to the steady rhythm of our ticking wall clock.

I woke to the familiar feel of Evan's warm lips against my forehead. "Hi," I whispered, dragging open heavy eyelids. His skin was cool from the winter air, suggesting he'd come straight to find me after leaving his coat and boots at the door.

"Hey, Gray," he said. "Soup smells amazing. Did you have any?"

"I waited for you," I said, forcing myself to sit upright and wincing slightly at the weight I'd inadvertently put on my hand.

"Stay right there," he instructed. A moment later, he returned with two bowls of soup, spoons, and little round crackers. "I see you started the crossword." He nodded toward the paper, which had fallen from my lap to the carpet.

He set the page on the couch at my side, then took a seat beside the bag at my feet and dug into his soup.

The reminder burned away any dregs of fatigue. "I did. Look at this," I said. "It's so weird. Two across. You'd better blank. Eight letters. Two words. The answer is watch out."

Evan stuffed a full spoon of soup into his mouth. "This is delicious," he said. "What's in it?"

"Ground beef," I said. "Diced tomatoes, beef bouillon, onions, and bell peppers. I added a dash of salt and a spoonful of sugar to the pot to cut the acid."

"This might be my new favorite."

"Thank you," I said. "But isn't that weird about the crossword?"

"Why?"

I watched as he devoured the soup and crackers, waiting for him to mentally catch up. When he didn't get as jazzed about the puzzle as he should, I was forced to explain. "For the last two days the answer to the clues for two across were my name." I lifted a finger so I could tick off the facts. "First Holly." I lifted another finger. "Then White." I added another digit to the pair. "And today the answer to that same clue is watch out."

He set his empty bowl on the coffee table and turned to face me from his spot on the floor. "You think it's a threat?"

I raised my shoulders toward my ears and held them there for a long beat before relaxing them once again. "Maybe." Clearly Evan disagreed, which made me second-guess my concerns a little. "You don't?" I asked, hoping he'd offer some clarity on his position.

"I don't." He rose and collected my bowl and spoon before carrying our dishes to the sink.

I listened as he rattled around in the kitchen, and I grew impatient with each passing second.

"Why?" I asked, projecting my voice through the rooms. "Watch out is a definite warning. Normally you'd lose your mind over something like this."

Evan stepped back from his place at the kitchen counter, peering through the archway into the living room. "Normally, yes," he agreed. "But, at the moment, I think there was a recent murder and you're processing that fact. You've been through a lot the last few years, and I'm guessing you're anticipating a repeat of an unfortunate pattern. Which is completely understandable."

I didn't like the theory that my past traumas were impacting my current reality, but he wasn't wrong about my concerns.

Evan vanished for another moment, then returned to the living room with a mug of tea and passed it into my hands.

"Thanks."

"But wait, there's more," he said, producing an orange from his pocket and beginning to peel it for me as I sipped.

"So you're sure I shouldn't worry?" I asked.

"Not about the crossword," he said. "Clues one and two happened before the murder occurred. So, unless the killer planned the crime and made arrangements in advance with the *Gazette*'s puzzle designer, I'd say you can remove this from your worry list. Besides, how would the killer even know you do these puzzles? Or that you'd notice the pattern at all? Taking four days to make a threat feels like the slowest plan on earth."

I pursed my lips and accepted the peeled orange.

I supposed when he put it that way, it seemed a little silly to assume the puzzle had anything to do with me. "So, it's a coincidence," I said. "I thought we didn't believe in those."

Evan sighed, ever patient, but visibly exhausted from his day. "The clues are from a monthlong holiday-themed puzzle, and you have an extremely Christmasy name."

"I did," I teased. "Until you changed my name to Gray."

He snorted. "Touché. How was your day at the farm?"

"Good." I straightened and recapped the highlights of my time at Reindeer Games. "I bought kettle corn and roasted pecans to share while we watch Christmas movies." I pulled my bag onto the couch and dug for our snacks.

Evan opened the kettle corn immediately while I hunted down the pecans. "While I appreciate you limiting your curiosity to the internet and guests at your family farm," he said gently, "please remember that hundreds of people visit Reindeer Games every day. Anyone could've overheard your conversations in Santa's Village, and I told you I would talk to Kent George about the goat. You should've left him alone."

I overturned my bag on the couch, liberating my laptop, a spiral notebook, and a half dozen pens. The pecans toppled out last, on the heels of a single *Dead and Berried* postcard.

Evan snatched the cardstock rectangle from the cushion and stood. A slew of curses rolled from his tongue.

"What happened?" I asked, repacking my bag, now that the nuts were recovered.

He turned the postcard to face me with one hand while pressing his cell phone to his ear with the other.

A thick black X was drawn through each of my eyes in the image, and another covered my mouth.

My head swam as he relayed the information to someone on duty at the sheriff's office. I couldn't imagine when someone could've been close enough to put the postcard into my bag, but the paths between stalls were quite crowded.

He disconnected and snapped several photos of the postcard.

"Are you mad?" I asked, needing a hug more than a lecture.

"Not at you," he said, drawing me into his arms. "But this is exactly what I was worried about."

* * *

Evan drove me to Reindeer Games the next morning. We'd told my parents about the postcard, and they'd promised to keep an eye on me while Evan worked.

I didn't like being treated as if I needed a babysitter, but I appreciated the added care and diligence for Baby's sake. Clearly, I could use some help keeping a killer more than an arm's reach away.

The table at my usual booth was set for me when I arrived. A small plate with mini pastries waited beside a carafe of cinnamon tea and a tray with all the fixings. The morning paper awaited as well, already folded to reveal the crossword puzzle.

I poured a cup of tea and snagged a tiny gingerbread man from the tray while Mom prepared the Hearth for another busy day.

Cookie arrived seconds later on a gust of frigid wind through the front door.

"It's freezing out there," she called, unwinding her scarf and removing her mittens as she moved in my direction. "Hi, Holly! I came to visit with your mom. Lucky me, I get a twofer. What are you doing here so early?"

"Mom and Dad are babysitting me." I told her about the postcard, and Mom shivered behind the service counter.

"Jeez," Cookie said. "That didn't take long. Is that the morning crossword?"

I slid the paper across the table, and she took a seat.

Mom delivered a second mug so I could share my tea.

"Thanks!" Cookie exclaimed, fixing her hungry eyes on the puzzle. "I did the whole thing yesterday, but my name wasn't in it."

"Maybe today," I said. Hopefully the answer to two across would be something pleasant this time. If so, it would go a long way toward putting my mind at ease. Especially after finding the postcard.

Cookie bobbed her head to a merry holiday tune playing through hidden speakers while she worked the puzzle. "Did I tell you who I saw the other day?" she asked, setting the paper aside in favor of a little gossip.

I leaned forward, instantly engaged. "Who?"

"Remember Scooter?" she asked.

Mom hustled past us, setting refilled sugar containers on the tables. "I remember him."

"You do?" I asked.

Cookie swung her short legs beneath the table, rocking slightly. Her lips curled into a mischievous grin, suggesting her tea was piping hot.

I searched my mind for something to go with the name. "Scooter," I repeated, mentally flipping through the children of everyone I knew.

"You know," she said. "Caroline's schmoopy stalker."

I barked an unexpected laugh as the man's face and associated memories rushed back into mind. Scooter took a big interest in Caroline the year she opened her cupcake shop, and he stopped by every day to make a purchase and chat. He was polite and friendly, but not nearly the same caliber eye candy as her current beau. Though looks weren't everything, at thirty years old, his round Harry Potter glasses and orange puffy coat didn't do much to help his odds of gaining her attention. Caroline declared him a friend, and nothing short of a wizard's spell would've changed that. But it didn't stop him from putting in the effort. "Right! Of course. He's back in Mistletoe?"

Scooter had turned out to be a really nice guy, if a little overzealous where Caroline was concerned. He'd claimed to love our town and visit annually, but I hadn't seen him in ages.

"Sure is," she said, still sporting a wicked gleam. "He's been on assignment," she said. "With the space force or something."

Scooter was an MIT grad working in cybersecurity for the military, if my memory served, so Cookie's story added up. "How long is he in town?" I asked, immediately wondering what he'd think of finding Caroline in love. And what Zane would think of Scooter's dedication to her, if that was still a thing.

"I don't know," Cookie said. "I didn't think to ask. He did all the talking, then hurried away. But wait until you see him!"

"Does he look different?" I asked.

"Nope."

I frowned. This was far from her best story.

Mom appeared and took our breakfast orders, then told an engaging story about a woman from Indiana who won last night's

Gingerbread Goes to Hollywood contest and bought hot chocolates for the whole café. Now that was a good story.

"Have you seen Ray this morning?" Cookie asked when Mom left to prepare our meals.

"Not yet." But it was still early.

"He's supposed to meet me here, so we can brainstorm for next year's calendar. This year is a bust, and I don't want to miss two in a row."

"Brainstorming sounds like fun," I said. "I'm sure he's on his way." Punctuality wasn't Ray's strong suit, but I blamed his creative streak. It didn't take much to distract him, and Mistletoe at the holidays had plenty of opportunities for distraction. "When I saw him last it sounded as if you two had a plan."

She wrinkled her nose. "We need to keep the calendar content fresh, but there are only so many things a goat can do. He's already climbed Everest, gone skydiving, and parasailed."

I smiled, recalling the photos she'd mentioned. All fictional outings, accomplished with a green screen, some creative camera work on Ray's part, and the sincere suspension of disbelief by viewers. But she was right. After four calendars, Theordore had covered a lot of ground.

"I thought maybe, Goats in Space," she said. "We drafted some sketches, but the sun, the moon, the stars, the planets." She shook her head. "Felt redundant month after month. And he can't visit most of those things anyway and make it back in his lifetime."

"That is a problem," I said.

Mom buzzed past us several minutes later, barely stopping when she delivered our meals, and hurrying in the direction of arriving customers.

"Thank you," we called after her.

"You're welcome. Merry Christmas," she returned.

Our hot chocolates were topped with tall cones of whipped cream and sprinkled with red and green sugar crystals. She'd placed peppermint sticks into the mugs as stirrers and filled our plates with slices of quiche.

"How's Alice holding up?" I asked, cutting a bite of quiche with my fork.

Cookie wiped whipped cream from the tip of her nose. "She's still pretty shaken. She hasn't left the inn, and she spends all of her time in her room unless I go fish her out for meals. I don't think she'd come downstairs or eat otherwise."

My heart broke for Alice. "I wish there was something we could do to help her," I said.

Cookie set her mug aside and dotted her mouth with a napkin. "Her grandpa's coming over from Sweden to stay with her a while. That should help."

"Really?" I perked up at the thought of Alice having a family member at her side. Especially her grandpa. Was he the husband of the grandma who left her all the goats?

"Everything worked out really well because the couple who booked the room beside Alice's, and their friends who were scheduled to check into Alice's room, all came down with the flu. They canceled last night about ten minutes after her grandpa announced his trip. Normally I'd call someone from our waitlist, but Alice is already there and her grandpa is somewhere over the Atlantic right now, so—"

"Sounds like a Christmas miracle," I said. *Except, maybe not for the guests who came down with the flu.* "I can't wait to meet him. I wonder what he's like."

Cookie gave me a long, contemplative look. "I just hope he has a beard."

Chapter Eleven

Ray arrived as we finished our meal. He spotted us easily and headed to our booth with a box tucked under one arm and his work satchel slung over his shoulder. "Sorry I'm late," he said, hanging his coat and scarf on the hook fastened to our booth's side. "I stopped at Wine Around and bought a cheese board for my mom. Samantha asked if I'd see you today, and when I told her I was headed this way, she made me wait while she smashed all these bottles for you." He passed me the box, then slid onto the booth bench beside me. "That woman frightens me."

"You are not alone," I said, beaming at the imagery.

Samantha, my most passionate friend, collected the empty bottles from her monthly wine club meetings and donated the glass to me for jewelry-making. She bought and sold vintages from around the globe, often delivering colors and shades of glass rarely seen in Mistletoe.

I gave the box a shake and the sounds of broken glass rattled inside.

"She went into the back to get the bottles," Ray said. "The next thing I know, sounds of smashing and shattering are coming from the stockroom. I thought she might've dropped them, but the sound kept coming until she returned with a grin and this box."

Cookie smiled warmly. "I appreciate the female rage," she said. "Samantha owns hers. I think her temper is one of my favorite things about her."

Ray released a shuddered breath, apparently not sharing the sentiment. "There's an envelope in there with more orders for gumdrop jewelry," he said. "They're from the Winers."

The Winers were Samantha's monthly wine club members. Mom, Cookie, and I were members but rarely found the time to attend meetings in November or December.

I made a mental note to stop in and renew my membership soon. I'd thank Samantha for the glass while I was there.

"I ordered more of those earrings," Cookie said. "I'm gifting them to my swing dance group. The Swingers love your jewelry, and they want to be part of the new Detective Gumdrop trend."

"Gumdrop Gumshoe," Ray corrected.

I pointed at him in warning.

"It's a lot of fun," Cookie said. "People in town are really getting into it. I've seen folks pairing the gumdrop charms with little magnifying glasses. You should make those too and capitalize on the local interest."

"National interest," Ray said.

I rubbed my temple. "No, thank you."

He stole a little gingerbread man from my tray and wagged it at me. "Speaking of the podcasters and your catchy nickname," he said, "when are you doing that One Year Later interview you promised them? I'd like to take pictures when you do."

"They haven't given me an exact date and time," I admitted. "We talked, informally, about meeting the day after Christmas." Hopefully they forgot.

Ray turned his cookie upside down and dunked it in my hot chocolate before stuffing it into his mouth.

"I don't want to talk about the podcasters," I said. "What else is new?"

"I finished my Christmas shopping," Cookie said. "How about you?"

"Almost," Ray said.

They turned to look at me, a notorious last-minute shopper.

Ray reached for another cookie, and I slid the tray in his direction. "What are you getting Evan for Christmas this year?" he asked. "Now that you made all that extra money from your podcasting fame."

"I'm not sure," I admitted. I'd never had so much money to spend on a single gift, and I wanted whatever I chose to be fantastic. "Do you think he'd like a snowplow for his new truck?"

Ray nodded. "I wish I had a plow on my pickup, but the truck's too small, and plows are expensive."

"The sheriff's truck is huge," Cookie said. "I'll bet that one could handle it."

"We really want to build on the plot of Reindeer Games land my parents gave us," I said. "Evan won't want Dad and the crew clearing our drive when the day comes. He's still in awe of their generosity. He'll want to handle our drive himself and help however he can. I think he'd really like a plow."

Ray slung an arm across the back of the booth. "Let me know if you want any help shopping," he said. "I'd love to take a look with you."

"Deal," I said, thankful for the help. I knew less about snowplows than I did about pickup trucks.

"How's everything else going?" Ray asked.

I grimaced. "Not great."

"She's here getting babysat," Cookie said, relaying the words I'd shared upon her arrival.

Ray snorted a laugh. "What'd you do this time?"

I told him about the postcard then watched as his smile fell and the color leeched from his skin.

"How did that happen?" he asked. "I was with you the whole time."

"It was crowded," I said. "There were people all around us, and we weren't together every second. Even if we were—" I let the sentence drift. I didn't know how someone had put the postcard in my backpack, but that didn't change the fact that someone had.

Cookie folded her hands on the table and set her jaw. "I can't believe you're on another killer's hitlist."

"I am not on a hitlist," I said, hoping that was true. "For all I know, a fan of the show planted the postcard to rattle me. There were dozens of people asking for autographs that day."

Cookie and Ray exchanged a long look. "How's your blood pressure?" she asked.

I rested my head briefly on the table. "Higher every time someone asks me that question."

"What's this about?" Mom's voice lifted my head.

"Hi, Mom," I said. "Ray is eating my cookies."

She laughed, then patted his shoulder. "I know just how to remedy that. I'll be right back."

"Have you told your parents?" he asked.

"Yes," I said. Technically, Evan told them, but that was an argument in semantics. "That's why I'm hanging out here while Evan works."

"Aren't you always here while Evan works?"

I made a grumpy face at him. "Usually, I'm helping. Today, I'm staying right here." I patted the table.

"Is your blood pressure really getting higher?" Cookie asked.

"No." I sighed. "I check regularly and usually get the same reading as Dr. Bright. Never higher, sometimes lower. I'd probably get a perfect reading if I was left alone to enjoy my pregnancy."

"And if you weren't on a killer's hitlist," she said.

Ray pulled a laptop from his bag and set it on the table. "How about something to make you smile?" He logged into the machine and loaded a slide show with images of Theodore, Clementine, and a bunch of baby goats posed in space.

I laughed.

Mom returned with a mug of hot apple cider and a fresh tray of sweets for Ray.

"Thanks, Mrs. White."

She patted his head. "Anything for my daughter's brother-in-law."

The door to the Hearth opened and my gaze flickered to the newcomers.

Alice stepped inside with a slender white-haired man.

"Is that her grandpa?" I asked.

"He's handsome," Mom whispered, then waved an arm overhead. "Welcome," she called. "We're saving seats for you."

Ray, Cookie, and I scooted to make room for Alice and the man at her side.

The duo approached our booth arm in arm. Alice wore her long blonde hair in two braids. She removed her coat to reveal a black turtleneck and jeans.

"Hi, everyone," she said, looking happier than I'd seen her in days. "This is my grandpa. Grandpa, these are my friends. Carol," she motioned to my mom, then moved her hand around the table to introduce us one by one. "Ray, Holly, and Cookie."

We answered in a muddle of hellos and nice-to-meet-yous.

Mom promised to be back with something from the kitchen, then hurried away.

Cookie scooted along her bench, making room for Alice and her grandpa to sit.

"I'm Hugo Andersson," he said, hanging his black wool coat on a hook at the booth's edge before following Alice onto the seat. Hugo wore a cream sweater vest over a white dress shirt.

Cookie leaned forward, peering around Alice at Hugo. "That's a nice beard you have there."

He stroked the tidy facial hair along one cheek. "Thank you."

I glanced at Ray, who bumped his knee against mine under the table. "It's wonderful to meet you," I told Hugo. "We're all incredibly glad you're here."

Alice leaned her head against his shoulder. "Amen."

"Of course," he said warmly. "Alice needed me." He patted her hands where they rested on the table. "Tell me about your friends," he suggested.

She made our introductions once more, this time with a few details to help him understand our positions in her world. "And Cookie is the innkeeper at the inn where we're staying," she finished. "She's kept me company, entertained, and fed while I waited for you."

"Is that right?" he asked.

Cookie blushed.

"What do you do back in Sweden?" I asked.

He smiled shyly. "I'm retired now, but until a few years ago, life and lineage made me a goat herder. Third generation," he added.

Cookie sucked in a breath. "I love goats," she said. "Theodore is a pygmy and lives here on the property. He's recently married to Clementine, and she stays here too."

Hugo's eyes widened. "Fascinating."

"I married them myself," she said, a wealth of pride in her tone.

Hugo leaned his elbows on the table and strained to see around his granddaughter. "I'd love to meet them sometime."

Delight swelled in Cookie's expression until I thought she might pass out or float away.

Mom delivered fresh drinks and snacks to our table, then went to start the first Reindeer Game of our day. She returned to the service counter and powered up my childhood karaoke machine. Using the attached mic, she greeted the café guests and got things rolling. "I know it's early, but this is the third day of Christmas, and it's time to play a Reindeer Game!"

Guests chattered and chuckled as Mom's staff delivered game play materials to the tables.

"This morning's game is Bling That Gingerbread. You'll each receive a prepared gingerbread house, along with a blindfold and tray containing icing and candy décor. When the timer begins, you'll don the blindfold and begin decorating your house. When the timer ends, you'll remove your mask and bring your house to the front. We'll leave the decorated projects on display all day where others can cast their votes, and I'll contact the winner by phone tomorrow morning. So please complete the form attached to the tray."

I caught Alice's eye while the rest of our group made small talk and waited for the game supplies. "Have you been to the antique fair yet?" I asked.

"On opening night," she said. "It was nice. A bit overwhelming. I don't have plans to go back," she added with a humorless laugh.

I smiled. "Understandable. Do you know any of the collectors who are in town?"

She frowned. "No, but I met the event coordinator when I visited the show. He had a few items I recognized from Sweden, and we chatted about those for some time. I think his name was Arnold."

"Did you mention your Yule Goats?" I asked, adding Arnold the show coordinator to my mental suspect list.

Hugo tented bushy white brows at the mention of the goats. "Her grandmother loved those trinkets and figurines. I've never been so relieved to know they arrived here safely. It was an honor to round them up from family members and send them."

"They were the perfect gift," Alice told him. "I cherish them."

"Did you tell Arnold about your collection?" I repeated, still waiting for the important detail.

Concern formed in her eyes, and she gave a stiff dip of her chin. "I suggested he stop by the café sometime so I could show him."

"Did he stop by?" Ray asked.

Alice tensed, apparently following our train of thought. "I don't know," she said. "If he did, I didn't see him."

"But he could've come to the café without you knowing," Ray said.

"Of course." She nodded. "It's so busy, I can barely keep up this time of year."

"We could talk to your staff," I suggested. "Maybe share a photo of him."

Alice bounced her gaze from me to Ray and back. "I haven't opened since the progressive dinner, but I can find an image of Arnold online and send it to my staff by email."

"Smart," Ray said. "I can help if you want." He used his laptop to bring up images of the Antiques Showcase's coordinator.

Hugo's frown deepened as he followed our discussion. "Are you suggesting this man is a murder suspect?"

"Not yet," I said. "But if he knew about the items that were stolen, where to find them, and their extraordinary value, he can't be overlooked."

Hugo wrapped a protective arm around his granddaughter. "What kind of trouble has found you?"

Chapter Twelve

Mom delivered our game supplies, and Bling That Gingerbread kicked off a few minutes later. Blindfolds on, we worked by touch and memory alone to find and apply the icing from little cups on our personal trays to the gingerbread houses before us. After the icing was spread, we used the sticky substance as glue to adorn the little homes with candies. Each player received the same number of gumdrops, peppermints, licorice strips, and rainbow sprinkles to make their project the prettiest.

I'd performed these steps enough times in my life to get a decent result, but the process was always a bit comical. The loudly ticking clock didn't help the sense of urgency. Neither did Mom's minute-by-minute updates.

"Three more minutes," she announced, using the karaoke mic.

Then approximately ten seconds later, "Two minutes."

Panic rose and contestants squealed.

"One minute!"

Sounds of falling candies and raucous laughter echoed through the room.

Mom increased the volume on the holiday soundtrack to cover the occasional curse word.

The second buzzer sounded. "Time's up!" she announced.

We removed our blindfolds as instructed, and the laughter began anew. The reality of our finished products, versus what we'd envisioned as we worked, sent the lot of us into hysterics.

The confidence I'd entered the game with went straight into the snow as I reviewed my results. The icing I'd smeared so intentionally on the board around my home was barren. My gumdrop fence stood on the table, where I'd missed the board completely.

Alice had a similar problem, though her icing was applied thickly across her roof. A pile of sprinkles stood along each side of the house, either because she'd missed her target, or simply because the tiny décor didn't stick. "Darn!" She laughed. "I counted on the rainbow roof to put me at the top of the pack. Now the place is completely naked." Her attempts to attach candies to the walls hadn't fared any better.

Hugo chuckled. "At least the icing is white. It looks as if snow is on the roof. And a few of those mints are under the windows. Maybe your house was a candy shop that overflowed onto the lawn."

"Nice spin, Grandpa," she said. "I'll take it!"

He smiled. "You managed far better than me. Look." His pattern of alternating small cinnamon candies and peppermints went awry when the heavier peppermints slid off the roof, leaving thick stripes in the icing. "It looks like a big bear clawed my place."

Alice cracked up, and my chest warmed at her joy.

I was immensely thankful for her small reprieve in an otherwise terrible week. Her grandpa's presence made all the difference. He'd sparked visible hope in her, and he wore his love for her all over his face.

"That's not bad," Cookie said, still examining Hugo's work. "Those claw marks look intentional. You can pretend they were a design choice."

Ray popped a candy into his mouth and pointed to Cookie's house. "What's going on there?" he asked. "Smallpox? Poison oak?"

Cookie frowned at her creation. "How was I supposed to know they were all red?" she asked, having somehow managed to polka dot her home with a variety of red candy. "You're one to talk. You didn't even play," she said.

Ray's gingerbread house was void of roof décor, and his tray of accoutrements was completely empty. "I put gumdrop trees on the porch and a peppermint wreath on the door. It's simplistic."

"Low effort," she corrected, shaking her head.

He patted his flat middle. "Free candy."

I shook my head, unable to suppress a laugh. "You just sat there, blindfolded and eating candy, while the whole café scrambled to play the game."

"I played guess the flavor," he said. "You should add that to next year's Reindeer Games."

"Put it in the suggestion box," I told him.

"There's a suggestion box?"

"No." I pushed him toward the edge of the bench. "Come on. We have to take these up front and turn in our trays."

We delivered our gingerbread homes to the front for display, then returned to the table.

Mom arrived a moment later, looking delighted. "I saved the morning crossword for you again. I thought of a prank," she said, nearly fizzing with excitement. "Wouldn't it be funny if you finish this one before you and Evan do the puzzle in your paper later tonight? You'd know all the answers as soon as you read the clues." She snickered. "He'd be so confused."

"I should do that before trivia night sometime," Cookie said. "They never ask anything I know."

"Diabolical, Mrs. W," Ray added, tossing a gumdrop from my misplaced candy fence on the table into his mouth.

Mom pulled the crossword from her apron pocket and passed it to me. "Do with this what you will." She stage-winked, then hurried to help her customers.

I read the clue for two across, immediately thankful the answer wasn't another song lyric or title. "Whoville delicacy. Five letters. Blank beast."

"Roast," Ray said.

Cookie smacked her lips. "That sounds delicious."

"I could go for some roast," I said, unsure how I felt about the clue's answer otherwise. It seemed innocuous enough, but something in my gut said roast was definitely threat adjacent.

* * *

Evan picked me up at the end of his shift and helped me into his truck. The cab was warm and the sun long set as we motored away from the farm. "Hungry?" he asked. "Or did your mom stuff you full of her homemade sweets again?"

"Both," I said confidently.

He smiled. "How about a dinner date?"

I beamed. "Can we go somewhere that serves roast?"

Evan slid his eyes in my direction and laughed before returning his attention to the snow-covered road. "Sounds good."

We ate at the Holi-Glaze Grill, and I enjoyed a hearty serving of roast with baby potatoes, carrots, and rolls that melted in my mouth. Evan got the glazed fish and steamed veggies.

Afterward, the drive back through town was magical with falling snow and twinkling holiday lights.

"How's your new truck holding up to a Mistletoe winter?" I asked.

He ran a palm along the curve of his steering wheel, then gave it a gentle pat. "Like a champ," he said. "I'm so glad I gave in and spent the money. These rural winters and all the miles I drive between home and the farm were the perfect incentive. I don't regret a thing."

Evan had toiled with the desire to buy a new truck for a long while. His frugal side stopped him for several years, but once we'd married, the occasionally perilous trips from the farm to town had sealed the deal.

"How about the features?" I asked,

He shot me a disbelieving look. "This thing has features I never knew I wanted, and now I couldn't live without. I'd say it has everything."

My satisfied expression reflected in the passenger window. I knew exactly how to improve his ride. I made a mental note to start actively researching snowplows tomorrow.

We slowed near the town square, and I glanced around, attempting to understand the change in speed.

Evan initiated his turn signal, then he parked in an open space outside the pie shop.

"What are you doing?" I asked, hoping I knew the answer.

Evan climbed out, rounded the hood of his truck and opened my door. "I thought a piece of pie might be the perfect end to a terrific night."

If I hadn't already been in love with my husband, this unexpected stop would've sealed the deal.

I pressed a palm to my chest and let him help me from the truck. "Swoon."

"I try."

I eyeballed him as we walked along the sidewalk to the door. "You're in an awfully good mood tonight, Sheriff. Care to share the cause?"

He raised our joined hands and twirled me before opening and holding the pie shop door.

"It's just a five-star day," he said, catching me when I momentarily lost balance.

Inside, the air smelled of buttery, fresh-baked dough, warm apples, and cinnamon sugar. I leaned against him in the foyer as the line of waiting guests ambled forward.

Evan lowered his lips to my ear. "Every once in a while, it just hits me," he said. "How much I love this life. This town. This season. I moved here to find peace, and I did that, but I got so much more."

I grinned. "Like?"

"Like a best friend for life, who thankfully agreed to marry me. And now I get to raise a family with her."

"She sounds nice," I said.

He kissed me gently and he fixed me with a beautiful smile. "She has her moments."

The hostess seated us a few minutes later, and Evan leaned across the table to take my hands.

"How's this healing?" he asked, stroking my injured hand with the pads of his fingers.

"Well," I said. "It hurts less and less every day. I can use it for almost anything now. Making a fist still hurts, but how often do I do that?"

He smiled.

"Are you okay?" I asked. Something in his tone and touch had been extra cautious and less carefree than I preferred, despite the affection.

"I'm not complaining," I clarified. "Just curious."

"Aren't you always?" he muttered.

I cocked a brow. "Something else you want to say, Sheriff?"

Evan wet his lips and glanced around the crowded shop before turning a worried look on me. "I want you to know how much I hate that you found another dead body. I hate that your friend is involved, and that you received that awful postcard. On top of all that, we received incredible news from Dr. Bright. I don't want you getting mixed up in this thing with Alice and putting yourself or our baby in danger. I wish we could just enjoy this miracle we were given like other, normal parents-to-be."

I slouched, unsure what to say to that. I couldn't stop what had happened outside Alice's café, and I definitely couldn't make Evan and me normal parents.

He caressed the back of my hand with his thumb, probably waiting for a response.

Thankfully, the waitress appeared. She wore a pale blue and white vintage uniform and a red elf hat with jingle bells. "How are you two doing tonight?" she asked. "Looks like a date. Any special occasion?"

Evan maintained eye contact with me as he answered. "Just enjoying a night out with my wife."

She set a palm over her heart. "Aww. Well let me get out of your hair. Can I bring you anything when I come back?"

"Coffee," Evan said.

"Cinnamon tea, please," I added.

Evan stretched long legs under the table, bumping his knees softly against mine. "Alice's grandpa is nice, huh?" he asked.

"Truly," I said. "And he has a beard."

"So, Cookie is half in love?" he guessed.

The waitress returned with our drinks before I could respond. "There you are." She set our mugs on the table. "Will you be enjoying any pie tonight?" she asked.

I looked at Evan, unsure I could eat another bite but positive I would try.

"What do you recommend?" he asked.

"That's a tough one," she said. "We're celebrating the annual twelve pies of Christmas from now through New Years's Eve, and today's special is White Christmas pie, which is fantastic. But the Kringle Cranberry is a classic, and chocolate pecan is something to dream about."

"What's in the White Christmas?" I asked, intrigued by a pie name I didn't recognize.

"It's a baked crust with a creamy coconut filling," she said. "There's almond and vanilla extract in there as well, and the whole thing is covered in whipped topping." She performed a chef's kiss.

"I want that," I said. I loved a new pie, and White Christmas sounded like a holiday fantasy. Yes, please!

"Let's make it two," Evan said.

"Be right back!" The waitress spun on her toes and headed for the pie counter.

Evan opened his mouth in awe. "That pie sounds wicked good."

"Tell me you're from Boston without telling me," I teased.

He reached under the table and squeezed my knee until I threw my head back in laughter.

"Stop!" I panted. "No tickling in public."

He put his hands on the table where I could see them and grinned. "How's Alice doing?"

"She's good," I said. "A lot better with her grandpa in town."

He nodded. "Did she say anything interesting?"

I dropped a sugar cube into my tea and considered his seemingly casual question. He'd asked about Alice's grandpa only a few minutes before. "Why, Sheriff, are you buttering me up to extract sensitive information about your case?"

He worked his eyebrows. "Maybe I'm buttering you up for completely different reasons."

I cackled.

I let him stew for a few minutes while I sipped my tea, but it wasn't long before the gossip in me cracked.

"So this guy, Arnold," I said, "knew about the value of her grandma's Yule Goats and that they were at her café."

"And he's the event coordinator for the antiques show?" Evan confirmed.

I nodded.

"I'll follow up with him tomorrow," he said. "Thank you."

I beamed.

"Okay," he said. "Your turn."

"For what?"

Evan leaned forward, eyes tight. "I asked you a question about my case. You can ask me something too, if you want. I'll be as honest as I can, but I can't promise I'll be able to answer."

I broke into another wide smile. "Oh, I like this game," I said. "Let me noodle a minute."

The waitress returned with two slices of pie. A dozen tiny peaks of whipped cream topped each dessert.

We thanked her before digging in.

The tines of my fork sank through the creamy goodness and flaked the crispy baked crust below. I slid the first bite into my mouth and felt my eyes roll with delight. White Christmas pie was possibly even better than I'd imagined. I ate silently, reverent in the face of such decadence. The moment was far too perfect to discuss a murder.

Evan didn't repeat his offer, and I let the opportunity go. Happy to enjoy the night for what it was—a holiday dream date come true.

We spent another hour talking about our days, our friends, and our baby, while enjoying hot refills on our drinks.

When we rose to pay the bill, Libby's face appeared on Evan's phone screen. He tucked the device against his shoulder and answered as we walked to the register.

"Is everything okay?" I asked when he ended the call.

"Yeah." He tucked his credit card into his wallet and put our receipt into his pocket. "My little sister is uncharacteristically excited about inflatable snowmen. Any idea why?"

I shook my head and busied myself bundling up before moving outside.

"Apparently, she found a deal and bought two," he said. "She wants to set them up on our lawn tomorrow morning. Is that weird or is it just me?"

A spark of delight lit in me as we braved the cold to his truck once more.

"Gotta love a good deal," I said, equally excited about Libby's purchase.

I didn't need to get involved in a messy, dangerous murder investigation this year. I could help find a snowman thief instead!

Chapter Thirteen

Evan and I moved slowly the next morning. We'd stayed up late and allowed ourselves the indulgence of sleeping in—something we'd soon have few opportunities to do. Libby called after breakfast to confirm she was coming over with the snowmen, and Evan made his way outside to shovel the driveway and sidewalk before work.

Cindy Lou Who followed me through the house, meowing and complaining until I fed her fresh kibble.

"There's food in your bowl," I told her. She hadn't finished the meal I'd put out for her last night. She didn't like leftovers, and I hated wasting money. "Can't you see it?" I asked. "Maybe you need some little kitty glasses for Christmas."

I watched through the front window for Evan to come into view, then I grabbed my laptop and searched for snowplows.

A loud clatter in the kitchen drew my shoulders to my ears. "Cindy!"

She sat beneath the archway, cleaning her paws and glaring at me. Behind her, the bowl of last night's dinner was overturned. I pushed onto my feet and marched to the kitchen. I cleaned up the mess, begrudgingly. Then I scooped fresh food into her bowl.

"I'm putting what you don't eat into a container from now on," I threatened. "Then you can't do this every time you're mad."

Cindy gave her water fountain a long look, as if she understood more than she let on. And I wondered if I'd just been threatened.

I returned to the couch and my laptop while Cindy ate. I added the make and model of Evan's truck for compatibility, then narrowed my hunt for a snowplow.

"Holy snowballs," I whispered, certain the decimal point was in the wrong place.

I opened more browser windows and checked more sites, scrolling through the details on pricing, installation, and available options. Ray warned me that this was an expensive gift, but I hadn't expected to spend thousands of dollars. At least three thousand, to be exact.

I dragged my gaze from the laptop to the box of *Dead and Berried* fan requests for autographs and sighed. Ray was right about something else as well. It was time I embraced my alter ego, because the Gumdrop Gumshoe made my snowplow dreams possible.

Nostalgic thoughts of playing detective had me opening another window and clicking in the search bar. I debated whose name to enter first. After a moment, I chose Kent George. The man had been present for the attempted theft of Alice's copper Yule Goat, and he was on the farm the day that creepy postcard found its way into my bag.

Multiple pages of information returned. For starters, I learned Kent was an avid collector of international art, including sculptures large and small. His photograph appeared on blogs and websites with articles he'd written on topics like the modern-day cultural importance of art history.

His specialty seemed to be paintings, but he'd contributed to a Swedish art blog on numerous occasions. He probably knew exactly how valuable Alice's goats were, and he could've easily doubled back to retrieve them after the initial would-be thief failed. He might've even run into her when she made a second attempt. Maybe they squabbled, and he shut her up permanently before making off with the goats.

My skin crawled at the more recent memories of Kent on my farm. I'd introduced myself and asked about the night of the murder. Then he'd seen my face on the stall calling me the Gumdrop Gumshoe.

"Not good, Gray," I whispered. "Not good at all."

Next, I logged on to the Antiques Showcase's website and typed his name in the search bar. A hit came back immediately. Kent was listed as a seller at this event. I checked the location map to see where his table was located in case I had the chance to visit. I made a mental note to look up Arnold, the event coordinator's last name, so I could plug it into the internet as well. Then I navigated to the forums and searched for conversations about the Yule Goats, wondering why I hadn't thought of this before.

The term didn't create any results, so I tried a broader search, using only the word Sweden.

That gained more than one hundred results, and I wasn't sure if I should rejoice or cry. I didn't have time to read that many posts right now. Maybe not before Christmas.

I pressed a palm to my forehead and willed a better idea to take hold.

I opened another browser and typed the name of Kent's pixie-haired friend, Nancy Grace. A generic social media profile returned with her picture and extremely limited available information, unless I wanted to send her a friend request.

I did not.

Nothing else turned up under her name, at least not for anyone that fit her description.

What exactly was her area of expertise? International art, like Kent? She'd shown an interest in the goats too. Maybe she and Kent were a team in this event? Either at the antiques show or in the recent theft and murder.

A quick honk of someone's horn jerked my attention through the front window and my heart into a sprint. I spotted Libby parking at the curb and felt myself sag in relief.

Evan had reached the end of the driveway on his first pass with his snow shovel and greeted his sister with a hug. The process of removing last night's accumulation would take him at least thirty minutes, which meant I had time to chat privately with my friend.

I set the laptop aside and went to meet Libby on the porch with a box of prepackaged sweets.

Libby followed the newly cleared sidewalk to our porch and waved a hand at my little cart of snacks for delivery drivers and postal workers. "I love this," she said. "You're much better at the presentation than Ray and me. We just put a basket of your mom's cutout cookies on a bench with a piece of paper taped to it. Free snacks for delivery drivers," she said, drawing a wide line in the air before her. "Yours looks like a photo opp. The drivers probably pose for selfies after they pick their treat."

My little display was intentionally, dramatically aesthetic. Outlined in twinkle lights and topped with a black and white checkered bow, I'd angled the bright red cart beneath our doorbell, on a big black and white checkered rug. A smaller red Merry Christmas mat sat on top of that one, positioned before the door. Evergreen topiaries with additional twinkle lights and bows stood sentinel on each side of the steps, and a massive wreath, made from the boughs of trees at our farm, hung front and center on the window.

An assortment of drinks, sweets, and snacks filled each tier of the rolling cart. Taller items in back, shorter ones in front. Heavier drinks lined the bottom, bagged cookies and chocolate covered pretzels stayed on the top. A sign containing cartoon images of various delivery trucks, a message of gratitude, and an invitation to help themselves to refreshments completed the look. I'd even laminated the sign to protect it from the weather.

I wanted my effort to make drivers feel appreciated, and if someone took a selfie before leaving, I certainly wouldn't mind.

My heart went out to teams who persevered when their loads got bigger and their days got longer. When the temperatures grew colder and the roads became more fraught with icy and treacherous conditions. Despite my best efforts to shop small and spend my money locally, Mistletoe didn't have everything. My online ordering was likely to increase with a baby on the horizon.

I invited Libby inside, and we shared a quick cup of coffee. She dropped a large quilted tote bag onto the table.

"How are you feeling?" she asked.

"Very well," I reported.

"Is this caffeinated?"

"Yes."

"Is it safe to drink when pregnant?" she asked.

My mood soured slightly. "Yes, and I can safely have one or two cups a day," I said. "I spent a few hours at the Hearth reading about the first trimester in pregnancy."

Libby lifted her cup and sipped. "Cool. Evan told me about the postcard with eyes scratched out. You doing okay with that?"

"There were Xs on the eyes," I said, clarifying for my sake. "I'm still hoping it was a terribly timed joke. Maybe someone mimicking the low stakes threats I've had in the past. They could've heard about those on the podcast."

"Like an homage," she said.

"Exactly."

"Sounds more like a stalker."

I winced. A stalker was even worse than a killer trying to keep me out of their business. Stalking was personal. "Let's hope it's not that one," I said.

When our coffees were done, we bundled up and headed onto the front lawn. Libby retrieved her newly purchased inflatable snowmen from the backseat of her car and hauled them into the snow.

Evan waved as we unpacked and set up the bases, tethers, and power cords.

"Something on your mind?" Libby asked. She kept an eye on me as she worked.

I processed my thoughts as she twisted a stake into the ground, then gave the attached tether a tug. Anchoring the Frostys securely to the ground was our first order of business. We'd lose our bait if a strong gust of wind took the snowmen into town.

Libby paused and set gloved hands on her hips.

"Maybe," I said, feeling a little silly that I couldn't let the crossword coincidence go. "It's probably nothing."

Evan whooped beside us as he finished clearing the drive and carried the shovel into the garage.

"Okay." Libby straightened to her full height. "Out with it."

I gave into my need for camaraderie and told her about the crossword puzzle.

She crouched as she listened, securing the snowmen with the remaining stakes.

I went on to relay Evan's thoughts, but I hoped she'd side with me. "I understand what he's saying," I told her. "But my instincts say it's something more. And no matter how I dice it, "watch out" feels like a threat. So does "roast," for that matter."

Libby stood again, dusting the snow from her gloves.

"In the context of a possible threat, roast could mean fire," I said, my voice going low and quiet on the final word.

Her suddenly sad expression suggested she agreed with Evan and was likely thinking about some of the things I'd been through since we'd met. "What about today's puzzle?" she asked. "If the answer is green beans or mashed potatoes, it might help dampen your concerns."

I shrugged. "We slept in today," I said. "And it snowed all night, so Evan started shoveling after breakfast instead of playing the puzzle."

Libby extended an arm in the direction of my front door. "Let's go have a look."

We met Evan in the kitchen, where he'd shucked off his coat and left snowy boots on the mat. He sipped a mug of coffee and flipped through the morning paper.

Libby and I hung our coats on the backs of two empty chairs.

I kissed his head and thanked him for clearing the drive.

He smiled. "You two made quick work of the snowmen. I thought that would be a much bigger job."

Libby cocked her head and stared at her big brother. "Are you suggesting you thought we'd need your help?"

His green eyes danced with mischief. "I saw the instructions sheet when you opened the box out there. Looked like a lot to read."

Her fair skin reddened, and Evan hooked one ankle over the opposite knee. "It takes a bit of muscle to secure those stakes properly in the frozen ground."

"We managed just fine," she said. Her attempt to feign unbothered might've worked if the red from her cheeks hadn't spread to the tips of her ears.

"I didn't do anything," I admitted. "She wouldn't let me. Libby was the muscle on this project."

"Ah," Evan said. "I'll take a look on my way to work, make sure everything's secure."

"Very funny," she said, gripping the edge of our kitchen table with white knuckles. "Keep it up, big brother. It might be time for me to bring back the atomic wedgie."

Evan rose with an easy smile and left the paper on the table. "Always so easy to rattle."

"I've got your rattle."

He chuckled as he kissed my head. "I'm going to shower and get ready for work. Pack my lunch while I'm gone."

"Hey!" Libby called.

I laughed with Evan. Everyone knew I wasn't a qualified lunch packer. I'd become a charcuterie queen for a reason. No cooking necessary. "One bag of muffins coming up."

He disappeared up the staircase, still chuckling at his ability to get Libby riled.

"All right," she said, taking a seat at the table and flipping the newspaper to the crossword puzzle. "Which clue is bothering you?"

"Two across," I said, moving to watch over her shoulder.

Libby set the tip of her finger against the page and read. "Three letters. All Mariah Carey wants for Christmas."

"You," we said in perfect unison.

My limbs felt wiggly as I took the seat beside Libby. "The clues for two across so far this week have been Holly White watch out roast you. Five days. Five answers. And it still feels incredibly pointed."

Libby squinted at the puzzle. "I don't love it," she said. "It's a strange coincidence, and I'm not a fan of those either."

"Exactly!"

"But—" She set the paper down and turned patient eyes on me. "Planting clues in the daily crossword seems like a very slow and hugely ineffective way to threaten someone. How would they even know you do these puzzles?"

"Evan said all of that," I reminded her.

She crossed her legs and tucked long auburn locks behind her ears. "Have you done anything to provoke the person who killed Hannah Ford?"

"Of course not."

She waited, and I squirmed.

"Provoke is a strong word."

Libby's mouth opened and shut it with a snap. "Holly," she hissed. "What did you do?"

I made wild eyes and pointed to the ceiling, reminding her to keep her voice down or Evan would hear. There wasn't any reason to upset him. He was having his perfect Christmas.

"Nothing significant," I promised. But I had asked a few questions and checked out the antiques show's website. It was possible one of those small things had led to a problem. "I made an account online with the Antiques Showcase," I said. "I read through a bunch of stuff in their forums, then I talked to a vendor at Santa's Village who knew a little about how things work over there. And I ran into the guy from the night of the progressive dinner who told Alice her Yule Goats were valuable."

Libby blinked. "Jeez. Anything else?"

"I don't think so."

She gave her head a disbelieving shake. "So, the postcard thing could've really been a threat. Someone might've overheard you asking around about the murder at Santa's Village."

I blew out a long, weary breath. "I guess."

"Tell me about the website forums. Did you interact with anyone there? Ask any questions?"

"No," I said. "But I noticed today that everyone online is listed with a green dot, so it's possible that someone online at the same time as me would know I had an account there. Maybe there's something they wouldn't want me to read, or maybe the fact I was there was enough to make them think I'm investigating."

Libby guffawed. "How would they know it was you? You didn't use your real name. Did you?"

"Of course not."

"Good."

"I used 'Gumdrop underscore Gumshoe for you,' with a number 4 and a capital U," I said, realizing the problem belatedly.

"Be serious," she scolded. "You didn't."

"Holly White was taken. So was Holly Gray. And I didn't know I needed a secret handle. I just wanted to see what I could do with an account there. Besides, what was I supposed to pick? It's the internet. Everything is already taken."

"Did you try User one two three four?" she asked. "How about User five six seven eight? Literally anything that wasn't your name or nickname?" She made a disgusted sound and waved her hands aimlessly before dropping them to her lap.

"How was I supposed to know the website would list the online users like that? I thought I'd be one of a billion people who made an account in the past thirty years. A needle in a haystack."

"Delete the account," she said. "If you're going to snoop in there some more, start a new account. Make a fake email address to go with it so no one can identify the fake name by its associated email. Stop using Holly dot White at email dot com for everything you do online."

"I made that email in middle school," I told her. "It was smart too. Try getting your exact name online for anything these days."

Libby looked toward the couch in the living room, where I'd left my laptop after using it to peek into those forums only an hour ago. "Log me into your computer, and I'll help you set things up securely before I go."

"I'm already logged in."

She rolled her eyes. "Let's power up the snowmen real quick and make sure they work."

We went to the living room window overlooking the lawn, and I flipped the switch that controlled our outdoor outlet.

Cindy Lou Who leapt onto the windowsill and watched with us as the Frostys slowly swelled to life.

Soon they stood side by side near the sidewalk.

"Sweet," she said. "They look great. They're far enough from the house to tempt thieves, and they're in plain view of the window, along with most of the block in both directions."

"They're super cute," I said. "Is it wrong if I hope no one steals them?"

"Yes," Libby said. "I spent a hundred bucks on those guys. I need them to be stolen."

I sank onto the couch. "Fine." Maybe I could score some discounted snowmen at the end of the season and put those on the roof next year instead of the rusty sled.

"Grab my bag," she said. "I'll get started on your laptop."

I went back to the kitchen for her bag. When I returned, she'd knelt before the window. "What are you doing?"

She twisted at the waist and outstretched an arm as I approached. "The bear," she said. "Give me the bear."

I unzipped the bag and found an adorable brown teddy bear with a thick crimson bow. "Aww—"

She cut my admiration short by taking the toy from my hands. "It's the nanny cam," she said. "Brilliant idea, by the way." She seated the bear on the windowsill, adjusting him carefully from her position at his eye level.

Satisfied, she pulled the cell phone from her back pocket and swiped a few times. My front yard appeared onscreen.

I knelt beside her for a better look. "Cool!"

"The camera has a motion sensor, so it only records when there's movement," she said. "During the day, when traffic is moving, you have to keep an eye on the battery. It could need recharged frequently. I haven't used this more than an hour or two at a time. At night, though, when things are still, it'll capture every move that's made out there."

"Can I download the app and watch too?" I asked.

She shared the link, and I added the app to my phone. "As soon as the snowmen go missing," she explained. "We can download the feed from the cloud and review it for a look at the thieves. No need to sit around staking out the place."

Evan bounded down the steps in his sheriff's uniform, and I nearly jumped out of my skin.

Libby tucked her phone into her pocket as he approached.

Evan darted his gaze from me to Libby, then the bear. "What are you two doing?"

"Setting up a sting operation," Libby said. "This bear is officially in charge of watching those snowmen."

Evan snorted. "All right. I'm off to protect the town," he said. "I'll take a look at those anchors on my way out."

Libby went to the couch and grabbed my laptop. "Don't slip and fall on the ice," she called. "I haven't had a chance to check your work on the driveway."

"Feel free to come over and shovel anytime," he yelled back. "Let me know if you need anything today." He threaded strong arms into his black sheriff's coat, and I hustled into the kitchen to kiss him goodbye.

"Be safe today," he said. "I love you."

"Love you too." I grabbed the collar on his coat and pulled him down for a kiss.

My laptop dinged, and Libby swore. "Ev," she said. "Holly."

I released my husband, but he took my good hand as we moved to the threshold of the living room and waited.

"What's up?" he asked. "Is that Holly's laptop?"

Libby sighed. "'Fraid so." She spun the device to face us, but it was too far away to read the page clearly.

Ribbons of tension spooled from her, gliding across the carpet to meet us, and pulling us in. My stomach churned with nausea.

"Holly is logged into the Antiques Showcase's forums, and a private message just arrived for her," Libby explained.

I imagined bouncing the heel of my hand against my forehead. I'd forgotten to log out when Libby arrived. "Who's it from?" I asked.

"I don't know," she said, her voice suddenly weaker than I was accustomed to hearing it. The look on her face as we reached the couch nearly buckled my knees.

> BackOffWhite to Gumdrop_Gumshoe4U: This is none of your concern but keep going and you will find a reason to be concerned.

Chapter Fourteen

Evan promised to stay in touch throughout the day and let me know if he had any luck identifying the sender of the online message.

Meanwhile, I went Christmas shopping with my new babysitting team—Libby and Ray. The couple were given explicit instructions to keep me in their sights at all times and not to let me say a word about the murder investigation in public. If the killer was watching, it should be clear that I'd taken their advice.

Their job would be simple, because I had no intention of putting myself or my baby in harm's way. I hated that things had already gone so far.

But it wasn't too late to fix this.

I buckled into the passenger side of Libby's compact SUV, and she picked up Ray on our way to the square.

He drummed a beat against my headrest. "You sure love traditions," he said, making a not-so-subtle joke about my current predicament.

I twisted to look at him between the seats as Libby drove. "If you knew how hard I've worked to mind my business, you'd give me a cookie."

Ray reached into his pocket and unearthed a prepackaged cutout cookie shaped like a star.

I accepted. "Thank you. I've stayed on the farm every day. I haven't asked anyone about that night."

"Uh," Ray interjected. "The Yule Goat guy."

"No," I argued. "I only asked him if he'd heard about what happened after we left. That was a normal thing to do, especially after what we'd all witnessed. I wanted to see his reaction."

"Meh," Libby said, glancing my way. "Normal for you, maybe. I might've asked my friends, but I wouldn't have approached a stranger to gossip unless I wanted more information or to stir up trouble."

I gave her response a long moment of consideration. "You could be right. I've always been able to talk to everyone." Growing up on the farm, I'd interacted with strangers all my life, and my folks treated everyone as if they were longtime friends. Clearly, I'd developed a bad habit. "I'll work on it. No more talking to anyone about the murder," I promised. "But since I already did, I wish the guy would've said something useful I could've reported to Evan." As it was, that conversation might've been the one that led me to the threats.

Ray snorted a laugh, then patted my head. "How is the sheriff, anyway?"

"Fuming," Libby said. "Also worrying his tech department won't be able to figure out who left that message."

"Can't he just reach out to the show's producer and ask who's in charge of the website?" I asked. "Then contact the website administrator to learn who's behind the BackOffWhite handle?"

"He can try," she said, settling into the steady crawl of traffic as the town square came into view. "If we're lucky, the user's associated email has their real contact information. But if they created a throwaway email account with bogus details, and used that to create the handle with the show's website, it's a complete dead end. Just like we talked about."

"So what happens in that case?"

Libby adjusted the heater and vents, then lowered the volume on the holiday radio station. Thinking or stalling, I wasn't sure which.

"The website is unlikely to release personal information without a subpoena," she said, finally. "They're obligated to protect user information, and they will to the best of their ability, unless legally forced to divulge personal information. Evan can pursue a subpoena, if he can collect enough evidence to convince a judge it's justified, but that takes forever and might still lead to a dead end."

Ray leaned forward. "What about using the IP address of the user to locate them? That's what hackers do in movies."

"IP addresses only locate the computer that was used. Back-OffWhite could've used a library computer to send the message," Libby said. "If they have any tech savvy there are ways to hide the IP address as well."

"If they used a public computer, like one at the library," Ray said, "We could ask management to share security footage."

Libby lifted a palm. "If, and yeah, we could," she agreed, "but tracking down an online person is a shot in the dark. It's not easy. It takes time. And it will require other entities to cooperate and assist."

Ray released a long breath. "All right. Do we have a plan for our time in town?"

I looked over my shoulder in his direction. "Yeah. I have shopping to do," I said. "And if I spend another day pinned to the booth at the Hearth, I might explode."

"You sure you're up to this after being threatened so recently?"

I nodded. "I also plan to put on a show. Anyone who spots me in town will see a woman highly focused on the joy of the holiday and utterly uninterested in crime solving."

Libby parked in the alley behind Caroline's cupcake shop to avoid parking at the high school football stadium and taking a shuttle back to the square. The process was designed to streamline traffic when an increase in tour buses started blocking roads and causing fender benders all day.

She settled the engine and looked at me. "We have a couple of hours before we need to head toward Reindeer Games," she said. "We don't have to stay in our booth at the Hearth all afternoon, but I'd like to play a game or two. I've been so busy with work, I've barely visited in a week, and I promised Cookie we'd be there tonight for the toy wrapping party."

I'd forgotten the wrapping party was tonight. I sent Evan a text to ask him to pick me up at the inn after his shift. He responded immediately in agreement.

"Sounds like I have a full day of fun things ahead," I said, immensely thankful for the change of scenery and time with friends.

Biting winter wind assaulted us as we exited the vehicle. It wouldn't be hard to convince me to get out of the cold soon.

"Where are we headed?" Ray asked. He shivered a little as he walked. "We should streamline our path to avoid backtracking, wasting time, and freezing our tails off longer than necessary between shops."

"Agreed," Libby said.

"I need to stop at Wine Around for Mom's gift," I said. "Oh, Fudge! for Cookie, and the cupcake shop to see Caroline. She's swamped all the time too, and I miss her."

"That's easy enough," Libby said. "I just need to hit the coffee shop and candle store. Let's visit Caroline last so we know how long we can chat before leaving town. The sooner we finish picking up our gifts, the more time we have for cupcakes."

We started at the Beanerie, where we each ordered a specialty coffee. I requested my usual drink with decaf. Ray chose hot chocolate with hazelnut, and Libby ordered a peppermint mocha before buying coffee-themed gifts for her family in Boston.

"How are you feeling?" Ray asked. He held open the door for Libby and me to exit.

I raised the logoed cup to my face, inhaling the sweet steam. "Are you asking about my pregnancy or the recent—" I caught myself. "Message," I finished, avoiding any mention of the recent murder, killer, or investigation while in public.

"Both," he said.

Libby passed her shopping bag into his hand and gave us a warning look.

It took more brainpower than I'd expected to answer him without saying anything I shouldn't while surrounded by potentially listening ears. "As to be expected on both counts," I said finally.

"Are you nauseous in the mornings?" he asked. "Headaches? Fatigue?"

"Sure." I nodded. "I've been all of those things for a while." I'd chalked it up to the chaos of holidays in Mistletoe at first. Waking early to help my folks prepare the farm for the Christmas rush, then staying up late filling jewelry orders would take a toll on anyone. Some weeks I never stopped moving while on the farm, assisting the crew with twinkle lights along the perimeter fence and hauling bulk ingredients to the Hearth for Mom's baking. I even helped Dad with the layout for Santa's Village. "I was exhausted and probably dehydrated, which are known causes of headaches and nausea."

"Makes sense to me," Libby said.

Ray stopped to drop money into a donations box surrounded by children dressed as Santa's elves.

"Thank you!" they sang.

An adult overseeing the group, which was collecting money for another downtown restoration project, handed him a flyer with coupons to local businesses. "Merry Christmas!"

He lifted the paper in thanks, then tucked it into one of the bags. "Do you have any baby name ideas?" he asked, beginning to walk once more.

"Not yet," I said. "It's early, and we're still getting our minds around the concept of a baby on the way."

"No names?" Ray's hopeful expression fell, disproportionally disappointed. "Do you at least have a plan?"

"What kind of plan?"

"A naming convention of some sort," he said. "The way some families name all the kids something that starts with the same letter, or the names rhyme like in my mom's family."

I smiled. Ray's mom, Fay, had two sisters, May and Kay. And a brother, Gay. "No rhyming," I said.

"The Bridgertons went in alphabetical order. Maybe that's worth thinking about."

Libby shook her head. "Leave her alone."

"I'm interested," he said. "This might be my only niece or nephew."

"That's true," I agreed. Evan and I weren't getting any younger. Evan was thirty-six. I was thirty-one. One was enough for us and more than we'd imagined possible after months of trying.

"You could have twins," Libby teased.

"Or triplets," Ray said.

"First of all, never say that again," I told Ray. "Secondly, the only idea I have so far is for the baby to have a name with meaning. Preferably something Christmassy or relevant to our family. Like nicknaming them our little snowflake."

Libby's brows lowered with interest as we waited for a group of ladies to exit the store beside us, temporarily blocking our path. "I need examples."

Ray raised a hand. "How about Douglas for a boy?"

Not my first choice, but interesting. "Do we know someone with that name?"

He managed to look exasperated. "Douglas Fir," he said. "It's a kind of tree."

I smiled. "Of course. Sorry."

We made our way to the candle shop, and Ray opened the door.

"I thought we'd use one of our dads' names, or Evan's name, for a boy," I said.

Ray waited as we entered, then followed us inside. "Fair enough. What's a Christmassy name?" he asked.

"Something like Holly," I said. "Or my mom, Carol."

Ray laughed. "Christmas Carol is almost as good as Cookie Cutter."

"And her dad's a tree farmer named Bud," Libby added.

Ray's brow wrinkled. "How have I never put any of that together?"

I inhaled the heady scent of a hundred candles, warming tarts, and oil diffusers, and my stomach coiled. I moved along the perimeter in search of something easier on my nose, but the formerly heavenly scents made me want to vomit.

Ray stuck to my side while Libby hunted for gifts. "You okay?"

I nodded, nausea clawing at my throat. "I'm gonna wait outside."

He beat me to the door and held it once more, then played with his phone a moment while I sat on a nearby bench swallowing lungfuls of fresh air. "I let Lib know where we went. You need water?"

"No." I raised my disposable coffee cup to my nose and inhaled. Thank my stars and snickerdoodles, the drink still smelled delicious. If coffee became my enemy, I'd sleep through the rest of this pregnancy.

"Give me another example of a Christmassy name," he said. "Or something you're considering."

"I like Aspen for a girl."

"Are there aspen trees on the farm?" he asked.

I nodded and inspiration struck. "We could name the baby Winter and call them Winnie as a nickname."

He tipped his head side to side, not loving or hating the suggestion.

"I also like Angel and Noelle."

"Noelle is the epitome of a Christmas name," he said.

I smiled. Noelle was adorable.

Chapter Fifteen

Libby arrived a moment later. "I got most of what I wanted, but they didn't have Toasted Marshmallow Fireside in inventory. I have to order it online."

Ray took her bag. "Can do."

I stood, feeling much better in the icy air. "Where next?"

"Oh, Fudge?" she asked.

"Perfect." I turned toward the fudgery. "I buy Cookie the cherry cordial every year."

"You're lucky they don't sell out," Ray said. "That's one of their most popular flavors. Mom always places her order ahead of time."

"I'm hoping they held a pound back for me," I admitted. I was a habitual last-minute shopper, and the fudgery owners, family friends of mine, typically planned ahead, knowing I'd get there eventually.

We moved to the corner and waited for a horse-drawn carriage to pass by. A couple huddled under a lap blanket in the back. I smiled, recalling my first sleigh ride with Evan, a sneaky setup by Cookie. Something I'd never properly thanked her for. That ride didn't end as well as it began, but it brought me closer to my best friend and husband.

The sleigh passed, and Ray, Libby, and I moved into the crosswalk with dozens of others. Last night's snowfall had covered the rooftops and accumulated on windowsills, adding to the magical Christmas effect.

Ray beat us to the other side of the street and waited while the crowd that had momentarily swallowed Libby and me spit us back out. "Whatever happened with the inflatable snowmen?" he asked.

Libby leapt over a puddle of mostly melted, very dirty snow at the curb. "Nothing yet," she said.

"But we baited the trap," I said.

Ray adjusted the bags in his grip. "Good. I can't wait to see who's behind this. Stealing twelve-foot inflatable anythings is bizarre to me."

"I want to know what they're doing with them," Libby said. "I've notified local consignment shops. I'm stalking the ads on Craigslist, and monitoring every social media group used to resell personal items. No one's yard is slowly filling with twelve-foot snowmen, so they can't be keeping them, right?"

"We'll figure it out," I said.

Ray shot me a warning look that said I should watch my pronouns. "Does Evan know you're involved in this?"

"I'm not doing anything," I said.

He sighed. "Well, that's a big no."

Libby interjected, then filled him in on the specifics of our sting operation. She reassured him I was safe, so he had no reason to bring up the topic to Evan. "You'll just get him all wound up if you seem concerned," she said. "And wouldn't we all prefer Holly focus on this instead of the other thing?"

"I am right here," I said.

Neither babysitter looked in my direction. Instead, they continued to debate the pros and cons of allowing me to keep tabs on two inflatable snowmen via a teddy bear and app.

"All right," I said, tired of being left out of their conversation. "I have a question for Ray."

He scanned the throng of shoppers, then ducked his head. "Yeah?"

"Who's in charge of the crossword puzzle at the paper?"

He relaxed visibly. "I'm not sure. A consultant, I think. Why?"

I gave him the wiki rundown on that topic, and he gaped.

"That's wildly unsettling," he said.

"Thank you," I told him, waving a hand in his direction. "Evan and Libby think it's nothing, but my gut says these messages are meant for me. I'd like to ask the puzzle maker how they come up with the clues and design the game. That should put my mind at ease."

"I'll see what I can find out," he said. "I'll pass along the contact information on the puzzle maker if I can get it."

The next hour flew by as we chatted and shopped. We bought rich, decadent sweets at Oh! Fudge, and renewed my mom's annual membership and mine at Wine Around. Libby picked up a case of wine for Ray's family's New Year's Eve party, then we headed to the cupcake shop. Our last stop before making the trip to Reindeer Games.

The interior of Caroline's Cupcakes was a whimsical mix of soft cotton candy colors. Pale blue and white striped wallpaper covered the walls, and thick white trim and molding lined the floors and ceiling. A marvelous grandfather clock stood in one corner, its large golden hands marking the time. Scents of spun sugar and warm vanilla hung in the air, carrying me to the back of a long line before her service counter and glass display case.

I checked the corners of my mouth for drool as I admired the rows of fresh baked cupcakes in every perfect flavor. Festive sprinkles topped vanilla icing, and drizzles of caramel, fudge, or raspberry syrup zigzagged over chocolate. Little peppermint sticks, cookie halves, and gumdrops topped others.

Ray kneaded his hands. "Should we get one dozen? Or two?"

Libby scoffed. "We each get one," she said. "My pants are too tight as it is. This town is my waistline's nightmare sixty days a year."

"So, three for me, and one for you?" he clarified. "My pants fit fine. Ow!" Ray rubbed his arm where she pinched him.

I spotted Caroline at the service counter and raised an arm overhead to wave.

She smiled, then said something I couldn't hear to her customer.

A moment later, Alice and her grandpa stepped into view. They moved away from Caroline's register with cupcakes and drinks in hand.

"Hey," Alice said. "I can't believe we ran into you guys. Are you shopping?"

Ray lifted our bounty of logoed bags, and Hugo chuckled.

"Are you taking your desserts to go? Or will you stay a while?" she asked.

"We have a few minutes," I said. "I came to visit with Caroline, but I can see she's not getting away from that service counter anytime soon."

"That works out for me," Alice said, smiling. She scanned the dining space. "We'll grab a table while you place your orders."

Several minutes later, the five of us huddled around a tall table near the front window. Outside, the streets teamed with shoppers, eagerly scanning the window displays. I hoped one of them wasn't a killer.

Across from me, Hugo selected a cupcake and peeled away the blue striped paper. Pink sugar crystals glistened on vanilla frosting, swirled high atop a strawberry and cream cheese cake.

"How are you enjoying our town so far?" I asked.

His eyes widened as he bit into the little dessert, then his eyelids closed for a long, appreciative beat.

Alice beamed. "It's amazing, right?"

He nodded, pulling his eyes open and looking from Alice to Caroline behind the counter. "This is unbelievable."

Pride swelled in me at his compliment, and I bit into my double chocolate fudge treat. I'd made it my mission to try every flavor, thinking I'd find a favorite. So far, I had about eighteen favorites. Double chocolate fudge was definitely one of those.

Hugo set his cupcake down and sucked a dollop of frosting from the tip of one thumb. "I'm enjoying every minute with my granddaughter. Your town is almost as enchanting as this cupcake. The energy here is like nothing I've ever experienced."

"I'm so glad to hear that," I said, lifting my cupcake for another greedy bite.

"I'd rate the overall experience a ten out of ten, if the sheriff wasn't such a dolt."

My gaze snapped back to Hugo. Chocolate crumbs clung to my lips and fingers.

Ray choked.

Alice's fair skin went ghost white. "Grandpa."

Hugo balked. He swept a curious gaze from face to face around the table. "Well, he is, isn't he?"

Alice shook her head with fervency and grabbed her grandpa's hand where it rested on the table. "Sheriff Gray is Holly's husband."

Hugo frowned. "Holly White."

I wrinkled my nose. "Not for about two years now."

His features reddened. "I am so sorry—"

"It's okay," I said, in understanding.

"—that your husband is such an utter dolt," he finished.

Ray, who had only just recovered from choking began to cough anew. "Excuse me," he croaked, heading to the counter. Presumably for a cup of water.

Libby brushed a napkin across her red lips and fixed Hugo with a serious stare. "The sheriff is also my brother."

Hugo sat taller. "I guess you received all the brains in the family, because there clearly wasn't enough to go around."

Alice blinked.

I shook away the shock and intervened before anyone else said something unkind. "Where is this coming from?" I asked.

We'd had a lovely visit with Hugo at the Hearth on the day of his arrival. He wasn't mean or negative then.

Alice wadded her napkin, leaving her dessert untouched. "We accepted an invitation to visit Sheriff Gray at the police station today. He had a few additional questions, and Grandpa was offended when the sheriff didn't immediately exclude me as a suspect."

"No decent constable would suspect you," he complained. "Or make you seem like the villain when you're a victim." Hugo pushed another bite of cupcake into his mouth, clearly searching for his zen.

Alice inhaled a long, steadying breath, then refreshed her smile. "We stopped at the café afterward. Sheriff Gray said it was okay to clean the crime scene and order a new glass for the door. Grandpa and I did some baking while we waited for the company to arrive and measure for the replacement window. It was nice to work at his side, the way I had when I was small."

"That sounds lovely," I said.

Hugo raised a logoed café bag onto his lap. "We made risgrynsgröt." He removed a pile of shallow plastic lidded containers with red holiday bows. "Risgrynsgröt is a rice pudding and part of a Swedish tradition. There's one for you and another for your parents," he said, stacking two containers in front of me.

"Thank you!"

He set a third container in front of Libby. "For you and your husband. We have another for Cookie, but I can deliver that one when we return to the inn for the evening." His eyes seemed to twinkle, and Alice grinned.

I met Libby's gaze and thought, *Interesting. Did you see that too?*

She nodded. "What's the tradition?" she asked.

"An almond is hidden somewhere in the batch," Alice said. "Whoever gets it will be married in the new year."

"Fun!" I beamed. "I hope none of us gets it," I said, motioning to the three batches on the table. "We're already married."

"Maybe Caroline will find the almond," Alice suggested. "We gave a container to her as well."

My smile grew. I would love that for her, mostly because it was good fun, but also because she loved Zane, and he adored the ground she walked on. If they decided to marry one day, it would be the party of the century.

Ray returned with a bottle of water and an easy smile. "Sorry about that. I'm not sure what came over me." He took his seat and sipped gingerly from the bottle.

Libby folded her empty cupcake wrapper into a tidy square. She looked pensively at Hugo before turning serious eyes on Alice. "I want you both to know I will get to the bottom of what happened that night," she said. "At least enough to prove Alice didn't have a hand in any of it. Evan will let you know as soon as your name is clear. He doesn't want you on his list any more than you want to be on it," she promised. Turning her attention to Hugo, she added. "My brother is a good man, and he's one hell of a detective. You can count on that."

Hugo gave a sharp dip of his chin. He didn't argue. The fight had left him.

Alice's eyes misted with emotion as she processed Libby's vow. "I'm not going to lie, it was a little terrifying at the sheriff's department today. Answering all his questions made me feel like I might be guilty of something. I'm not angry, but I am rattled."

"He's just gathering facts," I assured. "He doesn't mean to make things more difficult for you."

She nodded, eyes shifting to Libby. "Have you made any progress at all?" she asked.

Libby wet her lips and gave the busy shop another scan. She leaned forward, resting her forearms on the table, and we all followed her lead. "The victim, Hannah, got into frequent arguments online with someone in the antiques show's forums."

I gasped. "Why didn't you say anything?"

"I told you to get a secret account," she said. "I had plenty of reasons for that."

I pursed my lips. "Seems like something you could've told me earlier."

"Anyway," she continued. "She and someone using the handle HistoryBuff14 had a lot of beefs in the forums and chat rooms. I'm looking into that now."

"So, she was BeenThereDoneThat14," I said, recalling the multiple debates I'd read online.

Everyone at our table looked at me.

"I was in the forums trying to learn more about the showcase," I said.

Ray shook his head at me, looking either peeved or disappointed.

I looked away.

"How do you know about the arguing?" Alice asked.

Libby looked toward the ceiling before offering me a cursory glance. "I peeked through Hannah's phone while we waited for first responders to arrive."

I gasped again, doubly as shocked as I had been a moment before.

"Stop that," Libby said. "I knew how bad things looked, and I knew Alice needed someone on her side. It's not as if I was downloading her photographs. I just flipped through her open windows. I wanted to know what she'd been doing right before she died."

"What was open?" I asked.

"Email, a few social media accounts, and the antiques show's website. I'd expected to find her most recent phone call or text message, but those weren't open."

"How'd you know her phone's password?" Ray asked.

Libby grimaced. "Face recognition. Her eyes were open."

"Ugh," I said, losing interest in my cupcake for the first time in history.

"Libby!" Ray scolded.

She silenced him with a sharp look. "I knew Alice was innocent, and I needed to get a jump on proving that."

"Thank you," Alice said, her voice barely more than a whisper.

Libby folded her hands on the table. "Hannah ran a small antiques shop in her hometown. According to her recent social media posts, the business wasn't doing well. I think it was more a labor of love than profitable in any way. She needed a win to keep it going, which might be why she was willing to make a grab for the Yule Goat. That kind of money could've changed her life, saved her shop, given the business a chance to grow legs and run."

"Is there any way to prove that?" Alice asked.

"Maybe," Libby said. "I made an appointment to talk to her business partner tomorrow. I'll be out of town most of the day, and I'll check in when I get back."

My muscles tensed at that news. I wanted to go. Wanted to listen in on the conversation and take a look at the store a woman might've unintentionally given her life to save. But Libby would never agree, and I shouldn't take risks like that anymore.

The thought saddened, then irritated me. I wanted a baby more than I wanted to solve crimes, but why couldn't I do both? Evan was going to be a father, but he didn't have to give up doing what he loved, even though his job was dangerous every day, not just annually when a murder occurred.

Libby checked her watch. “I hate to cut this short, but we need to get going. We’ll be at Reindeer Games later. If you feel like joining in on a game or two, come and find us?” she asked.

“Will do,” they agreed.

I hugged Alice goodbye and waved to Hugo. Then I went to the counter to tell Caroline to call me soon. I missed my best friend, and we had a lot to catch up on.

Chapter Sixteen

Caroline picked me up the next afternoon for a visit to the Antiques Showcase. She gave herself a long lunch break from the cupcake shop and made time to catch up on friend stuff. Getting ninety minutes in the middle of the workday was a Christmas miracle that I didn't take lightly. I started talking the moment I opened her passenger door so as not to squander a single second.

Evan reluctantly gave his blessing on the excursion. He wasn't thrilled by the thought of me leaving home or the farm without Zane, Ray, or Libby joining us, but they were all busy, and in the end I made my own decisions.

We nabbed an incredible parking spot outside Mistletoe's historic train station, the official venue for the Antiques Showcase's final destination.

"I haven't been inside this place since elementary school," I told her as we hustled through the freezing cold toward the front doors.

A portion of the massive structure became a railroad museum the year I was born, and Mistletoe third graders had visited via field trip every spring since then. The station's cavernous central section was often used for major events like our high school's annual graduation ceremony. Sometimes the space was rented for wedding receptions or business conferences. Today, it housed nearly two hundred antique dealers and hosted thousands of shoppers.

We scanned our phones on the way in, sharing the tickets we'd purchased online, then crossed the threshold into the warmth.

"Wow," Caroline whispered. Her eyes and smile were wide as she took in the bustling sight before us.

I imagined I looked equally impressed.

Built in the early nineteen hundreds with inspiration from Grand Central Station in New York City, the architect utilized a similar beaux arts style. Broad Roman columns greeted guests, then expansive marble floors carried them inward. Ornately carved ceilings arched high overhead, and a series of custom stained glass windows scattered rainbows over everything in sight.

Top tier acoustics blended thousands of voices with instrumental holiday tunes as we walked the aisles of a neatly constructed grid. Tables, booths, and makeshift shops stood side by side in every direction.

Thick boughs of pine garland hung in sweeps along the perimeter, red ornaments and white twinkle lights adding to the festive appearance. Eight-foot banners stretched upright from the floor near the entrance, printed with site maps, vendor lists, and schedules for the day. Panels on family crests, milk glass, and tea sets happened in adjoining rooms, along with rare coin workshops and quill writing demonstrations.

"This is unreal," Caroline said. The marvel and appreciation in her voice raised a smile on my lips.

"I didn't know you were such a fan of antiques," I said.

She turned big blue eyes on me and blinked. "I'm talking about this exquisite organization. It must've taken months to plan all this. There are so many moving parts," she marveled. "So much to coordinate. I love it!"

I giggled. Now, that was the Caroline I knew and loved.

"I want to find something for my mom," she said. "She's usually excited about anything older than herself, and bonus points if it's one of a kind."

"Looks like you're in the right place," I said. "Are you shopping for jewelry? Art? Furniture?"

"How about a beaded purse?" she said. "Mom's handbag collection is remarkable. She'd love something with a dramatic backstory."

"Mission accepted," I said. "We'll find the perfect antique purse for your mother," I added more loudly, in case the killer noticed my arrival and questioned my intentions.

I was completely finished meddling. No need to tell me again.

"Why are you talking like that?" Caroline asked.

"Hmm?"

"You're annunciating your words as if one of us is new to the language."

A forty-something man in a polo shirt and khakis did a double take as we unfastened our coats and strode into the middle aisle. He approached, hands clasped behind him, and an expectant look on his gaunt face.

Caroline tensed, probably frustrated by an inability to go anywhere without having to play her lifelong role as Mayor's Daughter.

I shot her a small smile for moral support.

People usually only wanted a moment of her time, and they were typically kind. The hard part was never being able to let her guard down. One slip up on her end could result in a drop in the popularity polls for her father.

The man coughed into his fist, attention fixed tightly, surprisingly, on me. "I'm so sorry to interrupt you," he said. "I can see you're enjoying a day with a friend, but—" He hesitated, suddenly appearing unsure. "Are you the Gumdrop Gumshoe?"

Caroline's made-for-constituents smile increased its wattage.

I tried not to frown but failed. "Yep."

He threw his head back briefly and clasped his hands before him. "Knew it!" His green eyes sparked beneath dark rectangle-framed glasses when he returned his gaze to me. "I've listened to all of your interviews on the show," he said. "They're terrific. I crack up every time."

"Thank you," I said. "They're fake."

He barked a laugh and shook a single pointed finger at me, assuming I'd spoken in jest.

I hadn't.

Tate and Harvey made a game of manipulating recordings of my voice and interspersing my spoken words into answers for their purposes.

"Thanks for listening," I said, not meaning it at all. "It was nice to meet you."

"Wait!" He pulled a pen from his pocket. "Would you sign something for my wife?"

I darted my gaze around us, hoping not to draw another crowd. Caroline and I were on borrowed time. "Sure. What do you have?"

He patted his pockets and turned in search of something useful.

Caroline passed him a brochure from the ticket booth. "Here you go."

His worried expression became one of delight. "That's perfect, thank you!"

I signed the pamphlet and excused myself.

"Good luck with your next investigation," he called.

I curled my shoulders forward and wished my hood was up as we hurried away.

"Not cool," Caroline stage-whispered, grabbing my sleeve and yanking me around a corner.

We rushed through a large section with toy trains and tiny landscaping. Sellers dressed as conductors sold stacks of metal tracks, old cars, and engines in brittle, yellowed boxes.

Further down the aisle, shoppers gathered around old washboards, flour sifters, and posters for household products from the turn of the last century.

Caroline didn't slow her pace until we'd made three more turns. "That guy nearly outed you."

"In fairness, he doesn't have a clue what's been going on," I said.

Caroline's shoulders drooped. "This was supposed to be a fun little outing."

"It is," I said, standing taller. "I'm still having fun. And look! I see a display of ladies' hats up ahead. The purses must be close."

She released a long breath, then linked her arm with mine and marched onward. "You're right. Let's focus on friend time. Tell me something I've missed."

I started with the daily crossword clues, which were fresh on my mind.

"That is weird," she said. "What was today's clue?"

"Twelve letters. Four words," I said. "Where chestnuts roast."

She tapped a pink fingernail against her lips. "Oh! On an open fire?"

I nodded.

Caroline cringed. "That's unfortunate, given yesterday's answer."

I couldn't agree more. "So far this week, the streak reads, 'Holly White watch out roast you on an open fire.'"

Caroline stuck out her tongue in a gag. "I don't like it. Did you tell Evan?"

"Yep."

She pulled her lips to one side in thought. "Here's to hoping this really is the world's worst coincidence."

I gave a half-hearted thumbs-up, and a familiar face came into view several booths ahead. "Uh-oh." My arm bobbed up like a railroad safety gate, stopping Caroline in place. "That's Kent George. I don't want him to see me." I curled my fingers around her wrist and hustled into an adjacent aisle.

A large sculpture of a man with lots of muscles and no arms cast a shadow on the tables beside him. I pressed my back against the cool surface to catch my breath.

"Who did you see?" Caroline asked.

"Kent George." I filled her in, and she nodded.

"Right. Sorry," she said. "I'm trying to keep the new names straight. Was it the guy wearing a blue dress shirt and khakis?"

"That was him," I said, heart hammering. I didn't know if Kent was the killer, but I didn't want him thinking I was here to investigate or meddle. I came to see the show and hang out with my best friend. If I happened to notice anything Evan might like to know while I was here, I'd certainly share the information.

Caroline strode back toward the intersection of aisles and peered in the direction we'd been going. She shrugged once, then returned. "I don't see him anymore. Hey, are you okay? You look pale."

"I'm just pregnant," I said. I meant the words to lighten the mood, but the truth of them hung in the air between us as our smiles grew.

Caroline pulled me into a hug. "I can't believe you're really pregnant!" She released me with a challenge in her eyes. "I bet I can find an amazing, one-of-a-kind gift for your baby at a place like this."

"A silver rattle?" I suggested. "Maybe a silver spoon."

Caroline wrinkled her button nose and groaned. "I had one of those, and it's a serious choking hazard."

I wasn't sure if she meant her words figuratively, literally, or both.

"Come on," she said. "Let's shop."

The tension eased as we moved along the rows, admiring hatpins and dresses from other eras, wondering how grown women once had waists so tiny. We talked about our relationships and our families. Our Christmas Day plans and where to celebrate New Year's Eve. For a while, time lost its meaning in the old train station, and my heart healed in the presence of my best friend.

Caroline found a petal-pink clamshell purse for her mom and an heirloom amethyst ring to tuck inside. She bought her dad a Civil War era judge's gavel in a pine box with brass hinges.

"I wish I knew what to get Zane," she said. "I'm wide open to ideas if you have any."

"I'll have to think about that," I said, but I didn't know enough about her boyfriend to make a decent suggestion.

Zane was strikingly handsome. He was Libby's business partner at the PI firm, and his private security team helped Evan with the crowds at Christmas. I knew nothing about his interests, other than his jobs and Caroline.

"How about a detective badge from the Eliot Ness days?" I suggested.

Her expression lit. "He is a big fan of justice served. Maybe I can find mobster memorabilia or something related to hang in his office!"

"Adding that to my mental shopping list," I told her.

"Did you order a snowplow for Evan yet?" she asked, homing in on a display of silk scarves.

"I'm still shopping," I said. "I hadn't realized how expensive they are, and now that we have a baby on the way, I'm second-guessing how to use the money."

Caroline met my eyes and tipped her head over one shoulder. "My opinion? I say, buy the plow. Do all the things. Enjoy every last moment before the baby comes. You and Evan are so in love, and it's beautiful. You'll never get this time back. Nothing will be the same soon. It might be different in a better way, but it won't be like this. So just focus on today and manage tomorrow when it gets here."

I slipped an arm behind her back. "How did you get so wise?"

"I'm learning to appreciate the present," she said. "It goes against every fiber of my plan-ahead personality, but I am trying."

I turned to a scarf display and ran a fingertip over the beautiful patterns.

"Do you like this geometric one?" she asked, holding the fabric to her chest.

"Absolutely," I said, taking notice of a man in a gray suit several feet away.

He was overdressed for a vendor and spoke quietly with the woman running the booth while we browsed. Was he important to the show? Perhaps the founder?

I reminded myself I was only here to shop, then I cast my gaze over the aisle, keeping watch for Kent George.

"Good afternoon," a male voice said.

I jumped and grabbed Caroline's elbow.

The man in the suit approached with a congenial smile. He'd slicked his thinning salt and pepper hair back with gel, creating a fresh from the shower look.

I was certain the strands would crunch if I touched them.

"Hello," Caroline said. She returned the scarf to the table and stood a little taller.

Caroline was willowy and beautiful, in a real-life porcelain doll sort of way. But when she squared her shoulders and meant business, most men bumbled, flopped, and saw their way out.

"Arnold Printz," the man said, offering her his hand. "I'm the event coordinator, and you are Ms. West? Mayor West's daughter?"

Caroline's smile softened. "That's right."

My knees locked, and my mouth went dry. This was the man I'd been told to find for information on the forums and ongoing debates among users. The one who apparently knew everything about international art.

"It's lovely to meet you," Caroline added.

"You as well," he said. "I recognized you from the photos of your family in the mayor's office. He's an incredible man. It took a sharp business mind and impressive creative thinking to pull this together." Arnold motioned to the bustling space around us.

"Thank you," she said. "I appreciate that. Have you met my best friend, Holly Gray?"

"Arnold Printz," he said, bowing slightly at the waist. "Lovely to meet you. I hope you're enjoying yourselves."

"We are," I confirmed. "I think we could easily stay all day."

"That's the idea," he said. "The scarves are one hundred percent authentic. If you're considering one, I can confirm their quality."

Caroline frowned. "Is that ever a question?"

Arnold gave a sad bob of his head. "A number of irreputable vendors have tried to sell knockoffs of every manner here, but I take quality control seriously. You can rest assured that everything you see today is exactly what it claims to be."

"Impressive," Caroline said. "You must be incredibly knowledgeable to perform that duty. There are items here from so many categories and eras."

"It's my life's work," he said.

I debated my next words, then gave in to opportunity. "Are you the same Arnold Printz who wrote a book on historical art?" I asked, recalling the information I'd gained from Alice.

Pleasure coursed over Arnold's features. "I am. Have you read it?"

"No," I admitted. "I just learned about it, but I can't wait to buy a copy and get started."

"Well," he said, chest puffing with pride. "Come with me. I have a supply available at the desk."

Caroline shot me a quizzical look but followed, leaving her geometric scarf unpurchased. "What's your book about?" she asked.

Arnold broke into a lengthy description that boiled down to historical art and its significance in various countries and cultures.

"We have a friend from Sweden who has a collection of Yule Goats," I said casually as we followed him toward the information desk.

A three-foot photo of his face stood beside stacks of paperbacks with his name on the cover.

He glanced in my direction, flashing a full-toothed smile. "Your friend is lucky. Those goats are a very special part of Swedish culture. Any made before the start of World War Two are practically priceless."

I feigned surprise. "Wow. Collectors must be willing do anything to get their hands on something so rare," I said, selecting a book from the stack. "Will you sign this for me?"

An emotion I couldn't name flashed in Arnold's eyes as he accepted the paperback. "Of course."

"My friend's collection was from her grandmother," I continued. "The pieces are priceless to her for nostalgia reasons. She'd never part with any of them, especially not the copper one. What was that called?" I pretended to ponder.

Arnold's pen paused as he signed. "The Copper Goat of Gävle."

"No, that's not it," I said, scrunching my brow and looking dim. "I think she said her grandma called it Peter during her childhood bedtime stories."

Charisma seemed to bleed from Arnold as he held the autographed book in my direction. "Good luck to your friend. Collectors are a driven sort," he said. "I suppose they're like hunters in that way."

Caroline blanched.

"Is that so?" I asked.

She flicked her gaze repeatedly toward the exit while I pressed ahead.

Arnold nodded in answer to my question. "I'm passionate about antiques as a look into history," he said. "All the little tangible links to our past."

I schooled my features into my most noncommittal expression.

"You might've heard that if we don't learn from our pasts, we're doomed to repeat them," he said.

Caroline's eyes bulged, and a chill wobbled down my spine.

I jerked back to my senses. "We should get going." I lifted my autographed book between us and gave it a quick wiggle. "Where do I pay?"

Arnold snapped his fingers overhead, drawing the attention of a woman behind the desk in an Antiques Showcase T-shirt. "Marissa will help you."

We said our goodbyes to Arnold, and he vanished into the crowd.

Chapter Seventeen

"Boy," Caroline said. "You really stole his chutzpa."

The woman behind the counter dropped the book into a paper bag. "He's moody like that sometimes. Don't worry. It wasn't you."

I offered a small, appreciative smile, thankful for the reassurance. "I'll bet there's a lot of tension around here," I said. "Or at least some intense competition."

The woman ran my credit card through her machine, toying with her necklace while it processed. "They aren't supposed to, but some of them go around after we close for the day, asking for the biggest sale at each table. They celebrate the largest overall. They make a big deal out of the highest profits. And the lowest." She returned my card and receipt, looking a little embarrassed by the admission, though it had nothing to do with her. "Regardless, it's a great event this year," she added, making prolonged eye contact with Caroline. "The mayor did a wonderful thing. A lot of locals, like me, will earn extra Christmas money this year by working this show."

Caroline's warm smile seemed to put the woman at ease following her confession. "Thank you for your kind words. And for making this event possible. It couldn't happen without your willingness to be here." She set a hand on my arm. "I want to run and grab that scarf I was looking at. Care for a quick jog?"

"I'll wait here," I said. "I'll only slow you down." More importantly, I felt safe at the desk with my new friend, and not at all like taking my chances in the aisles again.

Arnold's comment about repeating history left my stomach queasy, and I wasn't convinced that neither Kent nor the woman I'd seen him with was responsible for the threatening postcard.

"She seems so genuine," the woman said, watching Caroline hurry in the direction of the scarves. "I've seen her around, but I've never spoken to her before. She's the mayor's daughter, right? Caroline West?"

"She is, and I agree, she's pretty great." I extended my hand. "I'm Holly."

"Marissa," she said. "I know who you are too." She blushed. "Everyone does, and I swear I'm not being weird. You've just created quite a stir the last few years. Only people living under rocks could've missed it."

I cringed. "Would you laugh if I told you I'm not even trying?"

An elderly couple approached the desk, and Marissa slipped away to give them a map and directions to the antique holiday displays. She returned to me a moment later. "I've only worked here a few days," she said. "I was sorry to hear about what happened to Hannah. She seemed really nice."

My ears perked at Hannah's name. "You knew her?"

"A little. We met here a few times. That's all. She was kind, and I had no idea what I was doing, so her patience was appreciated. I think it's awful that she's gone."

"Me too," I said. "Any idea why she'd try to steal a valuable heirloom?" That was the million-dollar question, wasn't it? Had her failing shop driven her to commit robbery? Was it something else? If I knew those answers, maybe the rest of what happened that night would make sense too.

"I'm just an observer," Marissa said. "But I've learned that these vendors come from all around the country to participate in this and similar events. Some take out loans to cover the expenses and lose their jobs for taking off excessive time. I'm from Oklahoma, originally, and these folks remind me of the rodeo cowboys, who do the same things. They get addicted to the chance of hitting it big. At the rodeo, everyone's seeking that perfect ride. The glory. Here, folks are looking for that one thing to buy or sell that will change everything for them. And in my experience, desperation makes people do things they wouldn't normally do."

Her words pulled images of Hannah into mind. She'd tried to rip the copper goat from Alice's hands in front of a café full of people. But she'd been knocked onto her backside and forced to run away.

Yet she came back.

"Desperation is motivating," I agreed.

I turned my attention to the rows of vendors again, wondering how many of them felt the way Hannah had, and what they might be willing to do to hit it big.

Kent George stepped free from the end of an aisle. His brows and tone were low as he spoke animatedly with Arnold. His flailing hands stilled, and their gazes turned sharply in my direction.

A few feet beyond them, Nancy Grace, the woman with the white pixie-cut hair looked on.

"Uh-oh," Marissa said.

"What?" I squeaked.

"I'd better get busy and stop chatting, if I want to keep my job," she said.

An idea sprang to mind, and I turned to face the counter once more. "Wait." I pulled a map from the nearby stack and spread it on the counter between us. Then I pointed at nothing in particular.

Marissa looked.

"Neither of us can be in trouble if I'm just shopping and you're helping a customer," I said. "Don't be obvious, but do you recognize the man Arnold is talking with?"

Her eyebrows twitched as my words registered and realization dawned. "Oh. All right. Let me see." She turned her eyes toward the men, a cheery, customer service smile in place. "Yep." She looked at the map again, then me. "That's Kent. He and his cohorts sell things from the Norwegian Nordic territories mostly. A lot of nautical stuff. Maps. Oars. Winged Nikes."

Kent knew the value of Alice's Yule Goats, and he had a way to sell them. He'd made a name for himself in the world of historic international art. It wasn't a stretch to consider that as motive. And anyone who'd made it inside the café after breaking the front door glass had access to means—a knife from the café's kitchen.

"What about the woman watching from a few feet away?" I asked. "Long black wool coat. Short white hair."

Marissa took another look. "I don't see anyone like that."

My head turned on instinct. Marissa was right. Nancy Grace was gone.

"I'd better let you get back to work," I said. "I'm going to wait for Caroline near the entrance."

In reality, I planned to hide in the restroom and send her a text.

Marissa refolded the map with a smile. "If there's anything else I can do, just let me know."

I glanced one last time toward the place where Arnold and Kent had stood, but they were gone. I turned in search of them, suddenly recalling all the times I'd spotted but not killed a spider in my bedroom. Then I'd spend the whole night in bed wondering where it went and when it would return.

Panicked, I stepped backward and hit a wall of muscle. My heart beat in my ears, and for a moment, I imagined the killer was there.

"Holly?" a male voice asked.

Dark spots danced in my vision as I spun away from the man and nearly fell.

Broad hands grasped my shoulders, steadying me while my ears began to ring. "I can't believe it's you," the vaguely familiar voice said.

My frenzied thoughts slowed as the person before me took shape. "Scooter?"

He released my arms as I regained my footing.

The person who'd grabbed me wasn't a killer, or even my husband, come to scold me for asking too many questions during checkout. It was Caroline's schmoopy stalker.

"Hey," he said. "It's great seeing you!"

I made a brief, strangled sound as I looked from him to the blonde at his side, still mildly confused. "Um."

The willowy woman on his right wore sleek black heeled boots and a designer wool coat over a creamy cashmere dress. Thick, magazine-worthy waves fell over her shoulders and bright blue eyes shone against perfect porcelain skin.

Caroline obviously lost a twin at birth. I'd just found her. Though based on the skating rink of a diamond on her left hand, Scooter had beaten me to her.

"Oops," he said. "My apologies! Holly White, this is my wife, Danica. Danica, this is the friend I'm always telling you about."

Perhaps I'd fainted when the black dots first appeared, and this was a coma dream.

Caroline's doppelganger came to life with Scooter's news. Her petal-pink lips formed a little O of surprise. "This is fabulous. I've always wanted to meet you. Are you still dating the sheriff?"

she asked. "I adore Scott's Mistletoe adventure stories. I ask him to repeat them all the time."

I led the couple several yards away from the desk on shaky legs, providing ourselves room to talk without blocking Marissa's counter.

"Scott?" I asked.

"Scooter's a nickname," he said. "Danica prefers my given name." He snapped his fingers. "Speaking of nicknames. I hear you have a new one."

"Nope—" I put up a palm. "Let's not talk about that, okay?"

Scooter and Danica giggled.

An interesting thought suddenly came to mind, and it popped from my lips before I thought better of it. "Are you still in the same career?"

Scooter's playful disposition vanished at the inquiry. He widened his stance and crossed his arms. "Tech? Yes."

I slid my eyes to Danica, then back. Tech was an extremely low-level way of saying military cybersecurity, but yes, I supposed that covered it. "Tech," I agreed. "The sheriff's department is working on an important case, but they've run into trouble on something you might be able to help with. Any chance you might want to assist? I can promise a free evening at the Hearth or a night at the inn to sweeten the pot. Offseason," I clarified. I wasn't a miracle worker, but surely Cookie could slide him into a cancellation spot eventually.

Danica rocked onto her toes. "That sounds wonderful! Scott loves to help everyone, and I'm going to have a Mistletoe adventure!"

His smile grew with her excitement and praise. "Sure. No problem. I'll reach out to the sheriff's department before we leave town."

"Or you can come to our house for dinner," I blurted.

No sense in leaving his plans open-ended when I could nail him down instead.

Scooter looked to his wife, who appeared doubly jubilant at new invite. "That sounds nice. Thank you," he said.

"Perfect. Do I have your number?" I asked.

We traded information, then the happy couple stepped away.

I lifted a hand hip-high in salutation. "See you soon!"

No wonder Cookie had been so entertained by her run-in with Scooter. On another day, I might've decided the fact he'd married Caroline's near-twin was creepy, but today, I had other breads to bake.

The steady click-clack of approaching heels drew my attention to Caroline.

"There you are!" she exclaimed, picking up the pace to my side. "You worried me. You weren't at the desk where I left you. I thought something happened." Her head turned as she spoke, tracking the path Scooter and Danica had taken. "Who were you talking to just now?"

I hooked my arm with hers. "I'm pretty sure that was you in another universe."

* * *

I drove myself to Reindeer Games when Caroline returned to the cupcake shop. The Hearth was jumping when I opened the door and slipped inside.

Three parallel sets of fast-play games were set up on the central dining room tables with hordes of guests gathered along the perimeter. The energy in the room was high, and the music selection was holiday pep at its finest. Adding to the Christmas game-show vibe, a mini light thrower cast images of snowflakes in big moving patterns over the walls.

I cut through the crowd and mouthed the words *thank you* to Mom as I removed a RESERVED sign from my usual booth. I'd arrived just in time for the show.

Cookie approached the microphone, and farm guests young and old took their places around the game tables, ready to test their mettle.

"Welcome to Reindeer Games!" Cookie called in her most authentic British accent. Green bubble letters spelled Ho Ho Ho across her white sweater, and endless layers of crinoline lifted a red swing skirt into a bell below her knees.

I recognized her dangling gumdrop earrings and the matching charms on her necklace and bracelet. All special orders from me over the years—before my goofy nickname made gumdrops my biggest sellers.

A few simple games posted around the café's perimeter gave everyone something to do while waiting for a seat or their turns in the competition. Pin the nose on Rudolph, and similarly, pin the bow on the present, were hits with the preschool crowd. Guessing how many marshmallows were inside a lidded container kept the too-smart teens, and more than a few men, busy. Christmas coloring sheets with the farm's logo, word search puzzles, and a scavenger hunt for items around the property were also available for good fun.

At the tables, however, things got serious, fast.

"Table ones," Cookie announced, pointing to the two tables where a half dozen players waited for instructions around each. Piles of bows were spread evenly over the playing surface. "Please put on your blindfolds." She waited while the participants followed the instruction. "Now, you may use one hand to hold the plastic mixing bowl before you. Remove the spatula from the bowl with your opposite hand. The goal is to transfer as many bows as possible from the table and into the bowl using the spatula. The two players with the most bows in sixty seconds wins. They will move on to table two! Everyone else goes to the back of the line and new players take their places."

She swung her pointed finger to the next pair of tables. "Next, the two winners from game one will stand across from one another and move down the long edges of the table with a party blower. The goal is to remove the green pompom from the top of each red plastic cup by puffing air into your blower until it unfurls and, hopefully, collides with the pompom. The first person from each table two to complete the task moves to game three."

Cheers and applause ensued.

Cookie increased her mic volume and pressed on. "The final challenge is to tie this belt around your waist." She lifted a felt and Velcro apparatus long enough to fit almost any size. "Position the string in front. The candy cane on the end of the string should be hook-down like this." She held the string and peppermint above her head before putting on the belt. "Then you go fishing! She moved to stand before a red cup filled with candy canes. "Without using your hands, you must swing your hips, bend your knees, and hook the other candy canes with your belt, then remove them from your assigned cup. First person with an empty cup wins!"

The crowd erupted with laughter as she swung her hips, and the candy cane, in demonstration.

"Winner gets free hot drinks and a cookie for everyone in their party, so let's cheer on your friends and loved ones!"

I clapped and whistled along with the other guests.

She removed her belt and held a hand in the air to get everyone's attention. "As each round ends, and the table clears, the next set of guests should take the empty spots, so a new round can begin. If we stay on task, we can have another winner every few minutes. Game play lasts for an hour in total, or until you're all worn out and call uncle. Are you ready?"

Mom slid onto the booth bench beside me, two steamy mugs in her hands. "I thought you'd enjoy a caramel hot chocolate."

I lifted the drink to my lips with a smile. "Goodness, yes. What did you get?"

"Wassail."

"Yum."

"I know," she said. "It's my favorite, and I might actually have a chance to drink it with Cookie running the show for an hour."

Cookie raised a leather strap lined in sleigh bells and shook them with her whole body. "Go!" she bellowed.

I caught sight of Alice and Hugo cheering and waiting their turns in the crowd.

Mom noticed too. "I'm so glad to see them participating," she cooed. "What's happened to her is extremely unfair. Have you heard anything more on Evan's progress?"

"No, but Libby's working the case from a personal angle," I said. "She went to talk to the victim's business partner today. I hope that conversation will unearth something useful."

Mom sipped her drink and studied me. "What do you think so far?"

The games ended an hour later, as I finished delivering my every thought and concern on the matter.

"Wow," Mom whispered. "That's a lot. I had no idea." She wrapped me in a hug. "I'm really proud of you for doing your best to stay safe."

I sat taller when she released me, buoyed by her words. "Thank you for saying that. At times I feel as if I'm running headlong into trouble like I have in the past. I swear, this year, I'm really not."

She cupped my jaw with one palm. "I believe you."

My phone dinged with an incoming text as she spoke.

Mom looked at the device, then around the room. Her staff moved quickly, clearing the tables of game materials and resetting them for food and drinks. "I guess that's my cue to get to work," Mom said. "All these guests need a cookie."

I laughed, and my phone dinged again.

"Can I get you anything else?" she asked.

I waved her off, then checked my phone in her absence. I swiped the screen to get a look at the message. Both texts were from Evan. Just checking in.

The device rang before I had an opportunity to respond.

"Hey," he said, sweetly when I answered.

We spoke for several minutes, catching up on our days while he drove back to the station following a call. I told him about shopping with Caroline and the upcoming dinner with Scooter and his wife.

Evan groaned. "I'm glad for the help, but wasn't that guy a little—."

"Quirky?" I asked. "Yes. Aren't we all? Luckily, he's also highly trained in cybersecurity."

Evan was quiet. Not completely sold on dinner with Scooter. "Can we invite Caroline and Zane?" he asked. "He really liked her, and two more people at the table will take the pressure off us to keep the conversation going."

I considered telling him about Danica's striking resemblance to Caroline, but decided it would be more fun for me to see everyone's expression when they knocked on the door. "Your way will definitely make things more interesting," I said. "I'll give Caroline a call."

I disconnected with Evan, and the phone buzzed before I'd set it down.

This time the message wasn't from my husband. It was a simple row of emojis.

A knife. A coffin. A woman. A magnifying glass.

Chapter Eighteen

I wore a red cable knit sweater and my comfiest jeans for dinner with Scooter, Danica, Caroline, and Zane the next night. The inflatable snowmen waved merrily from the lawn, thus far unbothered by holiday thieves and ne'er-do-wells.

I'd tidied the first floor, tossed a salad, and set the table while Evan made baked chicken, mashed potatoes, and steamed veggies. Mom, of course, contributed a pecan pie to the cause, but Evan and I had eaten our dessert before dinner preparations began. We shared the risgrynsgröt from Hugo, while we caught one another up on our days. The pudding was incredible, and though I was already happily married, I was a little disappointed not to receive the almond. Which would've felt like winning.

Now dinner was nearly ready. The house smelled amazing, awash with a mix of rich, salty scents from the kitchen and the fresh pine of our tree in the living room.

Tiny ornaments hung from the branches, representing so many things that Evan and I had done or experienced together in our few short years. A plastic ring inside a red velvet box commemorated our engagement. A glass heart, engraved with the date of our marriage, hung by a crimson ribbon, honoring our first Christmas as husband and wife. We added a similar ornament last year for our first anniversary, and we'd picked up two ornaments at the beach. One from our honeymoon, and one from Libby and Ray's destination wedding. Next year, we'd add a pair of booties, a bottle, or pacifier for Baby's first Christmas.

Time moved so quickly. I wished I could grip it firmly enough to keep it still once in a while.

"You doing okay?" Evan asked, probably noting my stillness. A tidal wave of nausea hit suddenly and set me quietly on the couch.

I nodded. "I'm learning morning sickness isn't limited to mornings."

He sat beside me and moved my lightly bruised hand carefully onto his big palm. "How's your grip now?"

I curled my fingers and squeezed his wrist. "Better every day," I said. "At this point, I think it looks worse than it feels."

He released a small breath of relief and kissed my head. "Have I told you how much I hate that you received that awful text?"

"Once or twice," I teased. "Maybe Scooter can look into that too."

Evan nodded. "Maybe."

"Any new leads?" I asked. "I'm not asking because I want to get involved," I added. "I'm just hoping this ends soon."

Evan's gaze drifted to the floor. "No. Until you told me about yesterday's text, I'd wondered if the killer took the goats and left town. We don't have much to go on, and the killer has to know my deputies and antiques show officials are watching for the stolen items to show up. I'd hated the thought of a murderer getting away. Now part of me wishes they had. At least then you'd be safe."

The doorbell rang, and Evan rose. "Here we go," he said, helping me to my feet as well.

I followed, feeling slightly less ill and smiling at the way our red sweaters and jeans made us look as if we belonged on a holiday card. All we needed were a couple of Santa hats to complete the vibe.

"It's Caroline and Zane," I said, seeing their car through the front window before the couple on the porch.

Evan opened the door and welcomed our guests.

Caroline greeted me with a hug and a holiday flower arrangement. "The florist promised these are safe for Cindy Lou Who if she tries to eat them."

"They're perfect," I said. "Thank you!"

I carried the vase to the fireplace and secured it on the mantle between the stocking hangers. Cindy was a menace where flowers were concerned. I was thrilled at the opportunity to enjoy the blooms without worrying she'd make herself sick this time. My last arrangement had to stay in the bathroom, behind a closed door to protect it.

Evan took the couple's coats and hung them in the little closet beside the door.

Caroline's gray tunic sweater and black leggings were the epitome of casual chic. Zane's black dress pants and a gray V-neck coordinated well.

He passed Evan two bottles. "We stopped at Wine Around and picked up a merlot for dinner. And sparkling white grape juice for Mama."

Evan accepted the gifts with a broad smile. "Did you guys have any trouble getting here? The roads are supposed to get bad tonight. I almost canceled so we wouldn't have to worry about that."

"Nah," Zane said. "Road crews are already out. Thanks for having us over. It's rare that Care and I can both get away at the same time. It feels good to have plans with friends."

We moved into the kitchen, and I gathered glasses for the drinks. I poured mine first, because I was partaking for two.

"We're glad you could make it," Evan said.

Caroline accepted her glass of wine and passed another to Zane. "How was the morning crossword?" she asked.

I glanced at Evan, who furrowed his brow.

We'd worked the clues together, and they held to the disturbing pattern. "Two across was Grandma got blank by a reindeer," I said. "Two words. Seven letters."

"Run over," Zane said.

Caroline wrinkled her pretty face into a look of disgust. "Ew. Not again."

"Again." I sighed. "Whoever the puzzle maker is, they definitely have a grudge against two across, because it's getting abused on the daily."

Zane sipped his wine. "Caroline just filled me in about this on the ride here. I don't think there's a reason to be concerned, but it's definitely a bizarre coincidence."

"I wish I believed in those," I said.

Evan accepted a glass of wine when I passed it to him, then he pulled me close and pressed a kiss to my head. "I am the world's worst husband, because I forgot to share important information."

I pulled back to look up at him, my mental wheels rapidly spinning. "What?"

"You haven't mentioned it in a few days, so after I spoke to the puzzle guy, I let it go."

My jaw dropped. "I haven't mentioned it, because the last time I brought it up, you dismissed it."

"I didn't mean to be dismissive," he said gently. "I didn't want you to worry without cause. And I wanted you to know I took your concern seriously, so I looked into it."

"When?"

"I went over to the paper that day and got the contact information for the consultant making the puzzles. It took a few tries to reach him. Apparently, game making isn't his main source of income. When we spoke, he seemed like a very nice man, no criminal record. He confirmed the clues and answers for two across had no relevance or connection to one another, and he hadn't even noticed the pattern until I questioned him on the matter. He creates the crosswords in bulk and works a month or two in advance. He had to pull them up on his computer to know what I was asking about."

I waited for the expected relief to come, but it didn't. "I wish you would've told me this," I said.

"I'm sorry." The sincerity was plain in Evan's eyes. He had a lot on his plate right now, and I hadn't voiced my fears again, so I willed myself to let it go.

I just wished I felt his certainty, because the gruesome consistency in the clues was beyond odd.

My phone dinged, and I grabbed it to check the text. Hopefully our other guests didn't run into any trouble on their way. "It's Libby," I announced, reading her name from the display.

"Everything okay?" Evan asked.

"Does she need anything?" Zane added.

I smiled at her brother and business partner. "She's fine."

"She should come over," Caroline said.

"She's already on her way." I hustled into the living room for a look through the front window. "Someone swiped the snowmen off the lawn!" I called over my shoulder.

The group hurried behind me.

Caroline reappeared at my side. "No way!"

"We just got here," Zane said.

Caroline and I peered through the glass, joined by our dates and their reflections a moment later.

"Well, damn," Evan said. "Doesn't this town know the sheriff lives here?"

"Maybe you need a sign," Zane teased.

"Aww." Caroline crossed her arms. "They were so cute standing out there. I'm sorry."

"It's okay. They weren't really ours," I said.

Zane filled her in on the sting operation, while I tried to recall the login to the nanny camera app on my phone.

A pair of headlights blazed a path across the snow-covered lawn a moment later. Libby parked in the drive and jumped out. Her black puffy coat and dark jeans were nearly invisible in the night.

Steam rose from her head as I let her inside. "Hello," she said, lifting a palm in greeting as she cruised past us and nabbed the bear from the windowsill. "At least this guy was watching."

I waited for Libby to log in. I'd forgotten my password. Not a shocker. Generally speaking, passwords made me want to chuck my phone into traffic. If she remembered hers, hallelujah.

"I'll grab you a glass of wine," I told her.

"Make it a big pour," she said.

"On it!"

Zane turned his attention to Evan as I passed. "Tell me about the other couple that's coming. Do I know them?"

"I don't think so," he said. "Holly ran into an old friend with some tech skills I'd like to borrow for that murder case we're working on."

I returned and passed a glass to Libby while she waited for her footage to download, and I lifted my sparkling juice for another sip.

Zane looked to Caroline. "What do you remember about this guy? Will I have anything in common with him?"

I choked, and the little group turned their eyes on me.

"You okay?" Evan asked.

"Mm-hm." I cleared my throat and gathered my wits. Zane had far more in common with Scooter than he realized. "Scooter's great."

"Scooter?" Zane asked.

"It's a nickname," I said. "His real name is Scott."

"Scott?" Caroline wrinkled her nose.

The doorbell rang, and I nearly broke an ankle jumping to answer. "I'll get it!"

"How do you guys know them?" Zane asked quietly, still attempting to gather information on the other guests.

Evan made a low, noncommittal sound. "I think he had some interest in Caroline a few years ago."

"Cookie called him my schmoopy stalker," Caroline said softly.

I opened the door with a flourish, wishing I'd gotten a look at Zane when the word "stalker" was used. "Hello! Merry Christmas!" I said, feeling my smile grow at the sight of them.

Scooter wore grey slacks and a black sweater. Danica wore a gray sweater dress with black tights. Their matching black wool coats were unbuttoned.

"Come in!" Evan extended a hand to each guest as they crossed the threshold. His tone was light, but I saw the twitch in his eye as he took in their appearances.

Zane just looked confused.

Caroline, however, gasped.

Libby moved into the space at my side as the others made small talk. She gripped my arm and locked her eyes on Caroline. "I don't think I've ever seen her look so flustered," she whispered. "I'm so glad I didn't miss this. I feel like I should thank whoever took those snowmen for their immaculate timing."

". . . married one year on Valentine's Day," Scooter continued.

I'd missed the start of the sentence but understood easily enough where it had begun.

"I saw her and I just knew," he said. "It was definite love at first sight."

Danica swooned.

Caroline's carefully poised expression morphed into blatant disbelief with a side of shock. Then she met Danica's gaze and froze.

"Ope," Libby whispered, readjusting her grip on my forearm.

Caroline looked to us for help, caught open-mouth gaping. "I'm so sorry," she said. "It's just that you—" She looked from Danica to Scooter, then back. "Both look so incredible," she managed. With effort. "Your dress is stunning." She linked arms with Zane and leaned playfully against him.

She was going to be super mad at me later for this ambush, but it was completely worth it. We'd talk about this for decades to come.

"Thank you," Danica said sweetly. "It's from Ellen & Taylor."

"I know," Caroline muttered, releasing Zane and moving slightly in my direction.

I stepped closer to Libby in case Caroline executed early revenge.

Libby watched in delight as Caroline drained her wineglass. "Five bucks says she owns that same dress."

"I do," Caroline whispered.

I longed to cackle but maintained composure.

Danica raised a bag I hadn't noticed from the space just inside our front door. "This is for you," she said, passing me a highly-poisonous-to-cats poinsettia. "You probably have a dozen already, but it was so pretty I couldn't pass it up. And what sort of guest would I be if I arrived empty-handed?"

I thanked her and accepted the plant, which was immediately on its way to the bathroom.

Cindy Lou Who lumbered off the back of the couch, where she'd spent her afternoon alternating between snoozing and chittering at passing birds. She performed a deep stretch with her round body and made her way toward my plant.

I lifted the poinsettia a little higher.

Libby shook her head at Cindy. "You probably watched my snowmen get stolen."

The cat yawned, a likely affirmation.

Evan opened his arms. "Let's move into the kitchen." He led the group to the next room where drinks and an assortment of cheeses, fruits, and crackers awaited.

I hung back with Libby and the teddy bear. "How long does it take to download footage from the cloud?" I asked.

"I don't know," she said. "I didn't exactly buy the top-of-the-line materials. It's a relatively low-stakes job."

Fair enough. I crossed my arms and leaned a hip against the wall, watching over her shoulder as she waited. "Did you get to talk to Hannah's business partner?"

Libby looked up at me. "Sit down. You're making me nervous."

I followed her request and hoped she had a story to share.

"Her partner was a guy named Baxter Tracey. I'm not a fan."

"What did he say?"

"Nothing useful," Libby said. "But he had the presence of a modern-day snake oil salesman. Everything about him felt false. His grief, his eagerness to help, and everything else he said during our chat. His whole personality seemed like an act he woke up and put on after his suit one morning."

"Yuck," I said.

"Yeah." Her brow furrowed in an exaggerated frown. "Worse, Evan had already spoken with him, and I hate when he gets to things before me."

I smiled. I'd had a similar thought once or twice in these scenarios.

"I am the sheriff," he called, stepping into view through the archway between rooms. "It's my job."

"Nothing wrong with your hearing," Libby said.

I wrinkled my nose. "That is absolute fact."

I used my phone to google Hannah's business partner, then turned the screen to face her when I found his profile on a head-hunting site. "Him?"

She examined the image. "Add a few years and about twenty pounds, but yeah, that's the guy."

Her phone buzzed. "Finally," Libby huffed, redirecting her attention to the screen. A grainy, pixilated version of my front yard appeared. The timestamp in the corner indicated the image was from approximately thirty minutes ago. "There!"

A shadowy figure moved toward the snowmen. The person stooped at the waist, making the gait awkward. For a moment, I lost visual as the thief moved between the snowmen and the window. Then in one fell strike, the snowmen were yanked from the ground, the material of each gathered into a wad, and the power cords unplugged.

Without the added light from inside the snowmen, the figure became little more than a shadow.

I squinted, concentrating as I tracked the white material in his arms until it vanished.

"Where did they go?" I asked.

Two small red dots appeared onscreen as I spoke. Taillights.

"Getaway car," Libby said. "They must've disabled the interior dome light. It didn't ignite when they opened the door and got inside."

A moment later, a small pickup truck zoomed away in the distance.

Libby closed the app and made a note on her phone. "Well, that's a start, at least."

"A start?" I parroted. "I saw nothing. Those snowmen practically imploded and vanished on their own."

Libby grinned. "This was a one-man show. Two tops, because that was a small truck. No extended cab. No room for more than two people and two snowmen, even if the latter were deflated. The truck was tan with a thick black stripe along the tailgate, and four big letters. F-O-R-D. I can use that information to narrow things down. Assuming the driver is from Mistletoe, even better."

I felt my eyebrows raise. "Impressive."

Evan cleared his throat nearby and I jumped. The look on his face when I spotted him said he wasn't a fan of my involvement in any investigation. Probably also that we had guests, whom I invited. And I should mingle.

I closed the distance to his side and slid an arm around his back. "I was just telling Libby we should grab a drink and visit with our guests."

Evan kissed the top of my head and steered me toward the chatter and laughter in our kitchen. "I would love that."

"Come on, Lib," I called, waving for her to follow. "We didn't catch the snowman thief, but Evan made dinner, and that's always a win."

"True," she said. "But I think I'm more interested in where you found a second Caroline."

Evan snorted. "I wouldn't mind knowing that too."

I tipped my head back and cracked up.

Chapter Nineteen

Evan and I shared coffee, fruit, and muffins the next morning. He had an early shift, and I had plans with Cookie, so we didn't bother making a proper breakfast. Quality time plus a little gossip was the goal.

"I can't believe you didn't tell me about Danica," Evan said. "I almost thought the whole thing was a prank."

I giggled, recalling everyone's stunned expressions. Priceless.

He pulled my feet onto his lap as he skimmed the newspaper. "I wasn't sure about asking for outside tech help at first, but I'm glad you invited Scooter over to discuss the possibilities. He seemed like he had a solid plan for hunting down the information I need without all the hoops and paperwork. I didn't ask how, but I'm dying to know."

"I'm sure it's for the best," I said. "I'm glad you suggested I invite Zane and Caroline. Watching the two of them try to process Danica's resemblance to Caroline was a special Christmas gift of its own."

Evan snorted. "What do you think Danica thought when she met Caroline? Because she didn't appear to think it was strange that they looked exactly alike."

I could not begin to imagine.

He squeezed my socked feet. "Do you want to take a look at today's puzzle before I have to leave?"

"Yes, please."

He folded the newspaper back to display the daily crossword, and my attention jumped directly to clue number two across.

"More lyrics," I groaned. "One word. Nine letters. The weather outside is this."

"Frightful," Evan said.

I balked. "To recap," I said, traveling mentally back to the day I found my first name in this position, then moving smoothly forward. "So far, in answer to clue two across, we have 'Holly White watch out roast you on an open fire run over frightful.'" I laughed, thankful it didn't make any sense.

Unless I was supposed to rearrange the words as a second step.

But that didn't seem right either.

"Okay. You win. I was overthinking, and this two-across thing was a coincidence."

"It happens to the best of us," he said. "Do you want to know what I was just thinking about?"

I turned my eyes to his. "What's on your mind, Sheriff?"

"My newest title."

"Dad?" I guessed.

He dipped his chin. "How do you feel about starting a new tradition that's just for us?"

"I'm a fan," I said. "What do you have in mind?"

"What if we open our Christmas gifts from one another on Christmas Eve night instead of Christmas morning? I'm going to miss all the time we have alone, and I hate how much you'll be alone with our baby because I have to work or can't get home from a shift. You're going to carry an undo amount of childcare responsibilities sometimes, but especially around the holidays in this town. I don't want your Christmas to become part of the blur. I thought setting aside an evening that's just for us could help preserve that. I can make it a standing schedule for me. I can't get Christmas morning every year, because it's not fair to the rest of the staff, but Christmas Eve night is far more flexible. I want you to have as much time as you need to enjoy the moments, and I want to be there when you do."

I kissed him. I would never fill my own stocking or wake to find an empty one so long as this man had breath, and I wasn't sure he understood how much that meant. "I think that's an incredible idea," I said.

He kissed my nose.

We talked more about how strange it felt, knowing this would be our last holiday alone, though it was impossible to imagine things any way other than they were. Then we daydreamed together about how incredible it would be to raise our family at Reindeer Games. As soon as we had the money to build a home on our plot.

When the coffee was gone, and the crossword puzzle was finished, I stretched onto my feet to help clean the kitchen.

"Can I give you a ride to the farm today?" Evan asked.

"No need. My ride should be here any minute."

He slid a curious look in my direction as he loaded the dishwasher. "When you said you were getting tea with Cookie, I assumed you meant you'd meet her at the inn or the Hearth."

"She's taking me out," I said.

"Where?"

I busied myself hunting for my hat, scarf, and gloves. "Hmm?"

The dishwasher closed, and Evan went silent. Waiting.

I peeked over my shoulder and spotted him with one eyebrow cocked high.

He rubbed his hands on a dish towel. "Out with it, Gray."

"It's nothing," I protested, then cringed at how guilty I sounded. "We're on our way to Cup of Cheer so we can support Alice," I added quickly. "She's reopening the café today and afraid no one will come, or everyone will come, but only because they know about what happened there."

The doorbell rang, and Evan walked along at my side to answer it.

Cookie beamed at me. Her smile dwindled as the door widened to reveal the hulk of protective husband at my side. "Oh, hello," she chuckled. "Fancy seeing you here."

"I live here," he said.

"Well, you're late for work."

He looked at his watch and cursed. "You're right about that." He kissed me chastely, then fixed Cookie with a pointed stare. "Stay out of the tea while you're driving. Doesn't matter how cold it gets. You're not the Gimbel's Santa."

I laughed at his reference to my favorite holiday movie. *Miracle on 34th Street.* Specifically, the original 1947 version.

She grinned. "Santa's my favorite. You know why? He's got a nice beard."

"You know who else has a nice beard?" I asked.

"Hugo," she answered. "And don't I know it."

Evan walked me to Cookie's new vehicle where it waited in our driveway. "I'll throw some more salt down before I leave. Be careful and watch for ice," he told me. "Call if you need anything."

"Will do," Cookie answered, climbing behind the wheel of the behemoth white four-by-four Hummer truck. She'd upsized when Theodore got a wife, saying she needed something large enough to haul his family. She'd also given credit to her lottery win for allowing her to afford what she called the goat life. Her personalized plate GOAT LF put the icing on the cake in my opinion.

She reversed out of the drive with ease and pointed the beast toward town.

I hoped Evan found some peace in the fact it would take a freight train to hurt us in Cookie's ride.

* * *

The parking lot at Cup of Cheer was full. Every spot held a parked vehicle, while other hopeful guests circled the lanes, waiting for an opportunity to present itself.

Cookie made a sound of irritation and drove onto a small hill of snow where a parking spot lived in warmer weather. On days like today, it was the area where snowplows pushed the parking lot snow to clear other spaces.

"Oh!" I gripped the small handle above my head as the massive truck rocked to a stop at what felt like a forty-five-degree angle.

"There we are!" Cookie said. "One more reason I love my new truck. It's big, but there's always room to park somewhere." She unlocked her door and it swung easily open, thanks to the position she'd parked. A moment later she disappeared.

"Cookie?"

"Yup!" She shot an arm up and her hand came into view. "Meet you around the rear."

Her door swung shut with some effort, rocking me slightly once more.

I hoped Evan didn't drive past and see me plummeting from the Hummer, parked halfway up Snow Mountain like the new Wranglers at our local Jeep dealership.

I landed on my feet a moment later, realizing from the safety of Earth that I wasn't quite as high up as I'd thought while still inside.

Sunlight reflected off snow-covered land, cars, and buildings all around us.

Cookie squinted into the brilliant day. "Goat's still standing." She pointed to the twelve-foot straw structure outside the café's door.

"I wonder how she'll take it down," I said, joining Cookie as she crunched her way across the lot.

"Hard to say, but I still think Theodore would love a crack at it."

Several yards away, a white-haired woman in a black wool coat exited Cup of Cheer with several others. Every member of the party was a stranger to me, but I'd recognize the woman's pixie cut anywhere. "That's Nancy Grace, the woman we saw with Kent George during appetizers," I told Cookie. "She was on the farm with him too, on the day I received the postcard threat. And I saw her at the antiques show when I went with Caroline."

"I wonder what brought her back to Cup of Cheer," Cookie said.

I tracked the car with my gaze as it made its way to the exit. "Hopefully just the food."

The woman locked eyes with me through the passenger window. She held my stare until continuing would've meant removing her seat belt.

"She sure got a load of you," Cookie said. "What do you think that was about?"

"I wish I knew." Hopefully, she recognized us from that night and nothing more. "I tried to look for her online and came up empty. Her social media accounts are private." I couldn't help wondering if she participated in the antiques show's online forums, perhaps as BeenThereDoneThat14.

I picked up my pace to the café door and held it open for Cookie.

Inside, Cup of Cheer roared with the merriment of happy guests and a team of staff spinning like tops throughout the dining space.

Alice and Hugo alternated greeting guests at the welcome stand and walking them to their seats.

"Doesn't he look handsome," Cookie whispered. "I like the way his beard is white, but his eyebrows are mostly black. They match his belt and shoes. I wonder if he dyes them?"

"His shoes?" I teased.

She shot me a get-serious look. "I'd do it if I had more eyebrows. I overdid the plucking in my twenties and by forty the hair stopped growing back. I guess I should've plucked my legs."

I considered reminding her she could wax her legs, but instinct told me that would open a can of worms.

Hugo returned to the stand, noticed us waiting, then wholly abandoned his job. "Cookie, Holly," he said, hurrying in our direction. "You ladies look marvelous," he told us, but based on my giant down coat and wool hat with earflaps, I suspected the compliment was meant for Cookie.

He straightened, looking dashing in his pale blue sweater vest and silver tie. "Alice didn't tell me you were coming. I would've saved her best booth."

Cookie worked the buttons of her swing coat free, revealing the royal blue velvet jumpsuit beneath. A silver sash tied around her middle. "We match!" she said, touching a fingertip to his tie.

From where I stood, their pink cheeks matched even more closely than their outfits.

"Hello!" Alice called, waving from the welcome desk. "Seat them in the kitchen, and I'll meet you there," she called.

Hugo straightened. "Of course! Follow me."

We followed Hugo into the busy kitchen, then along a wall of cubbies, cupboards, and compartments to a small round table on a little stage, just one step off the main floor. He motioned us up to the chairs.

"Alice built this little nook to honor her grandma," he said. "She says it's a place for her to sit and watch as Alice's dream unfolds. My Ellie supported and championed this future for Alice every day of our granddaughter's adult life. Now, Ellie has a front seat to the show. When Alice and I have coffee after closing, we sit here too."

I rested a hand on my chest above my heart. "That's such a wonderful story."

"She was a wonderful woman, just like Alice," he said. "And the two of you. She was sick a long while before we lost her. She's been gone more than a year now, and she's missed every day."

"I'm sorry," I said.

He shook his head, smile small and sad. "Her dementia took her years before she went. I think parts of me started the grieving process long ago. But she remembered Alice as a child, those goats, and long days of working in the kitchen to the very end."

Cookie took the chair closest to where Hugo stood. "I'm a baker," she said. "I was never the cook I wanted to be. I admire that in Alice."

"Maybe you can bake for me sometime," he said. "I'd love to cook for you."

She sat taller. "That sounds nice."

They looked at one another for so long my stomach growled. And I'd just had a boatload of muffins.

Hugo chuckled at the sound. "I'd better get the two of you some menus." He tapped the table, then went back through the swinging kitchen doors.

"This is fun," Cookie said. She smiled at the activity all around us.

Men and women in logoed shirts and aprons buzzed through the space in a well-choreographed dance, plating foods and clattering lids on pots and pans. Steam rose into the air in great puffs, along with the most mouth-watering smells.

My stomach growled again, and I felt my hair begin to frizz. My genetics weren't equipped for this level of humidity.

Hugo returned with a pair of menus and Alice. "I'll leave you to it," he said. "I'm on seating duty while you ladies visit and choose your meal."

Cookie didn't bother hiding her disappointment when he walked away.

I smiled brightly at Alice. "It's a shame no one showed up today," I teased.

She laughed nervously. "I guess no one's boycotting after all."

"Locals get more understanding every year," Cookie said.

I scrunched my nose. Sadly, that was true. Our town had gotten a little too comfortable with an annual murder, if anyone asked me.

"And there are so many tourists in town, most don't have a clue what goes on in Mistletoe outside the day they come to shop," she added. Alice toyed with the charm on her necklace, looking hopeful but unconvinced, despite the number of people in the dining room.

"Hey," I said gently. "This is going to be okay. It'll be over soon, and you can move forward. You'll begin to heal."

She nodded woodenly and refreshed her smile. "Ugh. I get in my head and imagine every worst-case scenario for my future. Or all the ways I might've been able to stop the break-in and murder from happening if I'd done something differently."

"Well, you can't do that to yourself," Cookie said. "We can't know what we don't know."

"That's right," I said. "And you had no reason to think someone would come back and break into this place."

Alice released her charm and a sigh. "Half the time, none of it seems real to me, even all these days later."

I looked at her more closely, noting her uneven braids and make-up free face. Typically, Alice wore mascara and lipstick. Her shirt had a small stain near the pocket, and it hung more loosely on her than I recalled. "How are you doing otherwise?"

I asked, slowing my speech and softening my tone. "Besides the overthinking?"

She scratched the back of her head. "Not great. I can't sleep. I can't eat. I don't want Grandpa to leave. I don't know how to live here alone anymore."

Cookie tented her thin white brows. "You don't have to rush back to your apartment," she said. "There's a room open at the inn as long as you need it. And when there isn't, you can always bunk with me."

Alice smiled sweetly. "Thank you, Cookie. You're a good friend."

Cookie glanced at the door to the dining room. "Is your grandpa going home soon?"

"Not until after the new year," she said. "But he can't stay forever."

Cookie chewed her lip.

Alice stepped closer to the table, her attention fastened on me. "Have you heard anything more from your husband?" she asked. "Libby is working hard to clear me as a suspect, I know, but it comes down to whether or not Sheriff Gray has enough evidence to arrest me. They have my knife," she whispered.

I followed the flicker of her gaze to a row of knives stuck to a magnetic band above one counter.

"I haven't heard anything more," I said. "Please don't worry. I know it looks bad and feels scary from where you are, but Evan's gathering more information every day." I pushed thoughts of his recent confession from my head. He didn't have any leads, but I couldn't bring myself to tell her. She needed hope, not more reasons to worry. "He knows you aren't a killer," I said instead. "Trust him to get to the bottom of what happened. He won't let you down."

She nodded, but the fear in her eyes remained.

I leaned in her direction as a new thought took hold. "I saw a woman leaving as we arrived. She has short white hair. She was here the night Hannah tried to take your goats during the appetizers. She spoke to you with Kent George. Did you see her today?"

"No."

I sighed and glanced at the menu, but I wasn't satisfied. "You mentioned talking to the antiques show's event coordinator. Has he stopped by the café?"

"Once," she said. "Before the progressive dinner. I haven't seen him since then."

Interesting. Could Arnold have been surveying the Yule Goat situation and making plans to return later?

While I was thinking about my suspects, I grabbed my phone and showed her Baxter Tracey's photo. "This was Hannah's business partner. Does he look familiar?"

Alice looked for a long while before speaking. "Maybe," she said finally. "The man I'm thinking of was older and heavier, but he wore similar glasses, and the smile is the same."

A shiver cracked down my spine. "When?"

"A week ago, I guess. We talked about my life in Sweden and all the heirlooms and keepsakes Grandma sent me—" Alice covered her mouth with one hand. "You don't think he put Hannah up to stealing? Then killed her?"

"I don't know what I think," I admitted. "But I'll let Evan know he was here. It could be highly relevant."

Hugo returned, and Alice started. "Grandpa!" she scolded, then laughed. "You scared me!"

"I didn't mean to," he said. "I wanted to see if these two had time to select something from the menu."

I'd barely glanced at the menu, but everything at the café was delicious, so I couldn't lose.

"I'll try your grilled salmon sandwich and a cup of vegetable soup," Cookie said.

"Have you tried our scones?" Hugo asked. "They're the best in town. I can attest. I'm a bit of a connoisseur."

"Then I'll take two," she said.

Hugo ginned. "Sweets for the sweet."

I slid my gaze to Alice, who seemed puzzled by the interaction.

"I'll have what she's having," I said, when Hugo pried his eyes off of Cookie long enough to look at me.

Hugo lifted a finger into the air, then hustled into the action and started working on our sandwiches.

Alice turned wide eyes on me. "Did he just—are they flirting?"

I lifted my shoulders in a quick shrug.

"You can bet your sweet scones," Cookie said. "I can't let a nice beard like that go to waste."

Chapter Twenty

I rode with Cookie to Reindeer Games after lunch. The farm was overrun with visitors, and the crew actively redirected tour buses to excess parking. The added hassle for guests was assuaged with free horse-drawn sleigh rides to the main activity site. A savvy, and strategic, trade-off. Dad wouldn't exhaust the horses by expecting them to do this and perform their usual sleigh ride duties, where people paid for the experience, which meant he lost those perspective sales. But using the rides as an enticement for all the extra guests to come to the farm—even if they had to park far away—meant more sales across the entire farm. A definite win.

I smiled as we motored past Dad on our way to the inn. Lumberjack, businessman, devoted husband and father. Bud White had set the bar high for five decades strong.

"Everyone adores him," Cookie said, as if reading my thoughts. "Your mama did good. You too."

"I did, didn't I?" My smile grew.

"Hmm."

I waited, but she didn't elaborate.

"Zane's a hot hunk of a fella too," she said, parking in her designated spot.

"Are you okay?" I asked. Did women go boy crazy again after a certain age?

"Ray's got a nice wholesome look. Some women like that."

"Cookie?"

"Hmm?" She shut down her engine and looked at me, but her eyes were a bit unfocused. "We only need eight more to make a dozen."

"A dozen what?" I asked, pushing her shoulder with my pointer finger. "Earth to Cookie. What's this about?"

She blinked. "A baker's dozen!" She cackled and a burst of excitement illuminated her face.

I imagined ways to ask for a look into her thermos without offending.

"We can call it the Mistletoe's Christmas Cupcakes Calendar."

"I still have no idea what you're talking about, but that seems a bit wordy," I said. "What happened to the baby goat calendar?"

"We don't have any kids yet, but we've got a lot of local cupcakes." She pointed through her window to Dad and a pair of farm crew members. "We only need twelve for a calendar."

I felt my mouth form a little O as a sharp bark of laughter burst free. "No!"

"Why not?" she asked. "I need something to top my Goat for All Seasons, and who doesn't like a cupcake?"

"Oh," I said, head shaking. "I was not complaining. I think this is hysterical."

She frowned. "It's not supposed to be funny."

"Trust me," I told her. "It is very funny. All the men you've named so far will change their names and move to Peoria before they agree to be next June's featured pastry." Another burst of laughter wrung free from my chest. I simultaneously longed to talk her out of the impossible mission and to fund the project myself. Or at least follow her around and film every potential cupcake's reaction to the request. Especially Dad's. Oh, my stars and snickerdoodles. He would turn red as Rudolph's nose and combust. Nothing but work boots and flannel left behind.

"You should definitely do this," I said, certain this was an out-of-body experience. She couldn't be serious.

Please let her be serious.

"I bet a cupcake calendar brings in the most money yet!" she said. "Those firemen calendars are what gave me the idea to start with."

"I remember."

We climbed out and headed for the inn.

"I'm going to get some tea and a notebook," she said. "I want to make plans and project the probable amount we can raise for charity before I approach anyone. Who can turn down a profitable act for charity?"

I lifted my giddy gaze skyward. "I don't know," I said. But hopefully no one!

Peals of laughter split the air and returned my gaze to earth. In the distance, dozens of small children in brightly colored coats and hats climbed a tightly packed hill of snow that had been carefully engineered into a slide. Others ran through a pint-sized snow maze, ducking and jumping at one another around every bend.

"That'll be you soon," Cookie said. "Chasing a jolly pink ball of energy around the farm."

"Pink?" I asked. I hadn't given much thought to the gender of my baby. I'd only imagined it dressed in tiny barn coats and Red Sox ball caps.

"Or blue," she said. "Or red or green. Pink was just the first color that came to mind."

A familiar face moved into view, and it took a moment for me to place it. "Oh, hey," I said. "That's Peggy!"

"Who?"

"I met her a few days ago when she was working at Santa's Village. She told me about her kids, and now she's here with them." Delight danced over my skin for her. "She was sad to be separated from them so she could be here, but it looks like she found a way to share Mistletoe with the little ones." I loved that for her.

"Holly!" she called, swinging an arm overhead.

"Looks like she spotted you too," Cookie said. "You made your first mom friend!"

My heart swelled as I let the concept sink in. I had a mom friend.

"I'm going inside to get started on the calendar," Cookie said. "Come see me when you're done, and I'll catch you up."

"Deal!"

Peggy approached with a broad smile. She wore a moss green wool coat with burnt orange hat and gloves. Her scarf was a floral mix of the two colors with thin lines of blue that matched her eyes.

A tiny version of Peggy marched steadily at her side. His sapphire eyes glowed brightly against his fair skin and pink cheeks. Only the circle of his chubby face showed beneath layers of cold weather gear, each printed with tiny cartoon dinosaurs.

An equally bundled baby viewed the world from the safety of a sling around Peggy's chest.

"Well, hello," I said, meeting her in the middle of the snowy field. "You look like you're having fun."

"We are," she said. "I can't tell you how much I appreciate all the free things for families and little ones to do and see here. My kids are convinced Santa has a part in all this magic."

"He does!" I tipped forward at the waist and grinned at the toddler. "You must be Henry."

His mouth opened and his eyes stretched wide. "How do you know that?"

"Santa," I said. "And you—" I stretched upright and spun for a better look at the cherub-cheeked baby. "Must be Margaret

Katherine Calliope Cranston the Twelfth. Queen of the Seven Gables."

"No," Henry sang, dragging the small word into long, laughing syllables. "That's my sister!"

"Ah! Eloise! I didn't recognize you all wrapped up like a burrito!!"

Henry cracked up and collapsed on the ground.

Peggy laughed too. "You're good with kids," she said.

"Because I am one," I admitted. "Life on a Christmas tree farm is a little like Neverland in that way."

"Are you a lost boy?" Henry asked.

I spun. "How do you know about lost boys?"

"Bedtime stories," Peggy said as I recalled the fantastic collection of children's books at her booth.

"Aren't you lucky?"

He swung his arms and legs in wide arcs, making a small angel in the snow.

Peggy's expression grew thoughtful. "I hope I'm not overstepping, but your friend bought something for a baby the last time I saw you."

My right palm moved instinctively to rest on my middle. "It's early," I said.

She nodded. "I thought so. You're glowing."

"Well, life is good. Mostly. According to my doctor, I had slightly elevated blood pressure at my last visit, but I'm monitoring it, and everything is looking good. Though my friends seem to think I'm a walking time bomb." I shook my head. "That was so much more than you asked."

"No, I get it," she said. "Being a mom is a little overwhelming." She laughed. "Usually in the good ways. Having friends who care is priceless. If you ever have any questions, even the weird ones, you can ask me anytime. I've probably experienced it too, or I know someone who has. And if Mistletoe has a new-mommy group, you should join. Everyone there will become your biggest ally. Moms are like that in my experience."

I didn't know if Mistletoe had a group for moms, but I planned to find out. I loved making new friends, and I had lots of questions. A double win.

My gaze returned to the floral scarf at Peggy's neck, and I couldn't help asking one non-mommy-related question before she went back to playing with her kids. "Have you been to the antiques show? I think I saw that scarf earlier this week. My friend, Caroline, spent at least twenty minutes examining an entire table of similar prints and patterns."

"Yes!" Peggy groaned. "Why were there so many to choose from? And why can we only wear one at a time? It killed me to leave the rest behind." She adjusted the sling's material to shield her daughter from a blast of icy wind.

Henry moved on to building a little snow fort at our feet.

"I wished I could've stayed longer," Peggy said. "The show was a lot bigger than I'd expected. These two lost patience shortly after I spent way too long choosing this scarf. It was naptime, and they were overstimulated. I am not going to lie, shopping loses some of its appeal with a tiny entourage in tow."

"Someone should warn Caroline," I said. "She's not expecting, but she'll want to take that information into consideration beforehand. Right now, she only has to put up with me getting bored and wanting snacks."

Peggy chuckled again. "Oh! I thought of you this morning while I went down my usual online rabbit hole over coffee. Have you logged on to the antiques show's website today?"

"No." In fact, I'd been doing astonishingly well at staying out of Evan's murder investigation, I realized. *Good job, Holly!* I thought.

"It was a circus," Peggy said. "The coordinator was in multiple forums having a meltdown about vendors trying to pass knockoffs as originals. A few users assumed the rant was passive-aggressively pointed at them and clapped back, which put Arnold on the defensive. Others chimed in, concerned about which things were frauds, worried someone would sell what they were selling for a lower price, which meant they'd lose sales. I started typing out a comment and realized I am officially too invested in drama and nonsense that has absolutely nothing to do with me. Which is how I ended up here, taking a break with the kids and reminding myself what really matters."

My mind raced with memories of Arnold mentioning something similar to me at the antiques show. He said it was up to him to discern fakes of all kinds. I still had no idea how he could do that.

But I didn't want to get into a conversation about anything related to the murder investigation in public. So I chose a safe response. "I'm glad Reindeer Games could give you the break you deserve," I said. "Time with these little ones would cheer up anyone."

Henry tugged her coat sleeve. "Mama, can I slide again?" He pointed to the snow slide behind them.

"Of course."

"I'll walk with you," I offered, not ready to say goodbye so soon.

She smiled and tipped her head toward the slide. "I couldn't do Arnold's job," she said. "It has to be overwhelming. I felt a little bad for him this morning. I still do. If I had to authenticate every item in the show my head would explode."

"Pow," Henry said, miming an explosion with his hands.

Peggy pulled her lips into an exaggerated grimace and patted the top of his hat.

"It's hard for me to get my head around how anyone can know so many items well enough to spot an imposter," I admitted. "I wouldn't know if you handed me someone else's coat after dinner at a restaurant."

"You probably don't care about your coat half as much as Arnold cares about antiques," she said. "And I shouldn't care about any of this, but I heard that Hannah's business partner is bringing a bunch of stuff from their store to sell at the show, and it's irritating me. The guy took no time for mourning. No pause for grief. Not even a small hiatus to show respect for someone who's not just gone but who was m-u-r-d-e-r-e-d, probably by someone at the dumb show. He's just moving right along. Gotta make that money. And he doesn't even need it! She did."

"Dumb show," Henry said.

Peggy's expression pinched and she chuckled nervously. "I should really stop talking."

He made another explosion sound, and she covered her face briefly with one hand.

My mind got hung up on something else. "The business partner doesn't need the money?" I asked. "I thought their store was in danger?"

"It was," she said. "Hannah loved that place. It was her dream, but he has other stores and venues for selling and trading. She wasn't his only source of income. He was hers."

"Mommy?" Henry asked. "Now?"

Peggy checked our remaining distance to the slide. "Yeah. Okay, now, buddy."

Henry made a slow run for the back of the line, bogged down by his cold weather gear.

"Do all of Hannah's business partner's businesses involve antiques?" I asked.

"Yeah, but different kinds," she said. "His online store is thriving in the international market. I've been watching it grow for years. He sold other stuff with Hannah. The shops weren't competing for sales or anything like that."

"Well, that's good," I said, but my concern was something else entirely.

Could Baxter, the business partner, have encouraged Hannah to swipe the Yule Goat? Maybe he offered her an exchange she couldn't refuse. Maybe if she got the goat for him, he'd make sure her business didn't go under.

It was a lot of maybes.

I couldn't help wondering if Evan knew Baxter Tracey was coming to town. Libby hadn't mentioned it when she told me about her chat with the guy. Did she know?

Or did I get an inside scoop?

"I'd better get back to the inn," I said, taking a step in the opposite direction. "Thanks for hanging out for a while."

"Anytime," she said. "I meant what I said. Reach out if you ever have questions or want to go on a mom date." She patted her pockets and frowned. "I don't have my cards with me, but you can find me online at Peggy's Curated Collection, and I'll be back at Santa's Village tomorrow."

I smiled as I turned away. Cookie was right. I needed mom friends, and I was thankful for my first one.

I pulled my phone from my coat pocket and typed the news of Baxter Tracey's impending visit into a message, then paused. Would Evan think I was meddling? Would he be angry? Disappointed?

A long shadow fell over me in the sun, and I pulled my eyes from the phone screen.

Scooter approached quickly, only a few feet away now. "Hey, Holly. I hoped to find you here." He wore dark aviator sunglasses and kept his hands in his coat pockets as he moved.

"Hello," I said, putting my phone away for now. "What's up?"

He looked over my head, then back to my face before stopping only a foot or so away. "I have information on the topic you suggested. I'm delivering it to you, by mouth, to avoid being seen passing information to your husband. Also to avoid creating a trail. You can share this with him in person later. No record of the exchange."

I pressed my lips into a tight line. This was very James Bond. I was more of a Scooby-Doo. But here we were. "'Kay."

"The text message threat was sent from a burner phone bought over the counter at a chain store in the next town. I visited the store and asked the manager to use the phone's serial number to determine the day, time, and register where the product was purchased. He agreed, and we pulled up the receipt to check the name on the credit card. But it was a cash sale."

"Dead end," I said. "Bummer."

"There's a bank machine across the street," he continued. "And those always have security cameras. The bank wouldn't let me access their records to see who accessed the machine for money around the time the phone was purchased—rightfully so," he said. "I don't have a warrant for that information, but they did take a look at the security camera footage and confirm that their camera has a clear view of everyone entering and exiting the store."

My chest tightened, and my heart rate rose. This was it. Scooter saw the person who sent me the threat emojis. The coffin emoji. "And?"

"There's a six-minute span where a public bus blocks their view of the store's front door, and that coincides with the time immediately following the phone purchase."

I made a fist between us and shook it. "That was so unnecessarily stressful!" I complained.

"What do you mean?"

I balked. "You could've started by saying you didn't have anything useful to report, then offered details about what you did, instead of keeping me on pins and needles for nothing."

Scooter wrinkled his nose, dislodging his round Harry Potter glasses. "I thought that was what I did," he said, quickly adjusting his frames.

I rubbed a gloved hand over one eye. "Thank you for your help, Scooter," I said.

I needed to go inside and check my blood pressure. I moved my glove away from my face in a goodbye wave, then turned toward the inn.

"I've tried tracking the phone," he said, stopping me short.

I turned slowly back and stared. My gullible heart pounded anew. "And?" I asked, when he didn't continue.

"No luck."

I mashed my lips together and grunted.

"It's not online. Either someone powered it off or destroyed it. Neither would be uncommon in a scenario like this one. Sending threats and completing shady transactions are popular usages for these types of phones."

I waited. "Anything else?"

"Yes."

My muscles locked. "What?" I pressed.

"No luck getting user details on the handles in question at the showcase's website," he said. "All were made with throw away accounts."

All hope deflated impossibly further. "Is that everything?"

"Danica and I really enjoyed having dinner with you the other night. We don't have a lot of couples friends, so hanging out with you guys was a highlight of our trip."

I softened a little at that declaration. "Anytime," I said. "We had fun too."

Scooter glanced shyly away, reminding me of the guy I'd first met. "I've always appreciated how kind and welcoming you are, and it was nice getting to know Evan better. If the two of you ever want to get together again, let me know. Danica and I would really like that. Zane seemed great, but Danica wasn't a big fan of Caroline. She thought they looked alike, and I guess it really bothered her that Caroline's outfit matched with hers."

I tented my brows. "I noticed."

He sighed. "I just don't know why she'd do that. The Caroline I remember was so cool and independent. Dressing like Danica was really kind of weird." He looked at his watch. "I have to go," he said. "Thanks again for dinner. Let's do it again soon!"

I ran mentally backwards over the final wackadoodle exchange, unable to make sense of more than half. Then I went inside to check my blood pressure.

Chapter Twenty-One

Cookie invited me over for lunch the next day, and Evan cheerfully offered to drive. I suspected his enthusiasm to drop me off at the farm without a ride home had something to do with the gossip I relayed from Peggy the night before.

I'd shared the information gleaned at the farm with Libby via text message and with Evan over dinner. Libby hadn't responded, and Evan had changed the subject, then given me gratuitous side-eye throughout dessert. He didn't seem to care that Hannah's business partner was visiting Mistletoe soon. I couldn't understand why.

Oddly, Evan was more interested in the lack of results from Scooter's tech dive.

Thankfully, my blood pressure was normal when we checked it before bed and after breakfast. If it hadn't been, Evan might've tried locking me in his cruiser where he could keep an eye on me twenty-four/seven. The readings weren't perfect, but they weren't particularly worrisome either. Nothing to call Dr. Bright about. Yet.

I'd declared Evan's constant panic a contributing factor to my problem, and he'd gone to the basement to run on the treadmill before bed. His doctor had insisted his bulk consumption of antacids wasn't a good way to live and prescribed jogging as a healthier way to manage stress. Evan took the advice and lost ten pounds. He'd gained an impressive amount of lean muscle as well, which I wouldn't see anytime soon if I kept stressing him out.

So I doubled down on my resolve to stay out of this year's murder investigation.

"How are you feeling?" he asked, shifting the truck into park outside the inn.

"Good. You?"

He snorted, then abandoned the driver's position to open my door.

I accepted his offered hand and slid into the bright, snowy day at his side. "You don't have to walk me all the way to the porch," I protested.

"I'm coming with you," he said. "I wouldn't miss this." He pressed the doorbell before I could ask what he was talking about.

The inn's front door sucked open before his thumb left the button.

"Surprise!" Mom called.

A chorus of voices echoed the word behind her.

Evan chuckled and escorted me inside.

"What's happening?" I asked.

Mom pulled me into a hug. "It's your special luncheon! Remember? We talked about it last week."

I peered into the cluster of familiar faces behind her. Caroline. Libby. Cookie. Alice. Hugo. Ray. Zane. Dad. A collection of Mom's close friends. Dr. Bright.

Evan rubbed his palm up and down my back. "I told her you'd forgotten," he whispered against my ear. "It's to announce and celebrate your pregnancy."

A lump formed instantly, nonsensically, in my throat.

All these people had taken time out of their days at Christmas to celebrate our good news. My heart swelled, and I loved these people impossibly more.

"Come in! Come in!" Mom instructed, ushering us deeper into the foyer, then collecting our hats, coats, and gloves. "We're so excited to do this for you. Just wait until the baby shower this spring!"

I moved through the little crowd, thanking everyone for coming. The logical, practical, and superstitious parts of me wanted to run away, suddenly afraid it was too soon to have any sort of party. Too soon to spread the word. Far too many things could go wrong at this early point in a pregnancy. But hope and unparalleled joy told those concerns to take a hike. If something went wrong, all these same people would be here to hold and heal me. And a future loss wouldn't make this moment any less worthy of celebration.

I felt the sting of tears only moments before the heat of them streamed over my cheeks.

Mom and Cookie had arranged a beautiful spread of appetizers and finger foods in the dining room and covered the table in Chantilly lace and linens.

"Caroline baked the cupcakes," Mom said, pointing to a frilly white arrangement of Caroline's signature sweets. "We have teas and juices, bottled water, and coffee to drink."

Evan made his way back to my side and tucked me under his arm. "How'd we get this lucky?"

"I have no idea."

Libby stepped into view with Ray. They passed us an envelope. "This is for three nights at a ski resort about an hour from here. We got you a chalet with catered meals and a California king bed so you can stock up on sleep."

Evan accepted the gift, and I pulled Libby into a hug.

Ray hugged me when Libby let me go. "Don't try skiing in your condition," he warned. "And don't use the hot tub."

"Still studying the dangers and perils of pregnancy?" I asked.

"Knowledge is power," he said. "Also avoid soft cheese and undercooked meats."

"I do that anyway," I said.

Caroline and Zane were next to approach. Zane and Evan shook hands. Caroline handed me another envelope. "This is for my favorite spa," she said. "We booked you a couple's massage and three follow-up massages. One per trimester and one for after delivery. Also, I signed you up for a prenatal yoga class, so you can meet other moms."

Another round of tears appeared, and I laughed. "Sorry! I can't control these!"

She passed me a handkerchief, and I ran it under my eyes.

The gifts for Evan and me continued for what felt like a century. I wasn't great at being the center of attention, and every eye was on me, including my husband's. We received comfy sets of matching pj's. Fuzzy socks and bathrobes. Gift certificates to local restaurants and upcoming shows. A dozen different opportunities to relax and spend time together, enjoying this brief season of anticipation. My parents gave me a weighty gift card to a local maternity boutique so I wouldn't live in Evan's sweatpants during months six through nine.

They knew me well.

When we finally sat to eat, a group of servers I recognized from Cup of Cheer appeared with trays. Alice and Hugo followed, setting carafes on the table, before taking the final two seats.

"You catered!" I exclaimed. "You have so much going on already. How did you find time to do this?"

Alice smiled. "There's always time for friends. You taught me that," she said, dragging her gaze around the giant table. "All of you."

A round of "Aww" lifted from the guests, and Alice laughed.

Hugo took the seat beside Cookie, which I suspected was planned.

Our meal came in waves, each course served and removed by the Cup of Cheer staff, and often so smoothly I barely noticed as I listened and chatted with our friends. We ate pickled herring and meatballs with jam. Cheeses and crispbreads, and boiled potatoes with sour cream and dill.

The party began as a tribute to Evan and me, but around that table, it felt more like a recognition of family. Not the sort we're born into, though I'd hit the proverbial jackpot there, but the kind of family where the members choose one another and will stand by those choices to the end.

After lunch, we broke naturally into smaller groups and filled the inn's first floor with conversations and laughter. Many drifted to the kitchen, where desserts were arranged on the island before Alice's staff headed home. Some sat in the dining room, too comfortable to get up and move just yet.

I paced the foyer, attempting to digest, then I spotted Cookie and Libby in the parlor seated on a loveseat by the fire. "Hey," I said, helping myself to the tufted velvet armchair across from them.

Libby looked more at ease than I typically saw her. She sipped from a teacup printed with holly berries and tilted her head slightly when I sat. "I hear you're already out there making mom friends, Miss Congeniality."

I grinned.

Cookie crossed her short legs at the ankles. "I told her about the woman with the kids. They seemed like a nice family."

"They are," I said. "And thanks to Caroline's prenatal yoga classes, it sounds as if I'll meet more nice moms soon."

"I've never been interested in yoga," Libby said. "I don't know why anyone would want to be so . . . zen."

"When I was your age," Cookie said. "I did yoga on the beach in San Tropez. I was very bendy."

I laughed. "I've never been zen or bendy, but if it makes me healthier for the next six or seven months, I'll give it a try."

"That's the spirit," Cookie said. "Maybe your new friend can join you."

"She doesn't live in Mistletoe," I said. "She's here to sell her books and things to folks who came for the antiques show." I couldn't recall where Peggy lived, but it was within driving distance. That was important to her, and she'd gone home to pick up her kids for a day at the farm yesterday.

"Clementine might be a new mom next summer too," Cookie said. "Wouldn't that be nice?"

"Very," I agreed.

"Maybe the two of you could take classes together. People love goat yoga."

I slid my eyes to Libby, who promptly looked away.

Alice rounded the corner and smiled. "There you are. I sat too far from you at lunch, and I can't leave without a chat."

I reached for the nearby chair and dragged it closer to our circle.

Alice sat. "Perfect. What are we talking about?"

Cookie filled her in, and Alice looked to me.

"Is Peggy a blonde lady?" she asked, ignoring the goat yoga comment as Libby and I had. "Or maybe her hair is very light brown?"

"Yes. Do you know her?"

"I do," Alice said. "She and her kids came into the café once or twice. They seem like such a nice family."

Instant suspicion skittered down my spine. *Such a nice family.* Those were the same words Cookie used to describe them. The same words people on the news told reporters about serial killers and cults. "Did you ever see her with Hannah Ford?" I asked.

"I never saw Hannah before that night at the café," Alice said. "Why do you ask?"

"They were friends," I said, intuition still itching. "They went to college together at the University of Maine. Did you ever see Peggy with Arnold, the events coordinator?" I asked. "Or with anyone from the antiques show? Maybe with Kent George?"

Or the lady with the pixie cut that Alice hadn't remembered the last time I asked.

I silently cursed my exile on the investigation.

Alice pulled her chin back, brows furrowed. "What's going on?"

"Yeah," Libby asked, shifting forward. "What are you all jazzed up about?"

I mentally released the thread I'd hoped would unravel the whole case. "I was wondering if my new friend is connected to the murder by more than her relationship with the victim."

"Do you think that's possible?" Libby asked.

I wanted to say anything was possible, or scream something like *how would I know?*

Instead, I shook my head. "Just exploring all options."

Then something directly related to my frustration popped into mind, and my eyes narrowed on my sister-in-law. "Did you get my text yesterday?"

"No."

I pursed my lips. "That was fast. Not going to ask when I sent it or what it was about?" Almost as if she knew the answers to both of those questions. "You just didn't get it?" I pressed. "So, it what? Got lost in the ether?"

"I was busy yesterday," she said. "I might've missed it."

Cookie frowned. "Now I think I'm the one who missed something."

"Hannah's business partner has plans to visit Mistletoe," I said. "He's bringing some things from their store to try to sell at the show. Peggy thought it was in bad taste, not to mention not very nice, to press on with business as usual so soon after Hannah's . . . untimely passing."

Libby shrugged. "It's good business to unload as many antiques as possible while the show is in town. The shop was failing. He probably wants out from under it."

I understood that, but I saw Peggy's point too. For someone more concerned with human respect than a bottom line, it made sense to see the businessman as a bad guy. I couldn't help siding with her against the smart business move on this. If Baxter Tracey had other avenues for sales, as she'd said, then business could at least wait until the poor woman's body was released and sent home for a funeral. He could've sold their joint merchandise in other ways, at another time.

"All right," Libby said, though no one had spoken for several long beats. "I'll see if I can find him and have a chat about his motivation for selling right now. But I think we know the answer. He has a prime opportunity. Maybe he'll confess to killing her if I ask nicely."

"If only it was that easy," Evan said, causing the four of us to snap upright in our seats.

We'd leaned forward, toward the center of our circle, as we spoke, keeping the discussion private, but apparently not too quiet.

Darn his superhuman hearing.

"How long have you been standing there?" Libby asked.

"I don't know, Ms. Private Investigator. You tell me." He crossed his arms and leaned a shoulder against the door jamb.

Libby rolled her eyes. "I shouldn't have to be on my guard at a congrats-you're-having-a-baby luncheon."

"And I shouldn't have to patrol my congrats luncheon."

Cookie and Alice hopped onto their feet, talking loudly about something in the kitchen. They beetled out of the room without a goodbye.

Libby stood, stretched, then sauntered away behind them, leaving me to fend for myself.

Cowards.

I chewed my lip as Evan moseyed in my direction, a single cupcake in hand.

He offered me the treat without breaking eye contact. "How are you feeling?" he asked.

Exactly as if I was busted.

But I still took the cupcake.

Chapter Twenty-Two

I was back at the Hearth for Christmas Karaoke the following night. I'd made another trip to town with Libby and Ray and finished my Christmas shopping. With only three days left until Christmas, my holiday season had shaped up to be deeply normal for the first time in many years. All I had left to do was choose a plow for my husband's truck and wrap all the gifts before the big day.

The plow had a high enough ticket price to double as a second wedding anniversary gift. Considering I struggled miserably at choosing gifts for him, this was a win I could get behind.

Outside the café, wind whistled around the window frames and rattled the glass panes. Temperatures had rapidly dropped sixteen degrees from morning to afternoon, and a pending storm would add another six to ten inches of snow by dawn. Santa's Village was forced to close early when the wind chill became dangerous with prolonged exposure.

Dad and the crew made every effort to keep the vendors comfortable, arranging portable outdoor heaters and erecting wind barriers, but the brewing storm wouldn't be managed.

As a result, the Hearth was packed, and Mom announced a repeat of several indoor activities to keep guests happy, beginning with Holiday Bingo and Christmas Karaoke.

I'd barely thought her name and she appeared at the end of the table. "Finished?" she asked.

"Yup." I passed her the stack of thank-you cards I'd completed for attendees of yesterday's luncheon. Being trapped on the farm with a killer on the loose was great for my productivity. I'd sent a big box of signed Gumdrop Gumshoe merch with the postal worker at lunchtime, and Evan took a pile of completed jewelry orders to the post office after breakfast. Having a fully functioning hand helped too.

"How are you feeling?" she asked, tucking the envelopes into her apron pocket. "You look tired."

"I'm bored," I complained, then laughed at the ridiculousness of it. I rolled my eyes up to meet her gaze. "I understand why it's better for me to stay out of Evan's investigation, but is it wrong for me to miss the excitement?"

"Yes."

I jutted my bottom lip forward. "Boo."

I'd tried snooping from the safety of my booth, poking around online instead of in person, and where had that gotten me? Threatened.

Benched.

Unfair.

"Where is everyone?" Mom asked. "They'll keep you entertained once they get here."

"I hope they hurry up," I said. "They're already late. Isn't Cookie tonight's MC?"

Mom checked the clock above the door. "I'm sure she'll be here any moment."

The door blew open as if on cue and a curl of snow snaked inside. Cookie, Caroline, Zane, Alice, and Hugo followed in its wake, hooting and laughing as if the party started somewhere in the snow.

"There they are!" Mom said. She stacked silverware rolled in napkins at the end of the table, then went to greet our friends.

"What'd they do? Get a ride share?" I mumbled, feeling disproportionately grouchy.

I was still a little miffed at Libby, I realized, for never responding to my text message letting her know Hannah's business partner was coming to town. And for not giving me a straight response when I tried to corner her about it at the luncheon yesterday.

There was clearly a fine line between appreciating all the people who loved and cared for me, wanting me to be safe and healthy. And wanting to Godzilla stomp every time one of them treated me as if I was made of glass.

Or maybe it was the pregnancy hormones. If so, hopefully that symptom wouldn't last much longer. I missed not wanting to rampage in between irrational bouts of tears.

Cookie hung her coat on a hook behind the service counter and climbed onto the small portable stage in the corner. "Hello, hello!" she sang into the microphone, using her most British accent.

Caroline and Zane slid onto the bench at my side. Alice and Hugo took the seats across from us.

"Hey!" Caroline pulled me into a hug. "How are you? What's new?"

My mood lifted with the proximity to my friends. "I'm feeling better now," I said. "You were all late."

Hugo leaned forward, slipping out of his coat. "We ran into one another in the parking lot. We came from the inn with Cookie and spotted Caroline and Zane headed in this direction."

"Then we got to talking," Alice said. "It was freezing, and Cookie was late, which finally got us moving."

Mom returned to deliver bingo cards and mints for markers. "In case you want to play after karaoke."

"Thank you," we sang.

"What do you think of your neighborhood in town?" Zane asked. "I've talked to Evan, and he likes it, but he's never lived anywhere else around here. I figure you're the better one to ask."

The question stumped me for a moment. "You don't like your apartment?" I'd never actually been to Zane's place, but Caroline said it was nice, and it had incredible views of town from the mountains.

"I'm looking for something bigger, now that I know I'm staying for the long haul," he said, casting a charming smile to Caroline.

She beamed, and her joy filled me. I smiled too. "Our neighborhood is nice. The homes are mostly from the turn of the last century. Postage stamp yards. The demographic skews older, mostly retired couples." Which was great for security and convenience. Someone was always home to sign for packages and discourage petty crime. "What are you looking for?" I asked. "Something new? Historic? Move-in ready? A fixer upper? A cookie cutter?"

"Yes?" Cookie called on the microphone, pulling my eyes to her.

"Not you," Zane said. "Look-alike houses."

"Oh," she said. "Where was I?"

The guests in the dining area laughed, and I joined them. Life on the farm was so profoundly unserious. I'd been joking when I compared my childhood home to Neverland, but it wasn't wholly untrue. For that, and so many other things, I was immeasurably thankful.

Caroline pulled her long waves over one shoulder, eyes sparkling as she leaned against her beau. "We were thinking it would be nice to live close to town, but also in a neighborhood with people our age. So I suggested River Park between the square and the covered bridge. That would give us quick access to everything, short commutes to work, and put us within walking distance of the parks and hiking trails."

Alice patted the table. "That's not far from me and the café!"

I lifted a finger, stunned, but processing. "I'm sorry, did you say 'we'?"

Caroline stomped her boots beneath the table and smiled so widely, all I saw were perfect white teeth. "Zane and I are getting a place together!" She lunged for me and hugged me so tightly I thought I might pass out.

I gasped like a fish out of water when she released me. "You are incredibly strong," I croaked. "Congratulations! How can I help?"

"We'll let you know," Zane said.

"I'll throw you a housewarming party," I promised.

"Deal," Caroline agreed.

I lifted my hand to flag Mom or one of her staff members. "This news calls for dessert."

Hugo waved at me. "I've got this," he said, pulling a small stack of lidded containers from his satchel. "I brought more risgrynsgröt. I hope you liked it. We made far too much."

"This is from the original batch," Alice said. "We accidentally used the commercial recipe."

"Thank you," Caroline said. "I gave mine to an employee the day you stopped in. She was woozy after too many hours on her feet and didn't want cupcakes. She said the pudding was magnificent, but I've been bummed for missing out on it."

"Now you don't have to," Alice said, passing the rolled silverware around the table.

We unlidded our risgrynsgröt and dug in.

"Take me house hunting with you," I told Caroline. "Please? I love seeing the insides of other people's homes."

"Of course!"

Alice folded her hands on the table and leaned forward. "I must sound like a broken record, but if you don't mind, I must ask. Have there been any new findings on my case? Anything we can use to clear my name?"

All eyes turned to Zane, and I felt a pang of sadness. I selfishly missed being the one with information. All I had this year was FOMO. Fear of Missing Out.

And a baby, I reminded myself. I had a very good reason to stick to the sidelines this time.

"Are you feeling okay?" Caroline asked.

I straightened my expression. "Just hating that this case hasn't been settled yet."

"Evan hasn't said anything?" she asked.

I shook my head, and the group's attention returned to Zane.

"We don't have anything definitive yet," he said. "You were at the scene with the victim's blood on your hands. The murder weapon belonged to you, and you were seen fighting with Hannah that night. It's going to take something significant to erase all that," Zane said.

Alice closed her eyes, and Hugo ran a supportive palm against her back.

"That said," Zane continued. "There's been a lot of animosity and allegations of fraudulent items being sold as originals through vendors at the antiques show. The more I look into it, the more I find information that supports this as the reason the show is ending a thirty-year run, not a lack of funding or interest as they claimed. Anyone who spends an hour at the show can see interest remains overwhelming. Vendors and buyers are here from all around the world, and the former are paying top dollar for space to sell at the event."

"Corruption," I said. That was a decent motive for murder. "Who stands to gain the most from whatever's going on over there?"

"The sellers who are passing off trash as history, I suppose," Zane said.

I took a moment to let that settle and had another spoonful of pudding to help me think it through. "What did Hannah have to do with the corruption? Her shop was failing, so it wasn't as if she was making out by selling much of anything."

Zane paused, spoon halfway to his mouth. "The more I look at her shop's financials, the more I think the real problem there was the amount her partner charged her for his initial startup investment. Baxter Tracey was in the antique business for years before she approached him for funds in exchange for a cut of her sales. The margins were terrible, but she was young and hopeful. She had a history degree but needed a business degree to deal with that guy. He saw a way to make easy money from every one of her sales without doing any work, plus he charged her monthly interest on the repayment of his initial investment. The way they set it up, she'd never be out from under that obligation."

"Not without making an enormous sale or two," I said. "Enough to pay him back in one shot and cut him loose for good."

Alice straightened. "Would my Yule Goats do that for her?"

Zane put the spoon into his mouth, considering. "Possibly."

"If things were dire enough, I'll bet she would've been willing to try," I said. *Desperate people doing desperate things.*

"Oh." Caroline stiffened and reached a hand to her lips. "Sorry, I just—" she pulled an almond from her mouth and tucked it into her napkin and offered an apologetic grimace.

Alice and Hugo clapped.

Caroline's perfectly sculpted brows rose. "What is happening?"

"You're getting married," I announced.

Zane smiled. "When?"

"Next year," Alice said, then Hugo chimed in with details of the legend. Caroline found the almond, so she'd be married in the new year.

Caroline twisted to look at her boyfriend. "Strange way to propose, so I'm going to have to think about it."

"Understandable," he said. He laughed, then kissed her cheek and forehead.

The door opened again, and Libby blustered inside, cheeks pink and eyes searching. Her hands flipped up then down as she hurried in our direction. "I should've known I'd find you all here. There's a hellacious storm brewing, so why not get some hot chocolate and shoot the breeze?"

She hung up her coat and nudged Alice and Hugo to make room for her on their bench.

"Nice to see you too," I said. "Something wrong? Because you seem a little—" I waved my hands around my head, attempting to mime a tornado.

"I caught the snowman thief!" she said. "I've been dying to tell someone, but no one answers their phone anymore. Then I thought, where could they all be that no one hears their phone?" She motioned to Cookie, shaking her backside and belting out the lyrics to "Run Run Rudolph" through a microphone and my childhood karaoke machine.

Touché.

"Well?" Caroline asked. "Do we get details or what?"

"Was he arrested?" Zane asked.

Libby shook her head. "One thing I'm starting to appreciate about living in this itty-bitty community is the level of interconnectedness. I hated that at first, but it's been a real boon for business." She pushed masses of windblown hair away from her face as she spoke. "For example, did you know it's easy to identify a local by their ride? I took a still shot of the truck's tailgate from the grainy, low-quality, nanny cam video, and asked around until someone recognized it and knew the owner. Took me less than two hours to get a name and address. I went over there to collect the snowmen, but there weren't any on the lawn, and no one was home, so I knocked on the neighbor's door. Turns out, the kid who drives that truck is seventeen, a junior at the high school, and a good kid. I questioned how good, seeing that he was a petty thief, and I stuck around until he came home. Then I waited and followed him when he left again after dark, expecting to catch him in the act of his next theft."

"You didn't contact the parents?" Zane asked.

"Nope. Never saw them."

"Maybe they have a shop in town," I said.

Caroline pointed her spoon at me. "That would explain the long hours away from home."

Libby made a pipe-down motion with her hands and scrunched her face. "Wrong. I followed the kid to the local children's hospital, where I found about two dozen twelve-foot snowmen anchored in rows outside one corner of the building."

That was definitely not where I thought her story might be going.

Cookie appeared at the end of our booth, looking mildly out of breath.

A middle-aged couple in matching ugly sweaters shared a mic on stage behind her. They sang "White Christmas" while their friends snapped photos from their table.

"Keep talking," Cookie said. "I've got the gist so far, and I don't have to go back onstage until we run out of volunteers."

I wasn't sure how she heard anything over the chaos of Christmas Karaoke, but I was eager for the rest of Libby's tale, so I let it go.

Libby pressed ahead. "I went in and talked to the receptionist who told me the snowmen just keep appearing, and no one knows where they come from, but they're arranged outside the oncology wing."

I covered my mouth. Caroline and Alice covered their hearts.

Zane said, "Dang."

"Yeah." Libby's voice cracked on the little word. "The snowmen have become a real bright spot in the kids' days. They can't wait to look outside, to count them, to speculate over where they come from and how many will be there by Christmas. The parents and staff get immense relief and pleasure from their presence as well."

I wiped a tear. "My goodness, that's the sweetest thing I've heard all year. Maybe ever."

Libby nodded, cheeks red as she fought a display of emotion I couldn't seem to stop. "I waited for the kid in the lobby, then I cornered him to say I knew what he was doing, and I showed him the image of his truck. Told him I followed him. He panicked. He cried. He begged me not to tell his parents. He was a dam waiting to burst." She blew out a long, steadying breath. "His little sister has leukemia, and his parents only leave the hospital for work. Christmas is all but canceled for them this year. He's worried to death, and he's essentially alone. He's not the sick one. Not a parent. Doesn't have any other siblings to lean on. He's trying not to be a burden or get lost in his parents' grief. His friends don't understand. It's too much, and he's just a kid."

She stopped talking to compose herself again but failed this time.

Caroline passed her a handkerchief.

"Sorry," Libby said, mopping tears from her cheeks. "It's just that I remember when our dad was sick, and how hard that was. Evan was grown, trying to manage me, and I was so rebellious. I know what it feels like to be helpless and hurting. It killed me, you know? And this kid just wanted to do something to make those sick kids and their worried families smile."

Zane cleared his throat, visibly wrestling emotion of his own. "What'd you do about the snowmen?"

"I got the contact information on all the inflatables, and the kid, Tim, and I are going to contact the owners together tomorrow. He's going to explain what he did, and ask if they're willing to donate the items to his cause. He's planning to return all the snowmen after the new year."

A soft round of "aww" went up from our table.

"If anyone tells him no, I'll volunteer to buy a snowman to replace theirs," Libby said. "I bought him a burger and took him to see that McDougal guy with the lights display by the covered bridge. We told him our story, and McDougal wants to donate a portion of his proceeds this season to the construction of an outdoor lights display for the children's hospital next Christmas."

My tears began again, and I pulled wads of napkins from the dispenser to manage the deluge.

"And your dad has agreed to light up the sleighs and put on a parade of horse-drawn carriages for the hospital Christmas Eve night."

"What?" I wheezed, utterly failing to maintain any amount of composure.

"Free rides to kids and families who are able," she said. "A beautiful show for those who can watch from the windows."

I set my forehead on the table and lost it.

Caroline patted my back. "I volunteer cupcakes," she said. "I know my staff will come in and help me with a bake-a-thon. We can make enough to deliver to the staff as well."

"Count me in!" Cookie said. "I'll bet Carol will let us use the industrial kitchen here after hours to double up on quantity."

I dragged myself upright with significant effort and slumped against the back of the booth, exhausted. "I love this town."

Libby, long reluctant to say anything was better than her hometown of Boston, nodded. "Yeah."

"You know what else might be nice," Cookie said. "I can bring Theodore and Clementine around. Kids love goats, and I just bought those two new matching sweaters."

"Speaking of the kindest lumberjack around," Libby said.

I followed her gaze to my dad, brushing snow from the shoulders of his coat as he approached the booth with a warm smile.

"Here comes cupcake number seven," Cookie said.

I laughed as the others in our booth frowned but chose not to ask for details.

"Hey, kids," Dad said. "Caroline, I need a big favor. I'm about to take advantage of our relationship and exploit your connection to the mayor."

She laughed. "Sure. What's up?"

"If I arrange to move the booths from Santa's Village to the extra indoor space at the train station, do you think your dad would consider covering the cost of that rental? My crew and I can handle the relocation, and I can offset the rental fees by refunding the money the vendors paid to sell here today and tomorrow while the wind chill stays below zero. It would be a wonderful gift to the folks who can't sell now due to weather. I know many of them came a long way and rely on sales to keep their lights on at home."

"No problem," Caroline said. "I'll make the call."

Chapter Twenty-Three

The conversation with Libby and my friends stuck with me through the night, as did my deep desire to be useful in Evan's investigation. By the time I woke the next morning, an idea had formed.

I dialed Libby while Evan showered, knowing she was my best chance at an ally. If I could get her on board, she could help me sell the possibility to Evan.

She arrived in time for breakfast.

I waited at the kitchen table while Evan answered the door.

He wore a navy thermal shirt with dark-wash jeans and brown work boots. His hair still damp and mussed from the shower. "Libby, we don't usually see you this early," he said.

"Guess it's your lucky day," she teased. "Your wife has a good idea, and I came over to make sure you hear her out," she said, slipping past him and toeing off her brown boots. A navy blue thermal and dark jeans were visible beneath her unzipped coat.

Evan hung his head before closing the door, then turned and followed Libby to the kitchen.

I smiled at their matching ensembles, but neither our dear sheriff nor our newest PI seemed to have noticed that fun detail.

She took a seat at my side, and I passed her a mug of coffee. I'd filled three when Evan went to answer the door.

Evan stopped in the threshold, arms crossed as if taking one more step would mean joining our team. Unwise when he'd yet to determine what game we were playing. "All right," he said. "Spill it. What are you two up to this time?"

Libby pointed a finger at me.

"I have an idea," I said.

"I've heard," he groaned. "I'm hoping you will elaborate."

Libby sipped her coffee and grinned. "Maybe we should check his blood pressure," she suggested.

Evan ignored her.

I bit back a smile. "As Libby pointed out last night, while telling me how she caught the snowman thief," I began. "Our town is full of people who hear and see everything. We never know who's listening because most of the time there are dozens of people all around us. And news travels fast."

Evan sighed, then peeled himself away from the wall and took a seat across from us at the table.

I passed him the third mug of coffee.

He accepted. "Keep going."

"I'm thinking that if someone who is being warned to stop their amateur investigation made it clear, while in a public place, that they had the final piece of evidence necessary to name the culprit, perhaps access to a neighbor's doorbell camera near Cup of Cheer, that news would travel—"

"Holly—" Evan interrupted. His jaw set, and worry lines raced across his forehead.

"Psh-psh," Libby said. "Just give her ten more seconds."

He frowned and slid his gaze to me.

"Then if that same person happened to say exactly when they were meeting the neighbor to get that feed, the real killer would probably try to stop that from happening."

Evan raised a hand to stop me from finishing the sentence. He pressed the fingertips of his opposite hand to his temple. "I'm a little tired," he said. "And it's very early in the morning for my head to explode, so I'm hoping I've misunderstood what you're saying."

Libby shook her head. "I think you get it."

"No," Evan said.

"Why not?" I asked. "I've been so good, and I want to help. I think this could speed things along on your end. You've said it yourself. There aren't any leads."

His face went pink, then red as he glared.

"Is he still breathing?" Libby asked.

"I don't know. Are you breathing?" I asked Evan.

"You are asking me to use my wife and our unborn child as bait for a murderer," he said, each word so quiet and precise, I shivered a little at the menace.

"I'm not," I said. "I'm asking you to follow me on my fake appointment to meet a fake neighbor. Keep me safe and stop anyone who follows me for questioning." I'd tried to think of the safest possible route to reach my goal. Something that would remove Evan's concerns about my security and the baby's. This seemed like the ultimate compromise. We could drum up a real suspect without letting them in arm's reach of me. A definite win-win. If it worked.

He didn't respond, so I kept going.

"Maybe no one will follow, because the killer has already left town with the Yule Goats," I said. "Maybe they're halfway across Europe selling them to the highest bidder. Who knows? But if the person responsible for my threats and Hannah's death is still here, and we do things right, which of course we will, I'll never be in any real danger, even if the killer takes the bait."

Evan stood, flattened his palms on the table and towered over us, looking as frightening and authoritative as I'd ever seen him.

"The two of you had better listen very closely as I speak, because I will not say this again." He pulled in a long, slow breath. "Abs-so-lute-ly. Not."

* * *

Evan and I made a pit stop at the welcome desk when we arrived at the antiques show to carry out my plan that afternoon. After some additional persuading, Evan came around to my suggestion. After all, what wasn't to like? I'd never be alone, because he'd be following in a borrowed vehicle the killer wouldn't associate with my husband or the sheriff, and there was a good chance we could draw out the criminal. Why chase when we could attract? Much better than my usual situation at this point in the investigation.

We grabbed a map of the layout and vendors before heading into the bustling aisles. I wore a white turtleneck and jeans with my favorite coat and boots. Evan stuck with the blue thermal, and I hoped Libby had too.

The setting sun shone through stained glass windows, creating a kaleidoscope of color on the historic marble floors. It was hard to believe we were hunting a killer in a place so beautiful.

"This train station is huge," he said. "It doesn't look nearly this big from out front, and it catches me off guard every time."

That was true. The building was at least twice as deep as it was wide, stretching away from the road for more than a city block. The building had once been a major railroad hub for all of New England, with a myriad of old gates and platforms, long ago closed and sealed shut.

"Good thing we have this," I said, pulling open the map before us.

Evan scanned the area while I examined the vendor layout. "We're going to be here until they close, if we want to see it all," he said.

"I guess we'd better get started."

He set his palm against the small of my back and steered me gently forward.

We moved methodically through the grid, stopping at nearly every booth and table. He bought Libby a nameplate for her desk at the new PI office, and Ray a roll of undeveloped film in a canister marked with the year of his birth. He'd have the time of his life developing the photos in his rarely used darkroom. Thanks to the digital age, he didn't have many opportunities to work with film anymore, and he told us often. Evan found a hand-painted street sign with the words "Lovers' Lane" for the end of my parents' long gravel driveway, and he found a black and white photo from the club in Vegas where Cookie was once a cigarette girl.

"She's going to love that," I told him.

He added the photo and receipt to our growing collection of gifts and bags. "Any idea why she called the sheriff's department earlier and requested a meeting with me?"

"You know Cookie. Could be anything." Miraculously, I managed a straight face as I lied.

"Why doesn't that make me feel any better?" he asked.

I snickered. "You'll have to let me know how it goes."

"Will do. Let me know when you have more of your Gumdrop Gumshoe things for the post office," he said. "You've got a fan group down there."

I frowned, then worked to rearrange my face. "I have another box that can go out tomorrow, and I finally opened an email from the *Dead and Berried* publicity team. We're still on for that interview the morning after Christmas. They promised to be in and out before lunch."

Evan pulled me closer. "Tomorrow is Christmas Eve," he whispered. "And our anniversary. I love that I have double the reason to anticipate Christmas these days."

"Me too."

It stunk that we were out of time to catch the killer. Tomorrow was also the last day of the antiques show, and all our suspects would soon be gone with it. With a little luck, catching a killer wouldn't take more than an hour of our night.

We moseyed along, arms linked, and probably looking as casual as any two people fishing for a killer in public. "I think it's fun that my wife is known across the country for solving crimes," he said. The words wouldn't have sounded less natural if they'd come from Cookie's goat.

Don't give up your day job, I thought as we turned the corner.

"It feels nice to be appreciated," I said. "The fans are a good reminder that there's nothing wrong with being nosey if it puts criminals in jail."

Evan grunted.

"I've had fun helping with this case," I said, hoping this outing wasn't a flop.

Libby and Ray appeared at the end of our new aisle.

Ray turned his entire body to face us, lifted a finger in our direction and stated loudly, "Is that the Gumdrop Gumshoe?"

Libby smacked his impossibly flat stomach. "Leave her alone. I hear she's got something good to share with us soon."

"How does she do it?" he said, enunciating each syllable, hopelessly overacting again.

I rolled my eyes. "Looks like you guys have been here a while."

Ray lifted the mass of bags hooked in his right hand. "This place is a blast. I found gifts for everyone on my list and a bunch of people who weren't." His phone dinged and he passed the bags from hand to hand, struggling to retrieve the device from his pocket. "It's a text from Cookie," he reported. He swiped, then his smile faltered. "She wants me to meet her at the inn tomorrow for a chat, but she didn't say why."

"Maybe it's about the calendar," I suggested.

"The baby goats?" he asked. "I thought Clementine wasn't pregnant yet."

"She's not," Evan said. He led us into the next aisle. "Cookie left a message for me today too. Didn't say what it was about."

"Uh-oh," Libby said. "I smell trouble."

I turned my face away, pretending to admire an antique gumball machine as we passed. A flash of white hair in the next aisle reminded me of Nancy Grace. I saw her everywhere these days, but when the crowd parted, whoever it was had gone.

"Well, look who's back," a vaguely familiar male voice spun me on my toes.

Arnold, the antiques show coordinator, shook hands with my husband.

In the distance beyond them, Kent George spoke with someone selling antique Santas.

I wasn't sure which encounter to watch more closely.

"What brings you by again today, Sheriff?" Arnold asked. "Any news on the thing we've been discussing?"

Libby and Ray stole glances at me while pretending to browse the nearby tables.

I flicked my gaze toward the antique Christmas décor booth, willing one of them to notice the covert observer.

"Just spending a day out with friends," Evan said. "This is my wife, Holly." He pulled me closer. "She's been graciously signing your maps and pamphlets for shoppers. People keep recognizing her as a local sleuth." Evan's eye twitched, and jaw locked on the final words, forcing an unnatural pause in his speech.

"I believe we've met," Arnold said. "I don't believe she mentioned being the sheriff's wife."

I offered a little hip-high wave.

Evan shot me a look that suggested we'd discuss that later. "We're with my sister, Libby, in the leather jacket there." He pointed, and Libby waved. "And her husband, Ray."

Ray hefted his armload of bags. "I promise we're trying to leave something for the other shoppers, but it's not looking good."

In the distance, Kent adjusted his position by a baby step or two, moving until he casually faced my group as he spoke with the other vendor.

Libby noticed and took Ray's hand. "We need to see if that booth has any blown glass ornaments for my great-grandma." She motioned to the stall with antique Santas.

"Definitely." Ray agreed easily without removing his attention from Evan and Arnold.

"How are things going here?" I asked the event coordinator. "I saw some commotion in the show's website forums."

Arnold's smile tightened. "All is well," he said. "But I should let you get back to your evening out." He clasped his hands before him, then turned a pointed look on Evan. "Let me know if there's anything I can help you find."

I bit the insides of my cheeks. The offer felt more like a threat than I preferred.

My friends and I traded weary expressions as Arnold scanned the larger area. He seemed to take note of Kent in the distance, his gaze catching and sticking there for an extra heartbeat. Then he delivered a departing nod and walked away in the opposite direction.

I opened my mouth to ask the group what they thought of the oddly tense interaction, but Evan silenced me with a microscopic wag of his chin. A reminder that we'd talk about our time inside the train station after we were safely back at home.

I longed to open a notes app on my phone and type out reminders of all the things I wanted to say later. But I had no idea who might be watching.

A blessed collection of food and drink vendors appeared at the center of the antiques show grid. We stopped eagerly to refuel.

"Does that sign say funnel cakes?" Ray asked, grabbing Libby's hand and towing her in the direction of the deep-fried dough and powdered sugar.

Evan and I followed. We made our dinner selections as a group and stayed within an arm's reach of one another at all times. The space allocated for food sales seemed warmer and louder than the aisles of shopping. More possibilities to be separated. Or worse.

Two hot pretzels, five street tacos, and a footlong hot dog later, we carried our meals and a stack of funnel cakes to a round table with four folding chairs.

Evan left me in Ray and Libby's care, while he made a run for lemonades and sodas.

I split my attention between the food, the shoppers, and the couple at my table. I hadn't noticed Kent or Arnold again, but I couldn't shake the feeling of being watched. Maybe it was one of them. Maybe they were together.

Maybe too many years of doing things like this had made me unnecessarily paranoid. I tore off a hunk of pretzel and dunked it into a little cup of mustard as I swung mentally from confident to terrified with each new breath.

The group at the next table stood and collected their trash. A flash of white hair caught my eyes, and I stared past them, searching, as they walked away. Nancy Grace sat on a bench, sipping from a disposable cup, legs crossed, eyes locked on me.

"Drinks for everyone," Evan said, and I nearly swallowed my tongue. Mustard flew from the pretzel onto my white turtleneck, and a tiny curse word burst from my lips.

"Whoa," Libby said. She twisted on her seat, hunting, visually, for what had startled me.

Ray made a goofy face. "Someone is overstimulated."

My heart hammered, and I wanted to tell them that I'd seen the same woman twice since our arrival, plus all over town this week, and she'd been staring at me just now. But I couldn't say it. Not with so many listening ears. And I couldn't write it down and send it by text. I couldn't do anything that had a point-zero-one percent chance of being intercepted audibly or visually. So I sat there and trembled with excess adrenaline.

Evan mopped the mustard off my shirt when I made no attempt to do it myself. "You okay?" he whispered.

I fixed my eyes on the spot where the woman sat, waiting nervously as a group of people passed between us. When they were gone, so was the white-haired woman.

"Yeah," I lied, eager to finish our outing and leave this place.

I lost my appetite and abandoned my pretzel. My stomach flopped and fluttered, making it impossible to think of keeping anything down.

I spent the remainder of our time at the table with my head on a swivel, looking for signs of anyone watching me. In the end, I came up empty, which only frightened me more.

How long had the woman been sitting there before I'd noticed? Had she been in the area when we arrived? Or had she followed us there? Had she followed us all day? And I'd been none the wiser?

Eventually, the Santa's Village stalls came into view, and I released a breath of relief. This was the final section of the show. We'd nearly spread my presence, as well as news of my continued nosiness, throughout the venue.

In the process, we'd seen everyone on my suspect list except Hannah's business partner, Baxter Tracey. Of course, I wasn't convinced I'd recognize him if he stood right beside me. At least not if his online image was as drastically changed as others had stated.

I made a mental note to ask Libby if she'd seen him after we made it back to our house.

Part of me rejoiced, confident the outing was a huge success. We'd made a plan and executed it flawlessly. The rest of me thought we might be chum in water where the sharks were circling.

We soon reached the last vendor and turned around, preparing stage two.

Libby moved to stand beside me as we headed back through the aisles, perusing the tables once more. "Are you sure you don't want to ride with us to the parade at the children's hospital tomorrow night?" she asked. "I know you're exhausted, but it won't be the same without you."

It took a moment for me to realize this was part of our script. Libby was eerily good at acting.

"I'll be late," I said. "But I'll do my best to get there. I'm meeting one of the homeowners from the neighborhood with Cup of Cheer on my way. They caught something on their doorbell camera I want to see. If it's the kind of clue I think it is, I'll head over to the sheriff's department to tell Evan, then go to the party."

"You're not going with her?" she asked Evan.

He frowned. "No. I have someone I need to interview on this case, so Holly and I will stay in touch by text until we're finished with our commitments."

We continued the discussion aisle after aisle, attempting to make it sound as unscripted as possible.

"Oh! Holly!" A familiar voice called. A narrow arm waved wildly on the other side of a group of passersby. A moment later, Peggy came into view. "I thought I missed you!" she said, motioning us over to her table. "I had customers when I saw you the first time. Why is your dad so amazing? I can't believe he was able to get the entire village into the show!"

I laughed at her rapid-fire words. "Dad is pretty great, but he had help from my best friend, Caroline, and her dad, the mayor. Have you met my sister-in-law, Libby?"

"Nice to meet you," Peggy said.

"This is your new mom friend?" Libby asked.

Peggy's smile widened impossibly further. "Indeed."

"How far do you live from Mistletoe?" I asked. "A friend registered me for prenatal yoga, and it got me thinking about mom groups in the area."

"I'm just over an hour from here," she said. "Probably too far for a regular commitment, but not too far for coffee dates throughout the year."

Ray and Evan moved into the space at our sides, and Peggy's eyes widened at the sight of them. Ray remembered her from the farm and introduced Evan while I traded a goofy smile with Libby. Having drop-dead handsome husbands could be fun sometimes.

Ray leaned against the wall of Peggy's stall. "Any chance you want to bring the kids out to see McDougal's lights tomorrow night?" he asked. "Holly and Evan are meeting us there, then we're getting dinner with friends and family. They might be a little late, but the kids would love the lights."

I smiled, warmed by his offer.

Peggy smiled. "Rain check," she said. "It's a long round trip after being here all day, and once I get my arms around my kids, I think I'll stay."

"Completely understandable," I said. "Maybe I'll run into you at the antiques show."

"I'll come with," Libby said. "Sounds like fun."

I gave my sister-in-law a sideways look, then remembered she was on babysitting detail.

Peggy beamed. "I'll be there."

We chatted with Peggy a few more minutes, until a group of shoppers approached. Then we stepped away so she could make some sales.

"Remember," Ray called. "If anyone needs the Gumdrop Gumshoe tomorrow night, she'll be ditching all her friends and family to chase another suspect."

"You're so loud," Libby muttered, sending an elbow toward his ribs.

Ray caught her arm mid-swing, stopping her attempt with ease. "So predictable." He bent to kiss her, and she dodged it effortlessly.

"Right back at ya," she said, a look of smug satisfaction on her lips.

With a little luck, this year's killer was as predictable as those I'd met in the past. Because if they'd heard our declarations today, they'd definitely take the bait tomorrow.

Chapter Twenty-Four

I woke before dawn the next morning, stomach churning. I took my time in the shower, attempting to ease my nausea and relax my aching muscles. Morning sickness had kept me up all night, if that's what this was. Regardless, I didn't like it or need the added misery today. I was already utterly fatigued. I spent half the night in a ball, knees hugged to my chest, and the other half clinging to Evan as if I was drowning and he was my life preserver.

In the rare moments when I found sleep, I did not find rest. Instead, I dreamed of terror and physical attacks. A faceless friend invited me for tea, which was poisoned. A stranger said I'd dropped something on the sidewalk, but when I reached for the thing, it became a knife, and the stranger stabbed me. I dreamed the giant straw goat outside Alice's café was on fire. That my home was on fire. That the pickup truck used to steal the snowmen came back to run me over. Every manner of tragedy and aggression played on a loop in my restless mind.

Freshly showered and dressed in my softest, comfiest clothes, I had breakfast with Cindy Lou Who before moving into the living room. There, we watched the sun rise. Rays of gold and apricot climbed the windowsill and illuminated her calico fur as she purred from her perch on the back of the couch. I absorbed the precious moment, sipped a cup of hot tea, and asked myself repeatedly if I was sure I wanted to go through with my plan. So many things could go wrong.

After he woke, Evan told me over coffee that he had a lead, but I tried not to hold on too tightly. He'd let me know if it panned out.

I didn't mention my plan to my parents, Cookie, Alice, or anyone outside the circle who'd set the thing in motion yesterday. The stress of keeping something so big from the others I loved only added to my constant nausea.

Every muscle in Evan's body stayed tensed to spring until it was time for his shift. He turned Libby's forgotten bear on the windowsill to face the room, then went to don his uniform. He didn't mention his possible lead again and neither did I. If there was a way to avoid putting me in danger, I knew he'd do it. So, here we were.

I did my best to think positive thoughts. I just couldn't decide what to wish for. Did I hope a killer wouldn't follow me? Or did I want them to try so they could be arrested for their trouble? Either way, the timing was ruining my anniversary.

And knowing what to wish for was much more difficult today than yesterday.

Evan found me in the future nursery a few minutes before it was time for him to leave.

I had one hand on my unsettled stomach and a ball of nerves wedged in my throat. He wound his arms around me from behind and drew my back against his chest. "It's not too late to change your mind," he whispered, breath warm against my hair. "People change their plans all the time."

A dagger of determination appeared at his words, and I grabbed hold of it with both hands. "Will it be enough?" I asked, turning for a look into his handsome face. "If someone follows me to my fake meeting? Will it make the kind of difference we need it to?"

"Maybe," he said, cautiously. "If I'm sure they're following you intentionally, I will pull them over and question them. If I can search their vehicle, I will. If I need to take them in, I will. Either way, a deep dive into their background will follow, and I'll see if there's a connection to Hannah. But remember, this experiment you designed only creates the possibility of drawing out the killer."

I nodded. "I know."

It wasn't a crime to follow someone down the street, and there wasn't a way to prove their intent was to harm me. Moreover, wanting to harm me wasn't a crime. And it wasn't cause to arrest the criminal for Hannah's murder.

But it was a last-ditch effort to limit the suspect list and give Evan something more to go on. I couldn't bear the idea of Hannah Ford and her family not getting the justice they deserved.

Evan hooked a lock of hair behind one of my ears. His features and tone were soft and imploring. "It's unlikely that anyone will be arrested tonight. I'm confident you'll be safe, but why stress yourself out like this? I'm working on leads that could pan out just as easily as the plan you've suggested."

"Will I be safe?" I asked. The thought was nearly comical. "For how long?"

It seemed to me that the only way out was to go through with my plan. Either a killer would follow, because they heard me running my mouth all day yesterday, or they wouldn't. But if they did, and Evan didn't stop them, they would try again.

Somehow that seemed worse.

At least tonight I was aware of the possibility they'd come for me, and there was active surveillance in place. There wouldn't be tomorrow. Or the next day.

Evan held me tight for several long minutes without answering my question. I was nearly asleep on my feet when his phone buzzed.

"Time for me to get going," he said. "One of those leads I mentioned might've finally panned out." His smile was brilliant as he spoke. "If things go my way, we might not have to do your thing at all."

I yawned and stumbled a bit as he released me.

Plans for a quick nap formed as I walked him to the door. I waited while he put on his coat and hat, then I kissed him goodbye.

"I took all those broken bottles from Samantha to your workshop," he said.

"Thanks."

"I love you," he added.

"I love you too."

He peeled himself away from me and headed into the snow. "I'll give you a call if things go well," he called.

I waved, then watched through the front window until his truck disappeared around the corner at the end of our block.

Cindy Lou Who bumped my leg with her head as I crossed the living room to the couch and curled up with a blanket on my legs.

The doorbell woke me sometime later. I hadn't meant to fall asleep.

Cindy Lou Who stretched on the windowsill beside Libby's forgotten teddy bear as I planted my feet on the ground and checked the driveway for a hint at my guest's identity. I didn't recognize the car, but I caught a glimpse of a familiar moss green coat and smiled.

"Hello," I said, opening the door to Peggy.

She grinned and lifted a gift bag between us. "I can't make it to see the lights tonight, but I wanted to bring this to you before I head home."

I accepted her offering and stepped back. "Come in," I said. "I took an accidental nap, so I think I'm entitled to some coffee. Can I get you some?"

She dithered, brows knitting. "I hate to get started on my drive home any later than I already am. Oh! But I was hoping to buy a piece of your jewelry for my mom. She's always so willing to babysit the little ones when I need to attend events like this."

"Of course," I said. "But you can't buy it. I want to give it to you. You can pick it out."

Peggy tilted her head over one shoulder. "You are so kind." She sighed. "There isn't enough kindness in the world. You know?"

I pressed my lips together, unable to concur. My world was filled with the stuff.

"Wait," she said. "Open the gift!"

I set the bag on the arm of the couch and reached into the tissue paper. "A book!" I freed it from the bag and turned it over in my hands. The face of a chubby kid adorned the front of a bright red book. "Baby's First Christmas," I read. "Aw, it's a Little Golden Book."

"It's an original," she said. "1959."

"Thank you." I hugged it to my chest. "Are you sure you can't stay for coffee?" Evan wouldn't be home for another two hours, and I could use the company.

Peggy bit her lip. "Okay. One cup." She lifted a finger into the air between us. "But you have to let me pay for the jewelry."

"Never!" I motioned for her to follow and led her to the kitchen. I set my gift on the table and started the coffeemaker, then set my hands on my hips. "Join me in the basement?" I asked. "My new workshop is down there."

"Sure."

I opened the nearby door and flipped on the light. "Right this way."

The unfinished space beneath our first floor was clean and tidy with a cement floor and exposed cinderblock walls. A flight of wooden steps stretched down from the kitchen to the center of the rectangular area below. The washer, dryer, and a wall of storage bins claimed the right side of the basement, while a small glass workshop and inventory area filled the other.

Evan had surprised me with the workshop. He'd spent the day assembling white floor-to-ceiling bookshelves, and he'd filled them with glass bottles in every imaginable color. He'd added pretty linen baskets, plastic containers, and tools for safety like protective glasses and gloves. Bulk materials were easier to sort now, and the occasional mess of ten million tiny glass shards were simple to clean up with my new shop vac. A metal table and matching barstool completed the area. The set made a perfect place to melt and shape the broken glass into little candies and treats with my torch.

It was a perfect gift.

I hadn't gotten around to ordering his plow, and I made a mental note to get that done as soon as Peggy said goodbye.

A wave of nausea hit as I reached the bins of completed items, and a rush of fear followed. I'd been sick more often than ever before. Was this normal? Just morning sickness as I suspected? Or Was my blood pressure the cause? Most importantly, should I worry?

"This is so cute," Peggy said, following me into the shop. "The whole vibe down here reminds me of a bar I frequented on campus at the University of Maine. Small, homey, fun. I can practically hear Maroon 5 playing through hidden speakers." She made a throaty sound. "I miss those days sometimes. Reminds me how twenty-fourteen was more than a decade ago already."

My mind stumbled over the words. It took several long moments for me to understand the issue. "Twenty-fourteen?"

She nodded, looking horribly distraught.

I set a bin of finished jewelry and charms on my worktable, then pulled the phone from my pocket. "This is everything I have ready. Help yourself. Will one of these work for your mom?"

I pressed the speed dial button for Evan.

"I need you to put that away," Peggy said. Her tone was sharp, her voice deeper than I recalled hearing until that moment. "Now."

"Holly?" Evan's voice was distant and tinny as I moved the phone away from my ear.

"Hang up," she whispered.

I said a prayer, then disconnected the call.

"What tipped you off?" she asked. "One minute you're leading me into the perfect place to do this. The next minute you're turning green and calling for help."

"I'm nauseous," I said. "And you graduated from college in 2014."

She stared. "So?"

"You went to school with Hannah."

The two handles from the antiques show's website, the ones who argued all the time, both ended in 14. Did that matter? I really hoped it didn't matter. Maybe it was a coincidence like the crossword puzzle answers.

Peggy was too nice to be a killer. To kill her friend. For what? Why?

The soft creak of floorboards overhead stilled me. Was Peggy innocent, and the real killer upstairs?

I held my breath, straining to hear the sound repeat.

Maybe Cindy jumped down from something high, I thought.

My worried heart thundered in my chest, and the nausea I'd momentarily forgotten returned with a violent surge. My previously, slightly elevated blood pressure was likely off the chart.

My phone buzzed against the metal table. Evan's name appeared on screen.

"Don't," Peggy warned. "Please finish your story. I went to school with Hannah," she said, reminding me of when I'd stopped talking and started parsing facts internally.

I grabbed my small torch and turned to face her.

She narrowed her eyes and raised a knife into view.

I put the table between us and pulled an unbroken wine bottle from the shelf. My glass torch was arguably more dangerous, but I didn't want to have to use it. I slid it into my hoodie pocket and prayed I could make it upstairs and out the front door before she caught me. "Why do you have a knife?" I asked.

"Why are you holding that bottle like a baseball bat?"

The phone buzzed again. It barely stopped before another incoming call began.

I crept to the back of my workshop and into the dead space beneath the basement stairs.

My stomach coiled, and gooseflesh skittered across my skin, prickling like the legs of a thousand baby spiders.

My head lightened, and fear clogged my throat. How could I protect my baby if something went wrong and Peggy caught me before I made it outside?

Flashbacks barreled like steam trains through my mind.

I was chased through the snow.

Fleeing in my truck.

Running for my life.

Alone.

And terrified.

My ears rang and spots danced in my peripheral vision.

"I really didn't want it to be you," I said.

Chapter Twenty-Five

Peggy peered at me though the open stairs as I added distance between us. "Please don't make this any harder than it is."

My vision darkened with a wave of dizziness, forcing me to grab the wall for balance. "Why are you here?" I asked. "You could be somewhere far away by now. Why stay and do this?"

"Just uproot my family, take the kids and leave without my mom?" she asked. "Or tell her what I did and take her with me? Ask her not to tell or look at me like the failure I am?" She shook her head. "I warned you. Twice. The second time, you seemed to finally get the message. I was so thankful for a little while. But then, there you were, yapping all around the show yesterday, announcing to the world that you were on the case."

She rounded the table, heading beneath the stairs, as I cowered and hatched a plan for escape.

I couldn't hurt her. I didn't want to.

But with the spots dancing in my eyes, I wasn't convinced I could run.

My phone buzzed continually on the metal table. I prayed Evan knew I'd hung up because I was in danger and I needed his help.

"I don't understand," I said, resolved to buy time and keep her talking. "Stop right there." I pointed the empty wine bottle at her. "Don't come any closer. Tell me why you're doing this."

"I just told you why," she said. "Because you wouldn't leave Hannah's death alone, and I'm a mother. I can't just go to jail for the rest of my kids' lives." She wrinkled her nose. "That cannot—it will not happen. They need me."

"You're the one who sent me the threats?" I asked, circling back to put something together. Searching for anything that made the smallest amount of sense. "How did you arrange the crossword clues?" I asked. Did she know the consultant who made the puzzles?

"What crossword?"

My shoulders drooped, and my stomach twisted. The crossword really wasn't a threat? I hadn't gotten anything right this year. The baby must be sitting on my gut instinct, muddying up my intuition.

"Come out here," Peggy said. She shoved the stool to my desk out of her way and skirted around it.

"Stop!" I reminded her, extending my arms and the bottle fully.

She obeyed.

"You told me Hannah was your friend," I said. "Why would you hurt your friend?"

"Unfortunately, I realized too late that Hannah was no one's friend," she said. The look on her face suggested Hannah was the problem. "We met in college. Both history majors at the University of Maine. We did everything together back then. We could've been that way again. Our kids even had a playdate together last month!"

"Then why?" I asked, my voice too deep and slow, the sound barely recognizable. I willed myself to remain upright as the feelings of weakness and instability increased. I just had to last until help arrived.

"We were supposed to open a shop together," Peggy said. "Hannah and me, not Hannah and that greedy buffoon, Baxter Tracey. She thought she'd make more money with him at her side because he was already established in the market, so she tossed me aside. But he didn't care about her or her success. I would've fought for every single sale." She banged a closed fist against her chest, emphasizing the last few words. "I would've done everything in my power to see our shop thrive. But she was too selfish and backstabbing to care. She chose opportunity over friendship."

I swallowed bile and an increasing, chest-constricting panic. "Why have a playdate?" I asked. Would her story make more sense if I wasn't ready to collapse?

"I knew from the online forums that her store was in trouble, and I thought I could help her. I wanted her to admit she was wrong for leaving me behind the way she did after college, then I wanted her to accept my offer and be my partner like we'd planned." She shook her head and puffed air from her nose.

"She didn't apologize?" I guessed.

"Hannah told me to mind my own business," Peggy said. "Then she called me twisted and manipulative for setting up a playdate for the discussion. As if I have a choice. Not everyone has a perfect husband to watch the kids whenever they want." She took another step forward, and I waved the bottle, which had begun to droop from my sagging arm.

"She rejected my offer, again, but she made a grab for the Yule Goats, and I couldn't let that go. Why would she do something like that when she could've just agreed to partner with me? I couldn't let her fix her problems so easily. She needed to admit she was wrong."

I closed my eyes briefly, willing my stomach to settle. "So you went to the café to wait for her," I guessed.

"And she came, like I knew she would. So pathetic," Peggy scoffed. "She'd already broken in when I got there. I followed and told her to put the goats back. That I wouldn't let her take them. She said I couldn't stop her, and taking the goats didn't hurt anyone, but it would save her store and her future, so that made it okay. She said insurance would repay the owner for her loss. So, I tried to take them from her, but she was bigger and stronger than me. I pulled the knife from the wall to make her stop." She paused and chewed her lip.

I felt the first beads of sweat form on my brow.

"I was so mad," she said. "I told her she sounded exactly like the man she chose to partner with, obsessed with money, no matter the cost. She ran and I chased her. I'm faster, so we struggled in the snow outside. Then we fell. The knife wedged between us." She looked away, an expression of pure trauma on her pretty face.

I screamed silently for my hero to get his cape in motion. My pumping adrenaline and churning stomach made it impossible to move or think. The wine bottle slipped in my sweaty palm and bounced against the cement with a crack!

Peggy snapped back to the moment, tracking the broken bottle back to me. "I didn't mean to do it," she whispered. "I was so angry. If I just hadn't drawn the knife, we would've kept fighting until the police came. Instead—" She wiped a coat sleeve across her eyes. "I took the goats because I thought it would make the whole thing look like a robbery gone wrong. It was exactly that. Just not in the way people think. I made one stupid mistake," she whispered. "One. And now all this."

I bent forward at the waist, moaning as I drew my little torch into my hand.

"I don't want to hurt you," she said. "I didn't want to hurt Hannah. But it happened, and I can't let my children grow up without a mom. That's not fair. Their dad already left us. I'm all they have, and I have to be there for them. I will be. Whatever it takes."

I straightened and ignited the torch in a single, if jerky, move.

Peggy gasped and jumped away. The tears rolling over her cheeks glowed eerily blue in the light of the torch. "Why couldn't you just stay out of this?" she wailed. "I don't want to be this person!"

"It's not too late," I said. A sour taste climbed the back of my throat and sweat rolled between my shoulder blades. "You can be the woman your kids deserve."

Peggy's face reddened.

I'd said the wrong thing.

"What do you know about being a mother?" she snarled. "What kind of mom inserts herself into a murder investigation when she's pregnant?" Her voice grew louder with every syllable until my ears rang, and she lunged.

I waved the torch and she screamed. A flame raced up her coat sleeve.

Peggy dropped the knife and jerked free of the coat, stomping the fire into the cement with her boots.

"Freeze!" Evan's voice reverberated off the walls and he seemed to manifest at the bottom of the stairs. "Step away from your weapon," he demanded. "Mistletoe Sheriff's Department. You are under arrest for the murder of Hannah Ford, the theft of nearly one hundred thousand dollars in art, and the attempted murder of my wife. Who is," he added, "a damn good mother. She gets involved because she cares about this community and wants our baby to grow up in a safe place."

Libby raced down the steps and flung herself in my direction. She pulled me into a hug as Evan read Peggy her rights.

"How did you know?" I croaked.

"The teddy bear cam alerted me," Libby said. "I almost didn't look, but I remembered Evan was at work. I thought I should see who it was, just in case."

"Then you called me and hung up," Evan added. "I knew that couldn't be good. I didn't understand how bad until Libby called a minute later and told me she saw Peggy at our front door."

I worked his words around in my head, trying to make sense of them. "You knew she was a suspect?" Why hadn't he said anything sooner? I'd trusted her.

"My lead panned out," Evan said, handcuffing Peggy. "You told me a city bus blocked the footage we needed of the store where the cell phone was purchased. That was the time when the buyer would've left the store. I requested the footage from an hour before the purchase was made. Only Peggy and two others with any affiliation to the Antiques Showcase entered during that time frame. The other two paid with credit cards. I couldn't prove it was her, but I had reason to suspect and dig a little deeper."

Peggy openly sobbed while he guided her toward the stairs.

"Whoa," Libby said when I stumbled. She took the torch from my hands and pressed a palm to my forehead. "You don't look so good."

Evan stilled. "Is Holly okay?" he asked. His worried gaze jumped from me to his sister, then back. For a moment, I wondered if he might release the criminal in favor of getting to me.

"I've got her," Libby said. "I think she needs to lie down."

I opened my mouth to tell them I was going to be sick, but the little food I'd eaten this morning came out instead.

"Ew," Libby cried. She adjusted her hold on me, and the world went black.

* * *

Evan called a deputy to take Peggy to the station. He drove me to the hospital for an assessment. As it turned out, I was just pregnant and dehydrated. The long day with little sustenance and lots of stress, following a night without sleep, had been too taxing. According to Dr. Bright, the baby, who was fine, took what it needed and left me depleted. She promised more similar experiences in my future if I didn't take her instructions for self-care more seriously.

I promised to stick to her plan moving forward. I would prioritize rest and hydration, eat nourishing foods, and add gentle exercise. I did not want a repeat of how I felt under the stairs.

"I don't see why they're keeping me overnight," I complained to Evan, after Dr. Bright left my hospital room. "I wanted to sleep in our bed. It's our anniversary, and tomorrow is Christmas."

Evan kissed my forehead, then slid onto the narrow mattress at my side. "Due diligence," he said. "I appreciate it. Besides, I'm staying right here. Maybe not in this bed all night, but I'll be with you when you wake."

"Knock, knock." Dr. Bright returned with a bulbous white machine on wheels. "I know I said I would leave you alone to rest, but I think it would make us all feel better if we take a look at that little bundle of joy."

"Is that an ultrasound machine?" Evan asked, climbing off the bed and taking my hand. The surprise in his voice reflected in his eyes.

Dr. Bright smiled and nodded. "It is, and if there are no objections, I think we should check in on the baby."

"Joy," I whispered, looking to Evan. "Our bundle of joy," I said, repeating the doctor's words.

He grinned. "I like it."

"Me too." My heart soared.

We'd agreed on Evan or Bud for a little boy. Joy was perfect for a girl.

Our baby had a name.

Dr. Bright set up the machine and helped me get situated. A grainy black and white image appeared, along with a steady whooshing like the sound I'd heard in my ears while panicking earlier tonight.

Evan's hold on my hand tightened as the sound grew steadier and picked up in pace.

"Hear that?" the doctor asked. "That's your baby's heartbeat."

"It's too fast," Evan said. "Isn't it?"

We looked to her, a shared panic flowing between us.

She shook her head as she watched the monitor. "Not at all. This is very typical of a thriving life at this stage. One hundred fifty-one beats strong."

Her enthusiasm eased my tension and filled me with sudden peace.

The wand in the doctor's hand stilled, and a clear black circle appeared onscreen, a flashing dot at its center. "There it is," she sang. "That's the heart we're hearing."

The knowledge hit with a whack of joy so strong it brought tears to my eyes.

Evan sucked in an audible breath, then wiped a tear from his cheek.

The wand moved again, and our baby appeared. Peanut shaped with nubby arms and legs and a strong flashing heart.

I would've cheerfully spent the rest of my pregnancy in that bed if it meant keeping our little bundle safe.

* * *

I woke in the middle of the night with a full bladder, much thanks to an IV bag of fluid tapped into my vein and the pitcher of water served to me in plastic cups before bed. I'd dreamed of sleigh bells and a deep, familiar laugh before physical needs pulled me from my sleep.

Whatever I'd been dreaming, it was nice.

I eased upright and swung my feet over the bed's edge, adjusting my eyes to the dim light. My nausea was at bay, a Christmas Eve miracle.

"You okay?" Evan whispered.

I smiled. "I thought you were asleep."

"I was." He yawned, then pushed onto his feet. "I heard sleigh bells." He rubbed his eyes and laughed softly. "Let me help you with your—"

I pushed the IV pole in his direction and stilled as my eyes found the thing that had stopped him midsentence. "Are those presents?"

The door opened, and I nearly jumped out of my skin.

"Oh!" The night nurse gasped. "Everyone's up. I thought you were sleeping. I came to check your vitals."

I ignored her, assuming she saw the strange surprise as well.

A stack of gifts three feet high stood against the wall, each perfectly wrapped in shiny red paper and tied with a wide golden bow.

Evan beat me to the stack. "Hit the light."

Behind me, the nurse pressed a switch, illuminating the room.

"Are those Christmas presents?" she asked.

Evan touched one of the little paper tags, fastened to the gift by a wispy silver thread. Then another. "They're all for Baby Gray."

"What?" Tears stung my eyes as I shuffled forward, pulling the IV pole at my side. "All of them?"

Evan flipped the tags more quickly, moving through the pile. "Yeah. I think so."

"There's a card over here," the nurse said. "This one says Holly and Evan."

Evan straightened, and I turned back, wondering if I'd really woken to use the restroom or if this was actually a dream.

I raised the card from the nightstand and broke the familiar wax seal on the back. "It's from Christopher," I said.

The nurse went to check out the gifts, allowing us some privacy as we read the message in my hands.

Evan stood behind me, holding my back to his chest and peering over my head at the card.

Dearest Holly,

I hope you've enjoyed my puzzle. You're now part of a very tight circle. A very trusted *circle. A spot you have more than earned. I know you'll honor it as fiercely as I do.*
Happy anniversary, and a merry Christmas to your growing family.

With love,
Christopher

PS: My apologies for spoiling Baby. The Mrs. and I couldn't help ourselves.

"What did Christopher mean about the puzzle?" he asked.

"I don't know. He sent a letter a week or two ago saying he was giving me a puzzle, but I never received anything else from him until now."

"Any idea what circle he's talking about?"

I shook my head.

Another Christmas mystery.

The nurse returned to us, visibly stunned. "You must've been the first stop on Santa's ride tonight."

"What?" Evan asked.

"It's Christmas Eve," she said, a wistful note in her voice. "You sure have some great friends to surprise you like this. How about I come back to check on you a little later?" She slipped back into the hallway and pulled the door gently closed.

Chapter Twenty-Six

We headed home from the hospital later that day with a good bill of health for me and Baby.

Evan navigated the empty roads, devoid of shoppers. All the shops were closed for Christmas Day, but the world outside was rife with holiday spirit.

I settled in to enjoy the ride, but a need for answers kept me from getting too comfortable. "When you arrested Peggy," I said, pulling a bland expression across Evan's face, "you told me you thought the killer could be her, so you dug a little deeper. What did that mean?"

He considered the question for a moment before responding. "It took me less than an hour to learn she'd attended college with Hannah. From there, I learned they both belonged to the history club, and I was able to contact some other members from that time frame. I also reached out to Hannah's family on the matter. Everyone I spoke to remembered the friendship between the two women and how it went south after a series of arguments when Hannah accused Peggy of being too clinging.

I cringed.

He nodded. "By the end of the day, I'd spoken to enough people from Peggy's life to show a pattern of behavior since high school. She makes a friend and attaches to them. She becomes too much, and instead of backing off, she doubles down, then makes them out to be a villain. They all said she was the nicest person they'd ever met, until she wasn't. She doesn't have a criminal record or history of violence, but what I learned was enough for me to contact her parents. They were babysitting for her on the night Hannah died. They said she was in Mistletoe, so I asked where, and they told me. I sent my deputies to the motel while I kept watch over you last night."

A thrill ran through me as he laid out his process and the way his investigation came together. "Did your deputy find anything at the hotel?"

"When he requested security footage of the parking lot, they found record of her leaving and returning just before and after the time of the break-in and murder. Furthermore, when she returned, she's visibly shaken and her coat is stained."

I gasped. "Is that enough?" I asked. "That plus the recording from our house?"

"The real smoking gun was in her hotel room. We acquired a warrant to check for evidence this morning, and the deputies found the stained coat in a trash bag under the bed. The lab confirmed the blood matches Hannah's. Peggy's going to jail for a long time," he said.

"What will happen to her children?" I asked. The whole thing was just so sad.

"They go to her next of kin, I guess," he said. "I'm not sure in her case."

I bit my lip, hating the way a momentary loss of control, one terribly poor decision, could change the trajectory of so many lives. Hers. Her children. Their new caretakers. More proof, in my opinion, that we were all interconnected, and more reason it was imperative that we keep that in mind.

"Alice should have a much merrier Christmas now," I said, digging for a silver lining in the heartbreaking situation.

"No doubt," Evan said. "You know I never suspected her as a killer, right? I couldn't completely discount it, but I would've been shocked."

"I know," I said. "Unlike your wife, you have an excellent sense about people."

"You just have an incredibly big heart," he said. "You only see the good. A few years working a detective beat in Boston would help minimize that."

I snorted a laugh. "I'll pass."

"Good. I think you're perfect as you are," he said. Evan reached for my hand and raised it to his lips, where he pressed a gentle kiss against my knuckles.

"You know what's weird?" I asked, realizing another question remained unanswered. "This woman, Nancy Grace, was everywhere I went all week, and she stared unabashedly. It was creepy. I thought she might be the killer, but I guess she was just really weird."

Evan wrinkled his brow. "Her name is actually Sylvia Stewart. She's an undercover FBI agent tracking an art thief and some stolen goods."

"What?" I turned wide eyes on him. "No way!"

"It's true," Evan said. "You're going to love this. I got so sidetracked; I didn't tell you last night. Arnold was using his responsibility for verifying the authenticity of items sold at the Antiques Showcase as a way to get the stolen items in. Sylvia had been on to him for more than a year, and she finally got what she needed to close her case this week."

"That's wild. I really thought she was following me."

"Probably seemed that way," he agreed. "She was working a case involving the same group of people."

I laughed. "I guess she was."

We reached our neighborhood a few moments later, and I told Evan about Caroline and Zane's plan to move in together. He was as pleased as I was about that news. They made one another happy, and who wouldn't want that for their friends?

"Cookie had some good news as well," Evan said.

I raised my brows in question. "Oh, yeah?"

He grinned as he made the turn onto our street. "Alice's grandpa has decided to stay in Mistletoe a little longer than he initially planned. Seems he's not ready to say goodbye just yet."

"Interesting."

"Cookie certainly thought so," Evan said. "I returned her call while you finished your discharge paperwork. You want to know what else she told me?"

I puzzled for a moment. "What?"

His green eyes slid my way, an expression caught somewhere between amusement and exasperation on his face. "She says the two of you are planning something called a baker's dozen cupcake calendar for next year."

A rocket of laughter shot out of me. I'd temporarily forgotten that little nugget of fun.

"She wants me to be the Christmas cupcake if she can't get Christopher to do it, and she says that if I say no, I'm letting down the children's hospital, because that's where she plans to donate the proceeds."

"I hope you said yes," I told him between bouts of giggling.

"I told her I'd think about it," he said, as he pulled into our driveway.

"If it makes you feel any better, she's asking Dad, Ray, and Zane too," I said. "I'm not sure who else is on her list, but she needs twelve cupcakes."

"Thirteen," he corrected. "It's a baker's dozen."

I cracked up all over again. It took several long minutes for me to realize the street behind us was lined in familiar cars. "Oh, my goodness. Are we having a party?"

"Did you think your family and friends would let you come home from a night like you had without being here?"

"No." I smiled. "But I thought they'd have other plans. It is Christmas, after all."

Now that Evan had mentioned the children's hospital, however, I wondered if charity was a better choice than the snowplow for the money I'd made signing autographs. Donating the three thousand dollars I'd made as the Gumdrop Gumshoe could go a long way to helping with the lights and sleigh rides for next Christmas, which could, in turn, bring in more money for them in future years. I tucked the thought away for now and refocused on our house full of guests.

"Folks probably won't stay long," he said. "But they wanted to see you and let you know how much you mean to them," Evan said.

"Who's here?" I asked.

"Everyone," he said. "The podcast has called twice to confirm tomorrow's interview."

I groaned. "Why is that so soon?"

Evan climbed down from the truck and rounded the hood to my door. He helped me onto the driveway and held my hand as we walked to the porch. "They heard all about what happened last night, and that's the story they want you to share with their listeners now."

"Great."

"Yep."

Money for charity, I told myself. *These interviews are worth the trouble, because they bring in money that I can give to good causes.*

Evan opened the front door and a dozen faces turned in our direction.

Mom burst forward. "She's here!" she cried.

A round of applause rose through our home.

Soon, I was passed from body to body, hugged and congratulated, both for my baby on board and for my role in helping to trap a killer.

Unlike parties in the past, most of these guests left soon after welcoming me home. They'd only wanted to let me know they loved me and appreciated my willingness to do ridiculously dangerous things in the name of justice.

I didn't bother telling them the intention was for me *not* to be in danger, but that had gone sideways as usual. That somehow seemed irrelevant now. Caroline saw guests out when they said goodbye, returning their coats and thanking them for their gifts or prepared meals meant to make my life easier in the days to come.

Christopher arrived as a group of others headed out. His cheeks were rosy from the cold. His white beard sparkled with flakes of melting snow. "There's the happy family," he said. He made his way to Evan, my folks, and me. "I can only stay a minute, but I wanted to be sure you knew I was thinking of you."

Evan shook his hand. "Thank you for the gifts," he said. "How did you get them into our hospital room?"

"Gifts?" Mom asked.

"They're still in the car," I said. "I can't wait for you to see them." I hugged Christopher on impulse. "We can't thank you enough for your generosity," I added, noting that he hadn't answered Evan's question.

"It's a small thing compared to what the two of you do," he said, bouncing his gaze from me to Evan, then back. "Before I go—" he patted his coat. "This is for you." He passed Evan an envelope much like the one left in my hospital room.

"I'll see you again soon," he said. "I've had a big night and need a little shut-eye." He winked.

"Wait." I followed him to the door.

"Yes?"

"You mentioned a puzzle," I said. "I never got it." I wrinkled my nose in apology. I probably sounded greedy after receiving so many things for my baby just this morning.

He frowned, pulling his thick white eyebrows into a V. "In the daily crossword," he said. "I started with your name, then moved one clue lower every day. I was certain I saw you doing the puzzles."

I imagined bouncing one palm against my forehead. "I knew those puzzles were meant for me."

"Of course they were," he said.

"What's this?" Evan asked, joining us once more.

"Christopher arranged the crossword clues," I said. "I was just reading them wrong."

"I hate to rush off," Christopher said again, tapping the screen of his watch. "But Merry Christmas to all." He waved a hand overhead, drawing goodbyes from the room. Then he was gone.

The other guests followed Christopher's lead, until only our family and closest friends remained. Mom fed everyone dinner while Dad peppered Evan with questions about precisely what happened the night before. I hated that I'd worried them, but this time it truly wasn't my fault.

"I'm keeping the spy bear forever," I said. "He saved my life."

"I'd argue that you saved your life," Evan said. "You managed to call me while standing five feet away from your would-be killer."

I smiled warmly at the man who gave me too much credit.

Mom snuggled against Dad's side and looked around the room. "We really are a lucky bunch."

"For a whole host of reasons," Dad agreed.

Cookie topped off everyone's coffee mug with the carafe on the table, then presented me with a cup of winter berry tea. "I'm going to miss having Alice at the inn," she said. "She's a good egg. I like her grandpa too."

Mom offered a small smile. "I wish he could stay a bit longer."

Cookie nodded, then poured some tea from her thermos and took a dainty sip.

Now that I knew she was interested in dating, I hoped she'd find someone as fun-loving as she was and someone deserving of her time. Preferably someone who lived in our country, so she wouldn't have to say goodbye again so soon.

Mom shared a million photos from the Christmas parade outside the children's hospital. I hated that I'd missed it but vowed to take part next year. Evan and I could bring our baby. The thought filled me, and I reached for my husband's loving hand. With more time to plan, the event would be a massive hit and a fundraising opportunity for the hospital. I could already see the organizational planning sessions with Caroline at the head.

Caroline and Zane were next to leave. She promised to be back soon and help me take down the holiday décor. I didn't need her help, but I loved spending time with her, and she was unnaturally fond of organizing the storage containers, so I easily agreed.

Libby rose to her feet a moment later. She scanned the remaining faces. Cookie, Evan and me, my folks, and her husband looked curiously in her direction. "I have an announcement," she said.

"You're giving up the PI business," Evan said.

"Better."

"I doubt that," he said with a wicked grin.

Mom laughed. "Tell us," she encouraged. "We love happy news. It is happy, isn't it?"

Libby nodded and locked her gaze with mine. "Ray isn't obsessed with pregnancy symptoms and details for no reason."

Evan shot to his feet a moment before I fully understood. He wrapped his arms around his sister as the room exploded in shouts of cheer.

"You're pregnant?" I asked. "You're having a baby?"

"Yeah," Ray said, grinning from ear to ear.

"We found out around Thanksgiving," Libby said. "We were waiting until the end of the first trimester to make the announcement, then you made your announcement, and you had concerning blood pressure. We didn't want to jump in and tell everyone our news on top of yours. You deserved the time to let it settle."

"Then another murder happened," Ray said. "We just decided to wait for the new year."

Evan examined his sister. "How are you doing? Both of you."

"Good," she said. "I was pretty sick for a couple of months, but I feel fantastic now."

I blinked, stunned as the excitement in the kitchen subsided. "When are you due?" I asked, unable to manage the mental math through my hormone-induced brain fog.

"From what I've gathered," Libby said, "about ten days before you."

The room erupted again, and I cried.

Whenever I thought my life couldn't get more joyful, something even better happened.

Chapter Twenty-Seven

Tate and Harvey arrived an hour early for the podcast interview and brought an entire team of professional technicians with them. "We won't keep you long, considering it's barely been twenty-four hours since your latest run-in with a killer."

My parents, who'd arrived only minutes before the podcasters, groaned and headed for the kitchen. "We'll wait in here," Mom called.

My folks brought breakfast, and if history taught me anything, they would be extra clingy for a few weeks following my latest scare.

I forced a bright smile for the *Dead and Berried* team. "Ready."

Tate clasped his hands. "Excellent. Let's set up!"

Cookie rang the bell a few minutes later. "Look who I found," she said, stepping inside with Alice and Hugo on her heels.

"Hey! Welcome!" I hugged my friends and escorted them to the kitchen, out of the tech team's way.

We got caught up over Mom's sweets and tea. Hugo said he planned to stay an extra month with Alice while she got comfortable in her apartment again. Cookie nearly burst with joy.

Alice said it was strange to see the train station and its parking lot empty again, now that the antiques show had gone.

I thought again of Peggy and Hannah, brokenhearted for them both in different ways. And especially for their families this Christmas.

Then a stranger clipped a mic to my shirt.

I started, and the woman gave me an enthusiastic thumbs-up.

"All set," she said, before walking away.

Cookie leaned in my direction, unbothered by the mic lady. "Did you ever solve the puzzle Christopher gave you?"

I looked at Evan, shocked that we'd forgotten. "Not yet," I admitted.

"We're doing it tonight," Evan said. He pushed away from the table and stood. "I'll grab the papers from recycling, so we can start from the beginning."

The fact I'd forgotten something so important and special was a testament to the level of cuckoo my Christmas day had been.

Within minutes, my living room was awash with fluorescent lighting.

I sat on my couch with Cindy Lou Who stretched lazily along the back. Tate and Harvey took seats in armchairs across from me. They positioned their freestanding mics and open laptops on my coffee table. A woman raised a camera in our direction, then counted us down. "Three, two—"

The interview passed quickly, and I found myself laughing at the podcasters' surprisingly funny jokes. I recapped the few details I could in relation to the recent Mistletoe murder, but Tate and Harvey would have to come back next year for the full story. Today was simply too soon.

Maybe it was the Christmas spirit, being surrounded by family and friends, or something more, but the podcast content didn't seem to be as poor in taste as I'd previously thought. And maybe the way the duo paired recipes with crimes was more like comic relief from the gruesome content than a way to poke fun.

"One more thing," Tate said, as the interview wound to a close. "We and our listeners have something for you."

My peace immediately subsided. I prepared myself for the onscreen delivery of a goofy houndstooth cap or comically giant magnifying glass.

The show's assistant lifted a finger and hurried away.

Tate returned his attention to me. "How about one more question while we wait?"

I refreshed my smile.

Harvey leaned forward, elbows resting on his knees. "What are your plans for all that Gumdrop Gumshoe money?"

I laughed, relieved his question hadn't been another about Peggy. "Honestly, I planned on buying my husband a snowplow for his truck, but someone recently inspired me to give the money to our local children's hospital instead. We aren't an expensive-gift-giving couple. We choose things with meaning, and I want to pick something smaller in budget and higher in nostalgia." Like a horse-drawn sleigh ride around Reindeer Games like the one we took before we officially began dating, or the one we took to our romantic Christmas Eve wedding.

Evan smiled broadly off camera, and Cookie gave an enthusiastic thumbs-up.

Evan broke the seal on the envelope Christopher had given him as he listened.

"If you don't mind me asking," Harvey said. "How much are you giving the children's hospital?"

"Three thousand dollars," I answered without thinking. Was it inappropriate to mention exact dollar amounts like that?

Tate gave a hearty bark of laughter. "This town," he said. "Or maybe it's just you, but—" He waved the assistant forward, and they returned with a cartoonishly large check. At least three feet long and more than a foot tall, it was yellow and black with the general vibe of crime scene tape. A *Dead and Berried* logo wedged in one corner. My name stood in block letters on the line indicating to whom the money was intended.

I blinked, confused by the amount of zeros. "What is that?"

"This is a donation for a down payment on your new home," Tate said. "You told us last year about your plans to return one day to Reindeer Games, and we thought it would be fun to help get you back to where it all began. So, listeners around the country have been donating to that cause through a crowdfund page on our website, and this is the final number," Tate said.

He swung his gaze dramatically to the camera. "The final donation arrived last minute via direct phone call, for exactly three thousand dollars."

A collective gasp drew my eyes to a knot of my friends in the kitchen archway. Caroline, Cookie, and Libby looked as if they'd seen a unicorn. Their expressions perfectly mirrored my emotion.

Could this be real?

Evan cursed softly, and I turned to him.

Ray and Zane left the kitchen, cutout cookies in hand. They bookended my husband and peered over his shoulder at the letter in his hand, then at the giant check.

They also cursed.

People were going to have to control their language around my baby next year. I made a mental note to bring that up soon.

"Well, that about wraps it up here, folks," Tate said. "It's safe to say you've left the Gumdrop Gumshoe and her family speechless with your generosity. Don't forget to like and follow this podcast to keep up with all the Mistletoe, Maine, shenanigans, and our weekly true crime features. Until then, we pair this year's Christmas killing with Janssons Frestelse and glogg."

I thanked the podcasters and removed my mic in a hurry, then sprinted to the kitchen while the crew packed up after the show.

Caroline and Zane, Mom and Dad, Libby, Ray, and Cookie huddled around the table, Evan, and the letter from Christopher.

I wanted to freak out about the donations from the podcast listeners, but everyone seemed more interested in whatever was in Evan's hand.

"What does it say?" I whispered, sliding into the space at Evan's side.

He passed me the unfolded paper from inside Christopher's card. "I asked for a quote on building our home," Evan said. His voice was thick and low, his eyes misting with emotion. "This is our cost, based on some general details."

I whistled. The number was high. We knew it would be. We'd met with a banker last summer and set up a strategy for building in the next three to five years. With a steady savings and a good sale on our present home, we could do it.

"Then you got that check," Evan said, pausing to clear his throat.

"What?" I asked.

"Excuse me," the stagehand appeared in the archway with the giant check. "Do you want to keep this? If not, I don't mind throwing it away for you. You'll get a paper check in the mail in a few days."

I stared at the number written across the foam board, then looked again at Christopher's estimate. "We just received exactly three thousand dollars more than we need for a down payment," I whispered.

Evan nodded.

"We can afford to build?" I looked at the little crowd, all speechless and smiling widely.

Evan turned and caught me around the waist. He hoisted me off my feet with a growl of joy. "We can afford to build!"

"Hot dog," Cookie said. "Can you still buy the snowplow?"

"Yeah," Libby said. "With that last minute donation, right?"

I hugged Evan's neck and let the tears of joy flow. "Yes," I said. "And I can still give to the children's hospital."

Evan set me on my feet, and our friends closed in on us for a massive group hug.

"Well," Tate said, breaking us up. "We're heading out."

Caroline sprang into action, delivering a covered tray of goodies to the crew, retrieving everyone's coats, and walking them to the door.

Evan and I followed, thanking Tate and Harvey profusely for their incredible kindness and generosity. For the crowdfunding project that enabled us to build our new home years sooner than we imagined possible.

"Hey, we're just hoping for another interview next Christmas," Harvey said. "Our listeners love you. Obviously."

I smiled and nodded. "I guess we'll see you next year."

* * *

Hours later, when our last guest had gone, and Evan and I had shared a quiet dinner at home, we eased onto the couch to enjoy our beautiful, twinkling Christmas tree and a blazing fireplace fire.

"Ready for the puzzle?" I asked.

Evan delivered the last week or so of newspaper crosswords and spread them on the coffee table before us. "Do you think this will clear up what he meant by the inner circle?"

"We shall see," I said. I arranged the papers in chronological order. "According to Christopher, the clues meant for me were consecutive. Starting with two across."

"We already know that one is Holly," Evan said, writing my name on a sheet of paper. "What's next?"

I looked at the next day's paper. "Delightful."

"One word. Ten letters. The fire is so—" Evan said, reading the clue. "Okay, next?"

Lyric. One word. Five letters. Can't beat home sweet home if you want to be this.

"Happy."

Evan wrote it down. "Next?"

Title. One word. Eight letters. O Come All Ye—

"Faithful," I said. "Two more."

He pulled the next day's paper closer and squinted at the print. "Singular of blank who are dear to us."

"Friends," I said, hearing the melody in my mind. *Faithful friends who are la la la.*

"Last clue," Evan said, writing the previous answer on his sheet. "How would artist Eartha Kitt address the letter in her song 'Santa Baby'?"

"To Santa Claus."

Evan wrote the final word, then slid the new sentence between us on the coffee table.

Holly, delightful, happy, faithful friend to Santa Claus.

We stared at the message in silence for a long moment, then Evan slipped his arm around my shoulders and tugged me against him. He kissed my head and chuckled against my hair. "Santa Claus."

I wasn't sure what I thought about the message, but I knew my heart was full. I knew my life was filled with family and friends, love and laughter. A year from now, I'd be right here in Evan's arms, enjoying the fireplace, our Christmas tree, and our baby. My parents would live a stone's throw away, and I'd get to raise my family on the tree farm where so many generations were raised before me.

Life, like this moment, was perfect and precious. I didn't want to waste a single moment.

So I pulled my husband's lips to mine, and I kissed him. "Merry Christmas."